GRAVE

Debbie Viguié has been writing for most of her life
and holds a degree in creative writing from U.C.
Davis. Debbie loves theme parks and enjoys travelling
with her husband, Scott. Debbie grew up in the San
Francisco Bay Area and now lives in Florida.

Also in the Witch Hunt trilogy

The 13th Sacrifice

PRAISE FOR THE WITCH HUNT NOVELS

'ONE OF THE MOST **BEAUTIFULLY WRITTEN** AND SCARIEST
BOOKS I'VE EVER READ...ONE OF MY TOP TEN **EVER**.'
New York Times bestselling author, Nancy Holder

'IMPOSSIBLE TO PUT DOWN...**DEBBIE VIGUIÉ**
JUST KEEPS GETTING BETTER AND BETTER.'
USA Today

'[A] **HEART-STOPPING READ**. IT WILL HAVE READERS ON
THE EDGE OF THEIR SEATS...THE TENSION THAT VIGUIÉ
CREATES IS ENOUGH TO MAKE YOUR HAIR STAND UP...
HER NO-NONSENSE STYLE AND DARK, GRIPPING REALISM
ARE HARD TO BEAT IN THIS **EPIC THRILLER**.'
DebsBookBag.co.uk

'THIS, LADIES AND GENTS, IS **A TRUE THRILLER**,
COMPLETE WITH MASS HYSTERIA, BRUTAL MURDER,
AND ONE SCARY BADASS WITCH RAISED FROM THE
DEAD...**READ THIS BOOK**...YOU JUST MIGHT WANT
TO PLAN ON SLEEPING WITH THE LIGHTS ON.'
darkfaerietales.com

'I'D RECOMMEND *THE 13TH SACRIFICE* TO ANYONE ONE WHO
ENJOYS AN ON THE EDGE OF YOUR SEAT THRILLER WITH A
MAJOR CREEPY FACTOR THAT **WILL UTTERLY HAUNT YOU**.'
Abookobsession.com

The LAST GRAVE

Debbie Viguié

arrow books

Published by Arrow Books 2013

2 4 6 8 10 9 7 5 3 1

First published in the US in 2013 by Signet

Arrow Books
The Random House Group Limited
20 Vauxhall Bridge Road, London SW1V 2SA

Addresses for companies within The Random House Group Limited can be
found at: www.randomhouse.co.uk/offices.htm

The Random House Group Limited Reg. No. 954009

www.randomhouse.co.uk

A CIP catalogue record for this book
is available from the British Library

ISBN 9780099574569

The Random House Group Limited supports the Forest Stewardship
Council® (FSC®), the leading international forest-certification organisation.
Our books carrying the FSC label are printed on FSC®-certified paper.
FSC is the only forest-certification scheme supported by the leading
environmental organisations, including Greenpeace.
Our paper procurement policy can be found at:
www.randomhouse.co.uk/environment

MIX
Paper from
responsible sources
FSC® C016897

Printed and bound by CPI Group (UK) Ltd, Croydon, CR0 4YY

To my mom, Barbara Reynolds.

Thank you for all the times you took me to see the Big Trees in Santa Cruz!

ACKNOWLEDGMENTS

As with all books, there are always many, many people to thank. Of course none of this would be possible without my fantastic agent, Howard Morhaim, and my amazing editor Danielle Perez. Thank you also to the family and friends who always support me. I feel, though, that it is especially important in this book for me to thank those people who work tirelessly to ensure that we remember our past and embrace our future. To all those who work to make Roaring Camp a magical experience for so many, thank you. Also, thank you to the California Academy of Sciences for inspiring so many generations to embrace science and learning. I spent a lot of time at both places when I was a kid and have always appreciated everything I was able to see and experience because of both of them. I salute the visionaries who keep these things alive for future generations to discover and experience.

1

The shadows were alive, moving, slithering, crawling across the floor toward her and swarming across the ceiling above her. She stood, helpless and naked, as she watched them advance. In her right hand she held an athame, the only thing she'd been allowed to bring. She lifted it and touched the tip to the palm of her left hand. The blade felt cool against the skin. A circle. She needed to form a blood circle to protect herself from the things.

Blood bubbled to the surface of her skin as she dug the blade in. She raised her hand, ready to drip the blood onto the floor.

No! a voice shouted angrily.

She knew without looking it was her mother. She could feel her disapproval like a physical weight between her shoulder blades. The shadows surged forward.

You must, another voice said.

She began to shake, her terror of the shadows nearly greater than her fear of the adults who were commanding her. A shadow ran like spilled blood across the final inches separating her from it.

It touched her bare toes and she cried out and stepped back. Suddenly iron hands were holding her tight, pinning her arms to her body. She could feel them pushing her forward, her mother and the other woman. She struggled even as they hissed threats in her ears, but all she could hear was the other voice whispering in her head. That one was soft and oily and it promised . . .

Power.

More power than she could ever dream of. More power than she could ever use.

And the shadow once again touched her foot, which felt as if it had been enveloped in a cold, wet blanket. She didn't want to look, but another hand forced her head downward. She tried to close her eyes, but an invisible force held them open so she could watch.

The shadow wrapped around her leg like a snake and moved its way up her body. She sobbed as she felt it moving against her skin and then through her skin, into her body, filling her with cold and fear and dread.

And she could feel the promised power surging through her. But she didn't want it. She screamed as the shadow slithered up her thighs, wrapping every inch of her as it went.

And then it was circling her hips and stomach. Then her chest, until only her head was still her own. And when the shadow moved upward again, it filled her mouth and nose. It flowed into her ears and her eyes, turning everything to ice.

She was drowning. She was dying. She was becoming—

*   *   *

Samantha sat up with a scream. She was shaking and drenched in sweat. She swore she could feel the icy hands of the shadow wrapped around her still. Another nightmare that was far more than a nightmare. It was a memory from the childhood she kept being forced to relive.

Her fists were balled up so tight that her fingernails were cutting into her palms. Beside her, Freaky Kitty was blinking at her with great, round eyes. He mewed, and she reached out to cuddle him.

Freaky wasn't a real cat; he was an energy creation she had learned to make when she was a young witch, and had only recently remembered how. In the important ways, though, he seemed real. He had weight and warmth and was incredibly soft. He was inquisitive, mischievous, and loving. She could feel the sandpaper roughness of his tiny tongue when he licked her finger.

There was a knock on her door, and she waved her hand and dispelled the energy making up the kitten. The great thing about his not being completely real was that he didn't need feeding, he never got sick, and she could hide him with the flick of her wrist.

"Come in," she said as she swung her legs over the edge of her bed. She reached up a shaking hand and fingered the cross around her neck.

The door opened and a blond head poked inside. It was her roommate, Jill, who was even now staring at her with wide eyes, as though she were some kind of monster.

But I am. I'm a witch.

She wrapped her fingers tightly around the cross necklace, anger rising to the surface swiftly. *I'm not. That's not who I want to be.*

"Everything okay?" Jill asked.

"Fine."

"Sounded like a nightmare. Want to talk about it?" Jill asked, sitting down next to her and putting a hand on her shoulder. The contact only reminded Samantha of the hands that had held her, pinned her.

"No!" Samantha said, jerking away.

Jill shook her head. She might not like that Samantha wasn't a touchy-feely kind of person, but at least she seemed to be getting used to it.

"You've got real trust issues," Jill said. "Especially when it comes to women."

"Tell me something I don't know," Samantha snapped, instantly regretting her tone.

"It would make you feel better if you talked about it," Jill said, looking at her grimly.

Samantha squeezed her eyes shut. "Look, I get that you're trying to help. And I'm sorry that my nightmares are waking you up. But I really, really don't want to talk about it."

"Sometimes it helps to talk about it," Jill said.

Samantha bit back the urge to laugh. Talking about her problems didn't make them better. It only ever made them worse.

Her phone rang, causing her to jump. She looked pointedly at Jill, who gave her a perky smile and left the room.

"Hello?"

"We're up."

It was her partner, Lance Garris.

She glanced at the clock. "It's three in the morning."

"Crime waits for no man. Besides, what did you expect, coming to the big city? Everyone else is already on something else."

She gritted her teeth. Lance knew she was from Boston, but he kept acting like she was some hick from a small town. It wasn't the only thing about him that grated on her nerves.

"I'll pick you up in five."

"Ten," she countered.

"Seven and I won't look if you need to change in the backseat."

Samantha hung up and clenched her fists, forcing herself to breathe. A moment later, she stood swiftly, threw on a pair of black slacks and a white shirt. She tucked her gun into the back of her waistband and clipped her detective's shield to her belt. Then she put on a heavy jacket. It was mid-January, and while that didn't mean snow in San Francisco, it didn't mean it wouldn't be cold.

In the kitchen, Jill handed her a cup of a coffee and a bagel.

"Thanks," Samantha said, forcing herself to smile. It had been explained to her that bagels were to northern California what doughnuts were to the rest of the country. She'd have rather had a doughnut, but beggars couldn't be choosers.

She headed downstairs to wait for Lance.

It had been three months since she'd moved from Boston, following an undercover investigation where she'd taken down a coven that was murdering young women. She'd hoped that getting some distance would help her forget, but it just seemed like every night more memories from a childhood best forgotten bubbled to the surface.

Samantha had been raised a witch, and only the massacre of her entire coven had allowed her to escape. After being adopted by a kind couple, she had turned her back on her old life and embraced the Christian faith of her adoptive parents. She'd studied hard, joined the police force, and made detective. She'd put in a lot of effort to build a life for herself, only to have it torn apart again.

One of the most painful losses had been that of the trust and friendship of her partner, Ed. He hadn't been able to handle what he'd seen, what he'd learned about her and her past. None of the cops in Boston had wanted to look her in the eye after what had happened. It had been her captain's idea to get her a job on the other side of the country, a fresh start. After all, as one of the only people aware of her past, he had pushed her hard to use her powers to go in and take down the coven.

She took a sip of the coffee and grimaced. Jill always dumped a lot of crap into coffee, and this cup was no exception.

Is that cinnamon? she wondered.

Having a roommate was strange and dangerous. She was constantly on edge and aware of everything she did. Which in its own way was good. Her last case in Boston had been a nightmare. It had required her to go undercover in a dark coven and use magic. Being undercover and having to use magic had led her to backsliding quite a lot into her old ways. But having someone else in her apartment assured that she couldn't use magic as often as she wanted. She never wanted to use magic, Freaky Kitty being the one exception. She'd grown to need the little ball of fur more than she should have.

Of course, she hadn't planned on having a roommate, but it was so much more expensive to rent a place in San Francisco than it had been back home. A roommate had been a necessary evil. Jill was someone she'd known from college in Boston a few years before. They'd had a lot of classes together and had been study partners. Since then, Jill had been consistent in sending Christmas cards even though Samantha hadn't.

When Samantha had decided to move to San Francisco, before she'd met any of her new coworkers, she'd reached out to Jill just to ask her some questions about where she should try to rent a place. It turned out Jill was in graduate school now and in need of a roommate. Jill had been thrilled, still seeing Samantha as a friend from the old days. Samantha had never had many friends. Trust didn't come easily for her—that much Jill was right about. But this way she could afford to live in the city.

And it's just a bonus that Jill's presence keeps me from doing actual evil.

A silver car pulled up to the curb. She got in, rubbing her hands briskly. "Morning, Lance."

He grunted in reply and pulled away from the curb.

Lance was thirty, just two years older than she was, but his dark hair was streaked with gray. In Boston she'd been the odd one who'd had difficulty finding the right partner until Ed had come along. Here she'd quickly assumed that they were sticking Lance with her because she was the outsider. As it turned out, it was more the opposite. She was the one person he hadn't pissed off yet, so they had stuck her with him.

Her phone rang, and he swore.

"You need to have that thing on all the time?" he asked.

If only Ed could hear you say that, she thought sadly. She never used to carry her phone, and it had nearly gotten her old partner killed. Now it was like it was a lifeline.

She checked to see who was calling.

Anthony.

Her heart stuttered. She couldn't deal with talking to him, not right now. She declined the call and pocketed the phone.

"The guy back home who won't let you go?" Lance guessed.

"Something like that," she said with a sigh. Her relationship with Anthony was far too complicated to deal with, let alone explain, especially at three in the morning. What was it Anthony had said to her before she left Salem, about them having a great story? It was something like *Boy meets girl. Boy falls for girl. Boy tries to kill girl.* And now they were in the phase where boy was trying really hard to win girl back. But she had nearly gotten him killed, and even if he could get over the fact that the coven she was raised in had murdered his mother, Samantha wasn't sure she could. Even if she was constantly thinking of him.

"Who calls at three in the morning?" Lance asked.

"You do," she said.

She could see him rolling his eyes at her. "That's business."

The truth was, it was the first time Anthony had called so early. It made her wonder briefly if something was wrong, if he was in trouble. She was tempted to call him back, but, whatever it was, she was sure she didn't want to be discussing it in front of her new partner.

"Want me to tell him to get a life?" Lance asked.

"No, but thanks for the offer."

"You know what they say: 'protect and serve.'"

She smiled. "So, are we going somewhere, or did you just miss me?"

"Someone called in a disturbance at the California Academy of Sciences in the Natural History Museum. By the time officers got there, there was no disturbance, just a body."

"Lucky us."

There was little traffic on the streets, and they soon arrived at their destination. Officers had already cordoned off the scene, and one of them met Lance and Samantha at the car.

"What do we have?" Lance asked.

"Winona Lightfoot, local historian, dead."

"How?" Samantha asked as she moved toward the building.

"That's one for the coroner."

"Any witnesses?" Lance asked.

"Nah. Call about a disturbance was anonymous, and there was no one outside when I got here."

"No one? Not even the homeless?" Lance asked sharply.

"Not a living soul."

"So, where's the body?" Samantha asked.

"Inside."

"Was the alarm tripped?" Lance asked.

"No, but when we got here, a side door was unlocked."

Samantha paused and turned to look at the officer. His name badge proclaimed him to be Zack. "Zack, what made you go inside?"

Zack looked sheepish for a minute. "My boy and his Scout troop are having one of those overnights at the African Hall exhibit. When I realized the one door was unlocked . . ."

"You didn't feel you could not investigate, just in case."

"That's about the size of it," Zack admitted.

"Sounds like it's a good thing you did," Lance noted. "None of the Scouts heard anything?"

"No. Not a sound."

They entered the structure and headed straight back. "The body's in the Swamp area," Zack explained.

"What was she doing, filming a PSA? I'm proud to be a Native American?"

Samantha blinked at Lance, wondering what he was talking about.

Lance glanced at her. "When I was a kid, they used to make all these public service commercials there. All about being proud of your heritage."

"I'm proud to be an Italian American," Zack said with a grin.

"And with her red hair, clearly Samantha's proud to be an Irish American," Lance said.

"What does that make you?" Zack asked Lance.

"He's proud to be an Asshole American," Samantha snapped.

Lance jerked his head around to stare at her. She bit her tongue. She shouldn't have gotten on him. Lots of homicide cops had a macabre sense of humor. His joking was a way of coping with the death he saw every day.

Before she could apologize, he nodded. "I'm going to use that."

She rolled her eyes, fighting down her annoyance with him. Which was good, actually, because it kept her from focusing too much on her surroundings, which were spooky at night.

The Swamp was part of the aquarium complex. It was where they housed alligators. Poisonous snakes and spiders also shared the space.

"Someone didn't feed her to a gator, did they?" Lance asked as they got closer.

Zack shook his head.

Samantha had been through the museum complex, the California Academy of Sciences, once since she'd moved there. She'd gotten sick of having everyone she worked with suggest she see it, so she'd gone on a Saturday.

Now, with the sound of their footsteps echoing eerily and darkness reigning over much of the area, it was a completely different experience.

The body came into view, and Samantha caught her breath. The woman was well dressed, wearing a business suit. Her eyes were frozen wide in terror. And her arms were lifted straight up, hands clenched into fists that looked like they were clawing at something Samantha couldn't see.

"What the hell?" Lance said, stopping abruptly.

"We found her like that," the officer said. "Took us a minute to realize she was actually dead. I've never seen a body do that before. It's like she was frozen."

"I've never seen rigor mortis like this," Lance said.

Samantha grabbed a pair of gloves and slid them on. She knelt down on the ground and touched the body. The skin was warm to the touch.

"She's still warm. She can't have been dead more than a few minutes, so this isn't rigor mortis and she isn't frozen."

She pushed gently on the arms, then on the woman's stomach, and finally on her cheeks. Everything she touched was hard. It didn't even feel like she was touching flesh. She sat back, head reeling.

"What is it?" Lance asked, kneeling down next to her.

"It's like she's been petrified."

"Come again?"

"Like a tree. She's warm to the touch, but everything is hard as wood. There's no give in her skin at all," she said.

Lance put on gloves and touched the woman's cheek. "She feels like stone," he marveled.

Samantha stood slowly and backed a few feet away from the body. Something wasn't right. She walked a few more feet away, leaving Lance with the officers who had discovered the body.

She swept the ground with her eyes, looking for something, anything that could tell her what had happened to the woman.

You won't find anything, a voice inside her head mocked her. *Nothing natural, nothing rational.*

She hissed to herself, trying to silence the voice. She walked in the direction away from the African Hall. If the kids and their leaders hadn't seen anything, then there probably wasn't anything to find over there, and it was best to leave them alone anyway.

She stepped lightly, straining her senses to hear and see whatever she could.

Whoever had killed Winona must have left just as Zack and his partner arrived.

Unless they're still here.

She came to a standstill and struggled with herself. It would be so easy to reach out with her senses, see if she could feel anyone nearby.

But that wasn't going to help her fight the desire to use magic. And if she found something, she'd have to find a way that didn't sound supernatural to explain it to her new partner.

Her last partner hadn't been able to handle the truth.

She forced herself to keep walking and she reached the rain forest biosphere. She let herself in and then stood for a moment, letting her eyes adjust. It would be the perfect place to hide, and it would be easy to slip out in the morning after the Academy had opened.

She took a step into the darkness and felt a growing apprehension. Another step, and the birds that lived in the rain forest exhibit fell silent.

And suddenly she wanted nothing more than to be out of there and to be *anywhere* else.

It felt as though the trees were actually whispering her name.

The trees.

She had seen a petrified tree once when she was younger. People thought it had been hit by lightning, but she'd been able to tell that lightning hadn't killed it; magic had.

What killed Winona?

She began to sweat, and her heart sped up.

She didn't want to know the answer.

She tried to force herself to take another step forward when a large bird screamed and flew at her head, wings beating her face. She threw up her arm to block the bird and felt energy surging through her. It would be so easy to push the bird away with magic.

Too easy.

The bird flew away and she took a deep breath.

Something didn't want her there and she couldn't agree more. She backed out slowly. As soon as she exited the biosphere, her heart began to slow again and the feelings of dread slowly ebbed. She made her way back to the Swamp, feeling like there were eyes watching her the whole way.

When she got there, Lance was talking to a short, balding man who looked like he was shy several hours' sleep and a gallon of coffee. He had the look of shock people wore when they were woken in the middle of the night with bad news. He was wearing a name badge on his shirt.

He must be one of the people in charge of the Academy, she thought.

"I have no idea who could have done this," he said.

"No enemies that you know of? How about angry exes?" Lance questioned.

"Nothing like that."

"What about her family?"

"She has a teenage daughter. That's all that I know of. This is going to be terrible for her. Imagine losing your mother that young."

Samantha didn't have to imagine. But the loss of her mother had been her salvation instead of the nightmare most would assume.

What kind of mother were you, Winona?

"So, there was no one that had a problem with her?" Lance pushed.

The man shrugged. "She was a treasure, as far as many of us are concerned. Her knowledge of mission-era and even pre-mission-era native settlements was exhaustive. She worked tirelessly to preserve that heritage, that culture. She worked to get some historical sites officially recognized and protected. She even helped spearhead cleanup efforts at some of the ancient sea caves down the coast."

"Was she in the habit of working late here?" Samantha asked, easing into the conversation and trying to forget the feelings of foreboding that still swirled within her.

"No. In fact, she didn't technically work here. She was here a lot. Doing research. We would bring her in to speak at events."

"Was she talking to the Scout troop tonight?" Lance asked.

The man looked at them both blankly for a moment and then turned even more ashen. "There's a Scout troop here tonight? That's terrible. The kids didn't ... they didn't see anything?"

"No. They don't even know what happened," Samantha said.

"That's a relief."

"So, she wasn't supposed to be here tonight?" Lance pushed.

"No. Certainly not. She didn't have keys, so I don't even know how she got in here."

Samantha glanced down at Winona's body. The wrongness of it set her teeth on edge. This was no ordinary murder. She knew that, but she didn't want to know it. Why hadn't there been someone else free to take this case? The way the department worked, she might have never even heard about Winona Lightfoot.

No, people would have been talking about this one, she told herself.

"She live nearby?" Lance asked.

"Nah, she worked in the city, but she commuted in. She lived in Santa Cruz," the man was telling Lance.

Samantha gasped and reached for her cross.

"Is that a problem?" he asked, turning empty eyes toward her.

It was a huge problem. Because what had happened to Winona was unnatural. There was nothing Samantha knew short of magic that could have caused the petrification. And before she left Salem, Anthony had warned her that Santa Cruz was home to witches.

Samantha struggled to find words while Lance and

the administrator stared hard at her. Nothing came to her, though. All she could think about was Anthony's warning. Witches in Santa Cruz. Winona was from Santa Cruz. It should mean nothing. It should be a coincidence. It wasn't, though; she could feel it.

Finally Lance shrugged. "My partner doesn't like hippies," he quipped. "Now, I have a few more questions."

"Yes, of course," the other man said, turning back to look at Lance.

Samantha just stood there, struggling to listen, as she let Lance ask all of the questions. He glanced at her a couple times more, and she could tell from the look on his face that she was going to have some explaining to do.

After standing there for what seemed like forever, as frozen in her own way as Winona Lightfoot, Samantha forced herself to move.

She crouched down, ostensibly to examine Winona again. Soon the coroner would arrive and, hopefully, a logical explanation for the condition of the body would be presented. She forced herself to take several deep, calming breaths.

And what if the coroner did find an explanation? Would it be enough for Samantha? Would she be able to shake the feelings that were plaguing her? The months that she had lived here, she hadn't actually ventured outside of the city. She told herself that was because there was enough to see and do in San Francisco to keep her busy for years. In reality, though, a part of her had been heeding Anthony's warning about staying in the city.

Her hand reached for her phone. He knew so much about the occult. Maybe he'd heard of something like this petrification before. A moment later, she pulled away her hand. Even if she did get up the nerve to talk to him, doing it where others could hear was the height of stupidity.

Get a grip, Samantha. Pull yourself together, she demanded. She'd spent the last few months jumping at shadows, and now that she was faced with the possibility of a real threat, she was a basket case.

There's only one way to know for sure, a small voice whispered inside her mind.

She glanced up at Lance. Her partner had all his attention focused on the man he was questioning. His voice had taken on a bit of an edge. Lance had a way of making even routine questions sound more like an interrogation. At least they were both focused on each other and not on her. Zack and his partner were walking back toward the exit, probably getting ready to escort the coroner or someone else in.

It was now or never.

Samantha took a deep breath, closed her eyes, and let herself reach out. In a flash, she could feel everything around her—the animals, the plants, the electrical currents running through the building.

And around Winona, fading quickly, was the faint pulse of magic.

2

Samantha toppled backward, landing on her rump with a thud.

"What's wrong?" Lance asked sharply.

She looked up and was dismayed to see that now she had her partner's full attention. The administrator was looking at her too, but from his glazed-over expression, she was pretty sure he wasn't going to remember many details about this night.

"My foot slipped," she said, hurrying to stand up.

She could hear voices. The coroner and reinforcements to sweep the crime scene. They wouldn't find anything. At least, not anything that really mattered.

Samantha wrapped her arms around herself. She probably looked like a twelve-year-old girl instead of a police detective, the way she was holding herself.

But the fears of her childhood were hitting her hard. It was because she knew deep down what she had to do. Something hadn't wanted her in the rain forest, so that's where she had to go.

"I'm going to take a look around," she said to Lance.

He was still staring at her in a way that told her an unpleasant conversation was going to be part of her near future. That was, if she lived through her immediate future.

He nodded, and she took off quickly before anyone asked her anything she wouldn't or couldn't answer. She hurriedly retraced her steps to the rain forest, her pulse skittering out of control with every step. As she walked, she began to pray, feeling the weight of the cross necklace around her neck.

It was a simple silver filigree cross. It was the one she had bought herself in Boston just before moving out to San Francisco. It was a pale replacement for the one that witches had stolen from her, but it was still of some comfort.

The cross she'd worn since she was thirteen had held a secret compartment in it, a centuries-old design, and she had put a drop of her own blood inside as she vowed to God that she would do no more magic. The cross had been stolen from her before she'd had to break that vow. She desperately wanted it back, but the police, who had swept every location related to the coven and its members, had come up empty looking for it.

So she clutched the new cross and prayed fervently for strength, for guidance, and for the ability to do whatever she had to do without resorting to magic.

She arrived at the dome that housed the rain forest and stepped quickly inside. If she hesitated, she would give herself a chance to rethink her decision, and that would do no one any good. She took only five steps inside before she realized that something was different.

She stopped, listening. She could hear the call of birds and reptiles. The air was warm and humid, as in an actual rain forest, and she had the immediate urge to shrug out of her coat.

She took a few more steps and nothing happened. The darkness she had felt before was gone. She was both relieved and angry with herself for her earlier cowardice. Someone or something had been here, and she should have confronted whatever it was.

Even if it had meant having to leave San Francisco and go somewhere else to hide her identity.

I am not a witch, she reminded herself again as she stared around.

But a witch was here, and I let him or her get away.

Slowly she began walking the circular path, looking for anything out of the ordinary. There were a few dim lights on in the structure, just enough to see the path. She was crazy. It was too dark to find any clues. She would need to come back when it was daylight.

You could reach out, see what you can feel.

She rejected the voice that whispered inside her head.

No more magic. She stopped, ready to exit the exhibit and rejoin her partner.

Suddenly a whiff of something came to her. She turned her head slightly, closed her eyes, and inhaled deeply. There was definitely something in the air. Sandalwood, maybe? She walked a couple more steps into the rain forest and her foot came down on a leaf in the path.

She froze as her senses were suddenly bombarded, assaulting her, undeniable. The presence of magic was so strong, it nearly overwhelmed her.

She stepped back. There was something on the path. There had to be lights that could be turned on in the ecodome. She would just have to go get someone to help her find it. She took a step backward. That's what she'd do. She'd turn on the lights.

And suddenly she felt energy rippling through her body and then arcing out of her and into the structure.

"No!" she shouted.

Hissing and popping sounds surrounded her, and suddenly the lights nearby turned on.

"No," she whispered. "That's not what I wanted to do."

She'd wanted to find the light switch. Instead she had used magic to send currents flowing to the lights. And she was still connected to them. They would remain on only as long as she was sending out the energy.

Tears of frustration stung her eyes.

She dashed them quickly away, though, and turned to look at what was on the ground.

Leaves from the nearby trees had been ripped free and formed into words on the path.

The last grave.

She blinked. What could that possibly mean?

And then, as suddenly as she had turned the lights on, they winked off. She sagged, feeling the drain of the energy. It took a moment for her eyes to adjust again to the darkness. She bent down toward the leaves, thinking to scatter them before somebody else read the message.

Stop! What are you doing, Samantha?

She blinked as if coming out from under a trance.

Had she really been just about to destroy crime scene evidence?

She sucked in her breath as she straightened. Even if the killer was a witch, she shouldn't be destroying evidence, especially when she didn't know what it meant and it wouldn't require her to explain the realities of that world to her new partner.

"Idiot," she said to herself. "Just treat this like every other case. If you don't, you'll expose yourself and lose any chance to bring Winona's killer to justice."

A bird screeched by, and she couldn't tell whether the creature was agreeing with her or contradicting her. Either way, she knew it was time to leave the exhibit.

She hurried out and made her way back to the Swamp. Half a dozen more police personnel were there now. Lance appeared to have finished questioning the museum administrator and was crouched down by the body, talking to the coroner.

She moved to join them.

"Evening, Detective," Jada King said, looking up at her. The coroner's long black hair was perfect, as always. Her dark skin looked flawless, and there was even a dusting of eye shadow on her lids. Her fingernails were freshly manicured with French tips.

"How is it you look good even in the middle of the night?" Samantha asked.

"In case you haven't realized it yet, appearances mean everything in this big, bad world," Jada said, casting a disparaging glance at Samantha's attire.

Samantha flushed, realizing she'd walked into that

one. She had learned that Jada wasn't trying to be catty with comments like that. She just really believed in always being at her best. Which was ironic, since she saw people only at their worst.

"Anyway, I was just telling Detective Garris that I've never seen anything like this."

"So, any idea what could cause it?" Lance asked.

"No. This is a new one. I'm going to have to do some research, ask around, and find out if *anyone* has ever seen this."

Samantha was willing to bet the answer was going to be no. She had been raised a witch and she certainly couldn't remember seeing anything like this before. Of course, that didn't mean she hadn't. The holes in her memories of that life were still staggeringly large, the gaps in her knowledge numerous.

"Well, let us know when you have something," Lance said.

"Really? Because I was planning on keeping that information to myself."

"If we're done here, I found something else," Samantha said.

Lance nodded and stood up. "Lead the way."

Not sure where the museum employee had gone, Samantha borrowed a flashlight from Zack. She led both of them into the rain forest and then shone the light on the message.

"'The last grave'? What is that supposed to mean?" Lance asked after a second.

"It's probably a prank—kids, a disgruntled janitor," Zack chimed in.

"I don't think so. I thought I heard someone in here, but I couldn't find anybody. It would have been a great place for the killer to hide out while we were all busy in the Swamp," Samantha said.

"Okay. Zack, get the lights on in here. Grab a couple of guys and sweep this place. If there's even a remote chance our killer's still here, I want this place torn apart," Lance said.

Zack nodded and dashed off. Still using the flashlight, they looked around the area some more. "So, this is where you disappeared to?" Lance asked.

"Yeah."

"Mind telling me why?"

"I don't know. Hunch, I guess," Samantha said, striving to be vague.

Lance turned to look at her, and in the light from the flashlight he was holding, his face looked demonic. She forced herself to stand her ground, reminding herself it was only a trick of the light.

"What's the matter, spooked?" Lance asked.

"Something like that," she said.

The overhead lights flooded on, and she breathed a silent sigh of relief that it had nothing to do with her and that the darkness had been driven away. She helped Lance do a preliminary search of the area even though she knew they wouldn't find anything else.

She traced the paths through the rain forest. Had it been a witch hiding in here when she was here earlier? She was sure it had to be. But why leave the bizarre message on the ground, especially since it was nowhere near the body? Janitorial staff could have easily mistaken it for a joke and cleaned it up without the police ever seeing it.

She walked for another fifteen minutes, peering into dense copses of trees, but seeing nothing. When she returned to the beginning of the trail, she still had no idea why the message had been left with the leaves or what it meant. Some uniformed officers joined in the search, and a few minutes later she and Lance conferred.

"I think it's time we head out," Lance said.

"Agreed. I don't think there's anything else we can do here tonight. If the others find something, we can come back."

"You need to get some sleep?"

She shook her head. "We need to tell Winona's daughter what happened to her before she wakes up and realizes her mother isn't there."

"Worst part of the job."

"Always is."

They made it to Lance's car, and as soon as they were inside, he turned on her. "What the hell happened back there?"

"I don't know what you mean," she said, forcing herself to meet his eyes.

"Don't give me that. You froze up. You got a problem with Santa Cruz? Did the place personally offend you somehow? An ex live there? What?"

She took a deep breath. "A friend warned me that I wouldn't like it there."

"Because of all the hippies? They're harmless. Obnoxious, but harmless."

"No, I've just heard some unsavory things about other people . . . not hippies."

"Look, we're nowhere near Halloween, so there won't be a bunch of stupid college kids trying to perform satanic rituals and torturing cats."

"Are you kidding me?" she asked, revulsion flooding her.

"I wish. It's one of the reasons a lot of the local animal shelters won't adopt out black cats in the month of October. But like I said, none of that is going on for another nine months."

Her stomach turned, and she began to move her hands, then stopped herself just in time before she had conjured Freaky.

"But the fact that kind of stuff happens at all is enough to keep me from wanting to go there. Because those people might only be doing that stuff a couple of times a year, but they live there all the time."

"I know—it's sick. Like I said, mostly college kids, not the regular granola-eating, tree-hugging residents."

She didn't respond, and he seemed willing to drop the topic, which relieved her to no end. She couldn't help but wonder how many of those "college kids" were actually practicing real witchcraft and how many others were just jumping on the bandwagon. Some could even be the unwitting pawns of the real witches, who were using them and harnessing their energies.

Lance turned on the radio and classic rock filled the car. They left San Francisco and passed through neighboring towns and cities until they finally were in the mountains. The highway narrowed, and it seemed as if the trees were pressing in on either side. There were only a handful of other cars on the road and whole stretches where they saw no one.

"Where are we?" she asked at last.

"Santa Cruz Mountains. We're in the Redwoods."

A while farther on, they turned off the main road and climbed into the mountains. She caught glimpses of houses tucked away here and there.

"People here must love their privacy," she commented.

"You could say that again."

Finally, more than an hour after they'd left, they arrived at Winona Lightfoot's house. It was a beautiful cabin constructed in the Arts and Crafts style. The porch light was on, but the rest of the house was dark. They pulled into the driveway, and Samantha reluctantly climbed out of the car. She hated doing this, shattering someone's world. It was bad enough to lose a loved one to illness or accident, but to lose them to violence changed a person's view of the world forever.

The gravel on the walk crunched underfoot as they made their way to the porch. Three steps up and they were standing on a well-worn welcome mat, facing a heavy wood door inset with beveled glass.

Lance rang the doorbell. They waited a minute and then rang it again. Lights came on inside, and she could hear steps pounding toward the door. She heard the lock turn and a moment later a girl came into view.

The girl stood, blinking at both of them in surprise. Samantha could only stare back at her. She was about fifteen, very young looking, with long dark hair and wide, hazel eyes. And there was the thrum of power coming off of her. Samantha reached out and grabbed the doorframe to steady herself.

In turn, the girl looked at her, eyes wide with bewilderment.

"Who are you?" she asked after a moment.

They showed her their badges.

"Robin Lightfoot?" Lance asked.

The girl nodded.

"I'm Detective Garris and this is Detective Ryan. May we come in?"

The girl moved back, her face already turning ashen. They stepped inside the house, which was just as beautifully crafted as the outside. Native American pieces accented the walls and floors. Robin closed the door and led them into the kitchen, where she turned around, leaning against the counter with her arms folded across her chest.

"What's this about?" she asked, voice heavy with dread and suspicion.

Lance looked at Samantha, and she saw the pain on his face. She swallowed hard. He was a jerk a lot of the time, but no one wanted to break this kind of news to a kid.

Samantha looked Robin in the eye. "We are sorry, Robin, but something's happened to your mom."

"What?" Robin said, voice raising in a high squeak. "Is she . . . She's not—"

"She's dead, Robin," Lance said, his voice quiet.

The girl crumpled to the floor. Samantha dropped to

her knees and reached out, pulling the girl close. Robin leaned her head in to Samantha's chest and began to sob and scream. And even though she was struggling to shut out her sensory input, trying desperately not to use her powers and praying that Robin wouldn't inadvertently use hers, she could tell the girl was not surprised.

Usually there was that moment of shock, followed swiftly by denial, before a victim's family truly processed what you were saying to them. Robin had understood immediately, and there had to be a reason it hadn't come as a complete shock to her, even though the news was still devastating her.

"I can't believe they killed her!" Robin shrieked after a minute.

"Who killed her?" Lance said, and Samantha realized he was on the floor next to them. His eyes were wide with sympathy but, ever the cop, he was quick to try to gather information.

"Those people, the ones who sent her the letters," Robin wailed.

"Who sent her the letters?" Lance asked.

But Robin just started crying harder. She was clinging to Samantha so fiercely that the girl's nails were digging into her. The grief she was radiating washed over Samantha, smothering her, until all she could feel was the grief, fresh and harsh as though it were her own.

Samantha twisted her head just enough to glimpse Lance's face, and she could see the tears streaming down his cheeks. She would not have labeled him an empathic individual. Robin was radiating her grief, and it was so all-consuming and her powers were careening so wildly out of control that she was making them feel her emotions whether she intended to or not.

"You have to calm down," Samantha said, dropping her voice into its lowest register and willing it to penetrate the haze surrounding Robin's mind. It didn't work. If anything, Robin's grief was becoming wilder, more out of control. Next to her, Samantha heard Lance swear and slam his fist into a kitchen cabinet moments after Robin began pounding Samantha's back with her fists. Samantha fought back her own urge to hit something.

The girl was caught in a feedback loop of her own emotions, and she had trapped them with her. Words weren't breaking through to her no matter how much force and persuasion Samantha put behind them. Samantha took her left hand and focused her energies on it until she had built up an electrical charge. Then she put it on Robin's back, giving the girl a mild electrical shock.

Robin jerked and looked up at her, tears ceasing for the moment.

"You're going to be okay," Samantha said, seizing the opportunity to try to reach her. "Do you understand me?"

Robin nodded slowly. Samantha allowed energy to flow softly, subtly, from herself to the grieving girl. They couldn't have her collapsing on them. Not yet, at any rate.

The girl sighed and her eyelids drooped slightly.

"Now, is there a relative, a neighbor, someone you can call to come over and be with you?"

"I don't know," Robin said. Panic began to creep back into her eyes, and Samantha increased the sensations of warmth and calm that she was pushing through her own hands into the girl's arms.

"Where's your father?" she asked.

She shook her head. "He was killed in a car crash when I was little."

"Any aunts or uncles?" Samantha asked, keeping her voice level and steady.

"No. Mom was an only child. Dad too." Her eyes teared up again. "There's no one."

Samantha nodded. "It's okay. We'll help you think of someone."

Beside her, Lance was also reclaiming his senses. "Robin, who is it you think did this?" he asked, hastily rubbing his eyes on his sleeve.

"I don't know who they are, but I know Mom got some threatening letters and they really upset her."

"When was this?" Lance asked.

Robin shrugged. "I don't know. It was like a week or two ago. She tried to make out like it was no big deal, but I could tell they really upset her. I . . . um . . . made . . . her talk to me about it."

The girl flushed.

She used her powers to compel her mother to tell her, Samantha realized. *And now she feels guilty.*

That meant that Robin was aware of her abilities and could use them to a certain extent. The odds were good that her mother hadn't shared them or she should have been able to defend herself.

"What was in the letters exactly?" Lance asked.

"She wouldn't say. She just said she had made some people angry at her and they were threatening her with not nice things."

"Do you know who these people were?" Lance prodded.

"No. She wouldn't tell me, and she wouldn't let me look at them."

So, maybe not as much control of her abilities as she would like, if she couldn't get more out of her mom, Samantha thought.

"Do you know where she kept the letters?" Samantha asked.

"In her office, I think."

"Can you show us?" Lance asked.

Robin nodded and, with Samantha's help, stood up. She walked over to the sink and splashed some water on her face before patting it dry with a paper towel. When she turned around again, most of the ravages of grief had been wiped clean from her face. Her eyes were far more vacant than they had been earlier, though. Samantha wondered whether she had jolted the girl too hard.

Robin left the kitchen, and Samantha and Lance followed her. They walked toward the back of the house, passing the staircase to the second floor. The Native American artifacts scattered around were colorful, but Samantha noticed faint vibrations coming off a few items she was unfamiliar with. She wondered if they had been owned by magic practitioners and used in their rituals. In the very back, right corner of the house was a room walled off with French doors inset with more beveled glass.

Robin pushed the doors open, snapped on a light, and then stopped with a gasp.

Samantha looked around the girl and saw what she had seen.

The room had been ransacked. Papers were strewn all about. Books had been yanked off their shelves and dumped on the floor. Drawers had also been pulled out and upended, sending an assortment of paper clips, pens, and note cards all over the floor. The back of the desk chair was slashed, and paintings lay on the floor, some of them with broken glass.

"How did this happen?" Robin asked. "When?"

She turned frightened, confused eyes on Samantha. Samantha stared instead at the open window on the far side of the room.

"How heavy a sleeper are you, Robin?"

"Mom says getting me up is like trying to wake the ... dead," Robin said, her voice slurring slightly.

"You think someone did this tonight?" Lance asked.

Samantha moved toward the window. Her skin was tingling, and she could feel energy swirling through the room. Whoever had ransacked the room had actually used magic to do it. It made no sense. That would be a huge drain on a witch's energy, when they could have just as easily ripped the place apart with their bare hands.

She reached the window and put her hand on the casing. It was warm to the touch.

"As a matter of fact, I think whoever did this just left," Samantha said.

"What makes you think that?" she heard Lance ask.

She didn't answer. Instead she jumped through the window. Once outside, she flattened herself against the

wall as she strained eyes and ears to see and hear everything she could.

Someone had just left. She could feel it.

And as she reached out with her senses, she realized
that that particular someone was still nearby.

She plunged into the undergrowth before she could
change her mind. She had gone only half a dozen steps
when she heard a crashing sound followed by snapping
twigs to her left.

She was right; there *was* someone out there.

She angled her steps to the left and heard a low groaning sound followed by a higher-pitched whining sound.
The hair on the back of her neck raised on end, and she
glanced over her shoulder to see a huge tree crashing
down, coming right at her.

3

Samantha threw herself to the side, barely missing being crushed by the tree. It crashed to the ground. Branches whipped her face and body and knocked her off her feet. She could feel a hundred tiny cuts open up, and blood began to flow down her face into her eyes.

She shook her head as she staggered to her feet. She could hear Lance shouting. He sounded far away. Her ears were ringing slightly, and she spun in a slow circle, trying to reorient herself. She could see the lights of the house, the window she had exited through. The tree wasn't angled toward it, so Lance and Robin should be fine.

"Stay inside!" Samantha shouted, hating that she was giving away her exact location.

As soon as she said it, she moved, going farther into the woods. She could feel the power shimmering and rippling in the air in the aftermath of the falling tree.

It would have taken a lot of energy to fell that tree. She only prayed it had left the witch who did it weak enough to capture easily.

You can't catch a witch. All you can do is kill them. The voice was whispering inside her head. That had been true in Salem. She had known it going in. Getting a jury to convict a witch would be nearly impossible if they had their powers intact and were exerting their influence. And even if Samantha could sit in that courtroom for days or weeks, trying to counter the witch's influence, no jail cell could hold a witch.

I'll deal with that after I find him or her.

Samantha walked slowly, carefully, through the forest, wishing she'd brought her gun with her. She'd left it in the car, not wanting to introduce the weapon into the emotionally charged environment with the teenager who was finding out her mother was dead.

A wind sprang up, catching Samantha's hair and blowing it back from her face. Around her the trees and bushes moved and groaned. It would make it impossible to hear someone walking quietly.

"Why are you here?" a whispered voice sounded all around her.

Samantha turned quickly, looking for the source of the voice, but she could see no one.

"I'm here because someone killed Winona Light-foot," she answered, praying that it wasn't the woman's killer she was talking to.

"She had to die, but you don't have to," the voice whispered again. It was definitely coming from multiple directions, and this time Samantha could detect several layers to it, as though it were more than one voice speaking. "You can leave, but you must go now."

"Why did she have to die?" Samantha asked, then

moved swiftly to a new location. If the voice was coming from all around, hopefully that meant the witch didn't know exactly where she was. As long as she kept moving, made direction changes frequently, maybe she could find the witch before the witch could find her.

"We can still see you," the voices whispered.

Was it true or just a bluff?

Samantha unbuttoned the top two buttons of her shirt and pulled it to the side slightly so that the tattoo she'd had put on again a few months ago shone out in the moonlight. A dozen times she'd gone to have it removed and a dozen times she had stopped herself. She'd told herself she was being paranoid, that there would never be another need for her to identify herself as a witch, let alone a witch of that particular coven.

"We do not recognize this symbol."

They could see her. Samantha forced herself to stand her ground. She threw back her head and gathered energy in both of her hands as they hung at her sides, waiting for the moment when she'd have to use it.

"If you have not heard of this symbol, of my coven, then how can you call yourselves witches?" she asked, putting as much contempt into her voice as she could.

"We do not call ourselves witches," came the whispered answer.

A shiver danced up Samantha's spine. Something was wrong. There was something going on that she didn't understand. She breathed in slowly, trying to focus her energies.

"Why not?"

"Because we are not witches."

She turned, trying to catch a glimpse of the speakers but could still see no one. "Then what are you?" she demanded.

"Trees."

Suddenly something exploded upward out of the ground, writhing and twisting. *Roots,* she realized as they wrapped around her legs and yanked her off her feet. She fell on her back, cracking the ribs on her right side, where they landed on one of the roots.

Branches began to rain down on her, and she screamed as she brought up her arms to deflect them. The impact of the first two broke her arms. The third grazed her scalp, and everything went black for a moment. She kicked and screamed and tried to keep her arms in place.

Panic seared through her, outracing the pain. *The trees are alive!*

They were going to kill her. They had given her a chance to leave and she hadn't taken it.

She shook her head, trying to regain her vision. No, the trees might be attacking her, but it was done through magic. She had to fight it with magic.

She filled her hands with energy, struggling to think of what to do with it. More roots reached up, snagging her arms and pinning them to her sides. Leaves and twigs began to shower down on her face. She coughed and twisted her head to the side, trying to breathe, but the leaves kept coming, burying her head until she realized she was suffocating.

Her body spasmed, the built-up energy needing somewhere to go, someone to direct it. But her mind was flying apart, bursts of images and fragments of thought coming to her.

She could feel the energy building, revving her body higher and higher even as she was dying. Her hands were so hot, it felt like they were on fire.

Fire.

Fire!

The roots and leaves went up in flames.

Around her she could hear screams of terror and the crashing of more branches.

The flames burned hot, turning the roots, pinning her down to ash in a moment, singeing her own skin. She struggled to her feet, coughing and gasping for air. She held her hands ready, waiting for the next attack.

"Hey!"

She spun around, and a moment later white-hot fire exploded in her temple. She was knocked off her feet, and she lay on her back, feeling the blood pumping out of the wound even as the echo of an explosion faded away into the darkness.

She could hear more shouting, crashing of under-brush.

I've been shot, she realized.

"Don't move!" someone roared.

She looked up. Lance was standing over her, his gun aimed at her heart. His eyes were wide, dilated.

He doesn't see me. He thinks he's seeing someone else.

"Lance! It's Samantha!" she shrieked.

"Where is she?" he demanded. "If you've hurt her . . ."

And behind Lance, a woman appeared, dressed all in black. Before Samantha could shout a warning, the woman touched Lance's shoulder. A shudder passed through his body, and she stepped back, melting into the shadows.

"Samantha, is that you?" Lance asked, sounding bewildered.

"Yes," she said, her relief triumphing over her confusion.

"What happened to you?" he asked.

"You shot me," she ground out.

"What! No, I fired at someone else. It was this woman in black."

"Yeah, well, you might have been shooting at her, but you hit me."

He dropped down next to her. "Where did I get you?"

"Grazed my temple," she said.

She could already feel her body going to work, healing all the injuries. For most injuries witches had to actively heal themselves, but her injuries were so extensive that her body and subconscious had taken over. The bones in her arms were knitting back together, and the pain was overwhelming her.

"I'll call an ambulance," Lance said, leaping up.

"No!"

He turned to look at her.

"What?"

"I'm fine. Just give me a minute to catch my breath and then help me inside to clean up. It's just a scratch, and I really don't think either of us wants to deal with the officer-involved shooting reports and the investigation."

He swore under his breath. "Okay."

"Good. Now, like I said, give me a minute."

The ripples of energy had faded almost completely. It was quite possible the witch had left the area and what she was feeling now was actually Robin.

"So, did you get a good look at the woman in black?" Lance asked.

"No," she lied. "Did you?"

"Just a profile, but it was too dark to see any useful detail."

She wished she knew why the witch had lifted the spell on Lance and kept him from killing her.

You were warned, told that you had a chance to live. Maybe she was feeling generous.

"Time to get you up and take you inside?" Lance asked.

"Just about. Two more minutes," she said.

Finally she let him help her up, and they made it back to the house. Robin was waiting inside. Samantha could feel the terror coming off the girl, which only doubled when she saw the blood on Samantha.

"I'm okay. It's just a bunch of cuts and scrapes," Samantha said. "If you've got some bandages, I'll just borrow your bathroom and clean up."

"The intruder got away, but I don't like any of this," Lance growled.

"I called my great-aunt. She was my grandfather's sister. She's going to catch a flight out to come stay with me."

"Is there a neighbor you can call in the meantime?" Lance asked.

"Mrs. Braxton. She used to babysit me."

"Call her," Lance said.

Robin got Samantha some bandages and she headed

off to the bathroom to clean up. Inside the bathroom, she inspected the damage. Her shirt was filthy and torn in several places. The scratches that covered her face and arms were fading away. Hopefully, if she got all the blood off, she'd look better than she was.

A sudden knock at the door made her jump. "Yes?"

"I thought you might like a different shirt," Robin said.

Samantha opened the door and the girl handed her a black T-shirt with a shiny red rose on it. "Thank you. That was very thoughtful."

"You're welcome," Robin said, but she wouldn't meet her eyes. "What happened out there?"

Samantha hesitated, not sure how much she should actually tell the girl. "I chased the intruder. It was a woman. I lost her in the darkness. I tripped on some roots, fell pretty hard. Lance . . . fired a warning shot, but the woman gave him the slip too."

"What do you think she wanted?"

"I don't know. Maybe when you go through the office you'll be able to tell if anything is missing. That would help us tremendously."

"I'm not sure I'm going to be able to tell. She didn't talk a lot about work stuff."

"Anything you can come up with at all would be helpful. And if you find those letters you were talking about . . ." Samantha drifted off, realizing how much pressure she was putting on a girl who had just found out within the last hour that she'd lost her mother.

"I'll do whatever I can. I think she hid the letters somewhere."

Again Robin looked away, clearly not wanting to admit she'd been snooping around trying to find them before.

Samantha took a deep breath. There were other things they needed to discuss, but she didn't want to risk being overheard. Besides, she wasn't sure Robin could take any more at that moment. She looked so young and so fragile.

"Thanks for the T-shirt. I promise to return it in good condition."

Robin nodded. "Mrs. Braxton is coming over. She should be here any minute."

"Good. I'll be out as soon as I'm finished."

Robin left, and Samantha closed the door again behind her. She stripped off her shirt and washed up as best she could. By the time that she was done, even the scratches had faded. The wound from the bullet was down to just a small cut, and it ultimately required only one small bandage.

"Hardly the worse for wear," she muttered to her reflection.

She stood there for another minute, struggling to compose herself. She didn't want to leave Robin when there was a witch running around, but if the woman had wanted to hurt Robin, she would have done so when she was in the house. Hopefully, she'd gotten what she had come for and was far away by now.

Samantha tucked her ruined shirt under her arm and headed back out to the family room, where everyone was congregated. Mrs. Braxton was a motherly older woman who, despite the obvious shock she was in, was already making a fuss over Robin.

Lance looked up, and he visibly relaxed when he saw Samantha. "A little scratch—is that what all the fuss was about?"

She refrained from the urge to remind him that the little scratch had been his fault. Instead she just glared at him, hoping he got the message.

Samantha made sure that both Mrs. Braxton and Robin had her card. "Call for anything, no matter how trivial it seems," she urged.

When they walked outside to the car, the sun was rising.

"Going to be a beautiful day," Samantha muttered.

"Yeah, heck of a day to catch killers or sleep until sunset," Lance said.

She climbed into the car beside him. He looked as tired as she was. "It's been a long night," she commented.

"No doubt about that," he said, as he headed the car down the mountain. "Although I'm still confused about what happened in the woods."

"A trick of the light?" she suggested. She wanted to tease him with something sarcastic, but since she knew the truth and knew it had nothing to do with him, she held her tongue.

"Head okay?"

"Nothing that a giant bottle of aspirin couldn't fix."

"You think the kid's going to be all right?" he asked.

She bit her tongue on another sarcastic comment. "I think a lot depends on how the next few months go," she said.

"Yeah. That's a terrible thing, losing a parent like that. I'm going to give mine a call when I get home. You know, just to make sure they're still alive and batshit crazy."

Samantha couldn't help but laugh at that. He had been starting to sound so sentimental. She should have known he couldn't keep it up for more than a second or two.

"You going to check on yours?"

"My adoptive parents are in the middle of the ocean. Anniversary cruise. My birth parents are dead."

"Both?"

"Yeah."

"Sorry. I didn't know."

She shrugged. It was not the time for confidences such as the fact that her mother had been slaughtered, along with everyone else in her coven, while trying to raise a demon. *Everyone but me, that is.*

And her father . . . she still didn't even know what his name was or what had happened to him. Some days she thought about actually trying to find him, but she was worried that she wouldn't like what she found. And even if he was some nice, normal guy, how would he react to her popping up in his nice, normal life with the load of chaos that came with being her?

"Don't go all maudlin on me," he said.

"I think the guy who shot his partner in the head has no say in how I behave. At least not for the rest of the day."

He nodded. "Barely grazed the temple, remember? Hardly a scratch. But fair enough. Since the rest of our day is only going to consist of this car ride, I think I can agree to that."

"Good."

"But you got to admit that is the teeniest, tiniest little scrape in the world. I mean, you probably scratched yourself on a tree instead. For all we know, I might have actually wounded the cat burglar chick."

"Oh, trust me. I know the difference between a twig and a bullet," she said. "And you don't want me to start thinking too much about what happened out there, right?"

He swore, and she leaned back in her seat, smiling to herself.

She struggled to stay awake as they drove back. After a few minutes of silence, Lance put the rock station back on. Unfortunately, the driving beats felt like they were trying to drill through her skull. Lance must have noticed because he turned it off after a few minutes. She didn't want to jinx her good luck by thanking him for the consideration.

When they were a few blocks from her apartment building, he spoke up. "Shall we reconvene around five or so? Draft out a game plan?"

"Sounds like a good idea. Remember, though, you're going to still have to be nice to me."

"Nope. I agreed to be nice for the remainder of the day. Sun's down by then, officially making it night."

She groaned. "Seriously? You're going to play semantics with me?"

"Got no one else to play it with," he said, straight-faced.

She thought about hitting him, but despite the fact that her injuries were for the most part healed, she still ached everywhere, particularly her arms.

"Fine. After sundown you don't have to be nice anymore."

"That's better."

It was nearly nine in the morning when Lance dropped her off. She staggered into the apartment building and made it upstairs, dragging herself every foot of the way. When she finally got inside, Jill waved to her from the kitchen. She was poring over a stack of books at the kitchen table.

Jill was an archaeologist. She was finishing up her master's in anthropology at the university so she could eventually teach in her chosen field. A Bay Area native, she had taken a couple of years off between her undergraduate work in Boston and her graduate studies to work at various dig sites around the world.

Samantha waved back and headed down the hall to her room. Once inside, she put away her gun and badge and kicked off her shoes. She stared longingly at the bed but wanted to shower first.

Her phone rang and she grabbed it. It was Anthony. She wasn't ready to deal with him, but she needed someone to talk to, and who else was there, truly, who would be able to understand and maybe even help?

She answered the call.

"Hello?" she said. Was her voice shaking, or was it her imagination?

There was silence on the other end.

"Hello?" she asked again.

Still more silence. She pulled the phone away from her ear to see if the call had dropped, but they were still connected.

"Anthony, are you there?"

"Yes. I'm just shocked that you are."

"I'm sorry."

"Sorry for picking up, or sorry for all the times you didn't?"

"Both," she admitted.

She could hear him sigh heavily. "Well, at least that's something."

"Yeah, I guess so."

"How have you been?" he asked.

"Okay. It's strange here."

"San Francisco is its own kind of weird, that's for sure."

"How is Salem?"

"Back to its same old sleepy self. And I'm fine, by the way."

She winced. "Glad to hear it."

"So, why did you answer?" he asked.

She cleared her throat and fingered her cross. "I had a rough night. I had to tell a young girl her mother had been murdered."

"I'm sorry," he said, his voice suddenly sympathetic.

Of course, Anthony could relate. Doubtless it had been some policeman who'd told him the same thing when he was a child. Having your mother murdered by witches didn't lead to a happy life. She just hoped that Robin would have a better time of it than Anthony had.

"And the weirdness here just got a whole lot weirder."

"How much weirder?" he asked.

"Salem kind of weirder."

There was a long pause and then Anthony said, "That's not good."

"No. No, it isn't."

It felt good to talk to somebody she could actually confide in, someone who knew her, knew who she was, who she used to be. She closed her eyes and wished that he were there. She just wanted someone to hold her and tell her everything was going to be okay.

It was so crazy. She was pretty sure it was one of the only universally female things, that need to be held and told things were going to be okay. Even if it was a lie, it was good to hear those words when you were stressed out of your mind.

Of course, if it weren't for her being an idiot, Anthony might actually be here to do that very thing. There was amazing chemistry between them, but the history and the baggage of it were staggering. How did you have a relationship with a man when you knew he'd been hunting you for years, blaming you because you were part of the coven that sacrificed his mother?

She hadn't yet been able to move beyond that, and despite whatever he might say, she knew that Anthony hadn't either.

"So, you want to tell me about it?" he asked. "Is there anything I can do to help?"

"I've got a question for you. Have you ever heard of a body being petrified? Like literally?"

"Like wood petrification?" he asked.

"Yeah."

"No. I think I would have remembered that. I could do some research, though, if that would help."

It would, but she was even loathe to accept his help in doing that. She didn't want to see him get hurt. He had already been in the line of fire with her once before. Plus, she was afraid of breaking his heart. What if she could never really recover from everything that had happened to her, to them?

But then the part of her that was a cop took over. "Yes, please, that would be great. I need all the help I can get on this one."

"Anyone out there you can actually talk to about what's happening?"

"No."

"Well, I'm happy to do whatever I can, help you think through it, whatever."

"I appreciate that," she said.

"Anything I can do to make your job easier, let me."

"That's very kind of you."

"It's not kind; it's entirely selfish."

"You're not selfish at all," she protested. In fact, he had been nothing but unselfish and patient during this entire process. She was sorry she'd been ducking his calls for so long. It was just that she didn't know what she wanted from him and she didn't feel it fair to lead him on.

"You know, Samantha, I—"

She panicked as her mind raced ahead to what he might be about to say.

Suddenly Samantha heard a slamming sound and the earth began to shake.

4

Samantha stood for a moment, phone in hand and senses reeling. It wasn't just the floor; the entire room was shaking

Her panicked thoughts latched on to an explanation. *Witches! They've found me. They've come for me. They—*

"Earthquake!" Jill shouted.

Samantha threw open her door and stood in the doorway. Across the hall, Jill was doing the same, a grimace twisting her lips. Fear squeezed Samantha's chest. She had made the ground shake before and had witnessed other witches doing it as well. But this was totally different. This was wild and uncontrolled, Mother Nature showing humanity that she was still in charge despite its own lofty achievements.

The building was swaying; she could feel it. Jill must have read the panic in her eyes.

"The building is supposed to move," she said.

"Samantha, what's wrong?" She could hear Anthony through the phone.

And just as suddenly as it had started, it stopped.

Samantha slid to a sitting position in her doorway. "Earthquake. Everything's fine, but I have to call you back," she said to Anthony.

"Are you sure?"

"Yes. I promise."

She hung up and rested her head in her hands for a few moments.

"Your first earthquake, huh?"

"Yes."

"It was longer than most, but not too hard. Shaker, not a roller."

Samantha glanced up, and a retort froze on her lips.

Jill's hair was brown.

"You okay? It really rattled you, didn't it?" Jill asked, suddenly sounding sympathetic.

"Weren't you blond a couple of hours ago?"

Jill's eyes widened. "Blond? You have to be kidding. It's hard enough to get taken seriously as a woman without being blond. Nope. All natural—that's me." Jill crossed her arms over her chest and leaned against the doorframe she was still standing in.

And without meaning to, Samantha reached out, instinctively trying to sense if there was magic involved, a glamour, mind control, something. But it was still Jill and she was being sincere and Samantha didn't sense magic around her.

She closed her eyes again and leaned her head back against the doorframe. *This is what going insane feels like.*

"What's wrong?" Jill asked.

"Tough night."

"A homicide?"

"Yeah."

Jill paused a moment before asking, "Do you want to talk about it?"

Samantha thought for a moment. Jill rarely asked, respecting the necessarily secretive nature of Samantha's investigations. Given the victim and the location of the body, that information would at least be spread around by local press within a couple of hours, if it wasn't already on the news.

"A woman was killed. We had to break the news to her teenage daughter."

"That's terrible," Jill said. "I can't even imagine how you begin to deal with something like that."

Samantha opened her eyes and forced a smile. "Yeah, all the dead bodies you have to deal with are centuries old and there's no one to mourn them."

"That's why I'm an archaeologist and not a crime scene investigator."

"I've got to get a couple of hours' sleep before getting back on the case," Samantha admitted. Just the thought of trying to talk to Anthony about anything suddenly seemed overwhelming. "What's your day like?"

"I've got a meeting this morning with a woman. Part of the research for my thesis."

Jill was getting her master's in anthropology, and she was doing her thesis on the mission era in California and the effect of the Spanish settlements on the native populations, particularly relating to changes in religion and mythology. Jill was serious about her studies and had learned a couple of the oldest dialects spoken in the area as part of her program.

"Anyone interesting?"

"A friend of the family's. Colorful. She's a historian and a local celebrity. She knows a lot about the ancient lore of the area."

Alarm bells were suddenly going off in Samantha's head, and she sat up straight, spinning to fully face Jill.

"What's wrong?" Jill asked.

"You're not going to see Winona Lightfoot, by any chance?"

"Yes. Do you know her?"

Not again. Not twice in one night. Not when I'm so tired I just want to pass out here in the hallway.

"Jill, you might want to sit down here with me," Samantha said, patting the carpet.

"Why? What's going on?" Jill asked.

And her face slowly drained of color, because deep down, she already knew the answer. Samantha could see the flicker of comprehension in her eyes, followed immediately by dread.

"Winona was the one killed last night."

Jill pressed a hand to her mouth as her eyes widened even more. "No, that's not possible!"

"I'm afraid it is. Her body was found at the Natural History Museum."

Slowly, Jill slid down onto the floor next to her. "But I'm supposed to meet her today. She can't be dead."

"She is. That was the call I went out for last night."

Jill looked at her sharply. "Wait, what? The call you got? That's not possible."

"What makes you say that?"

"After you left, I was too wired to go back to sleep. I checked my phone and saw that Winona had texted me, asking if we could meet in the morning instead of the afternoon like we'd originally planned."

"What time did she text you?" Samantha asked, suddenly very alert.

"It hadn't been that long. I texted back agreeing, asking what time. And—"

Jill broke off and looked like she was about to start hyperventilating. Her cheeks had lost all color, and she was taking fast, shallow breaths.

Samantha grabbed her hand. "And what?"

"She sent me another text after that saying ten thirty."

"Jill, where's your phone?" Samantha asked, jumping to her feet.

"On the kitchen table next to my purse."

Seconds later, Samantha had the phone and was staring at the string of messages.

Jill joined her shortly. "What does it mean?" she asked.

"We didn't find Winona's phone at the crime scene. And these texts were sent after she was killed."

"What are you saying?"

"I'm saying that whoever was texting you, it wasn't Winona. It was probably her killer."

"Oh my—why? Why would someone do that?"

Jill's voice had risen an octave and she was going into a full-fledged panic. *So much for only dealing with centuries' old bodies.*

Maybe to kill you too, Samantha thought. She kept it

to herself, though, not wanting to frighten Jill more than she had to at the moment.

"I don't know, but I'm going to help you figure it out. And you could help us solve her murder."

Jill sat down at the kitchen table, and Samantha walked over to the fridge and got them both some orange juice. She set Jill's glass down in front of her and saw that tears were shimmering in her eyes.

"You got anything strong to put in it?" Jill asked, nodding toward the juice.

"Not right now. I need you alert and sharp. Can you do that for me?"

Jill nodded. "I'll try."

"Okay. I've just got to make a quick phone call and then we're going to talk about your meeting with Winona."

Samantha headed back to her room and then realized she was still clutching her own phone in her left hand. She called Lance and, a moment later, he answered.

"You better have a good excuse for calling me."

"I think the killer has Winona's phone. Someone texted my roommate, Jill, with it after she was already dead."

"Jill. Remind me—cute, petite brunette, yeah?"

"Yeah," Samantha said, shaking her head silently. Lance remembered her as a brunette and not a blonde. She must just be slipping.

"So, what's your gal pal got to do with the corpse? If the words 'pillow fight' aren't part of your answer, I'm hanging up and going back to bed."

"Stop being an ass," Samantha snapped.

"You know me—I'm proud to be an Ass—"

"Shut up! Okay, listen. Jill was set to interview Winona this afternoon as part of her master's thesis. Whoever has Winona's phone changed the meeting time from this afternoon to this morning—ten thirty, to be exact."

"That gives us, what, less than two hours? Okay, I'm awake."

"Good. See if we can track that phone. I'll text you the number. I'm going to talk to Jill again."

"And let's see just who shows up to this meeting," Lance said. "And what they want with Jill. Maybe it's something the two women were researching?"

"I don't know, but hopefully we'll find out. Unlike with Winona, the murderer seems to have picked a more public place, so hopefully they won't be trying to kill Jill."

"All right. I'll call as soon as I have something. But for the record, I think you're just trying to take advantage of my daylight agreement."

"You'll never know," Samantha couldn't resist firing back at him.

Hanging up with him, she turned and made her way back to the kitchen. Jill had her head down on the table and her shoulders were shaking. Samantha sat down next to her and rubbed her back.

"It's going to be okay."

"No, it's not. You're not the one who has to tell my mother that her friend is dead."

Samantha bit her lip. "If you need me to, I can. I have to do this kind of thing all the time."

"I can't even imagine."

"Look, we can talk about all this later, I promise. But right now I need to know what you were going to be talking to Winona about."

"Local legends and history, mostly. I just wanted to pick her brain. I attended a series of lectures she gave at the university about religion and folklore in the pre-mission days. We exchanged contact information, and I reached out to her because I wanted to use her as a resource while completing my thesis. She's Miwok, but she knows a lot about all the coastal tribes as well as the Sacramento-area tribes. She specialized in the mission time period, like I am, but she knows a lot about precontact culture as well." Jill paused. "Knew, rather. It's hard to think about her in the past tense."

"It always takes an adjustment," Samantha said. "So, had you already met with her about your thesis?"

"No. We'd just exchanged a phone call or two, a handful of texts. Today was supposed to be our first meeting."

"Can you think of any reason why anyone would want her dead?"

"She was an outspoken advocate for cultural preservation. Sometimes that leads to head-butting with land owners and developers. I don't know, though. She was very well respected in the community. She was viewed as a real leader, a force to be reckoned with, but a real person who could see both sides of a story and chose her side carefully."

None of that would explain why a witch had killed her. Samantha sipped her orange juice. She thought about the petrification and wondered if that had a special significance. The only thing she could come up with was deforestation and that didn't really help her any.

"I'm sorry I'm not more help," Jill said.

"Do you want to help catch her killer?"

"Yes," Jill said fervently.

"Good, because I have a way that you can."

"What can I do?"

"I want you to go to that meeting, pretend as if you didn't know Winona was dead. We'll have police all over the area. Then, if the killer shows up, we can grab them."

"Oh," Jill said, her voice trembling a little. "That sounds dangerous."

With a witch on the loose and possibly wanting something from her, it was far more dangerous than Jill guessed. But Samantha forced a smile as she lied to Jill's face. "You'll be perfectly safe. I promise."

And even though Jill should have known better, realized that Samantha couldn't possibly promise that, she started nodding.

Samantha curled her hands into fists on the table, wondering if somehow she had persuaded Jill with more than just words.

She didn't want to think about it. She was too tired and there was a killer to catch.

No rest for the wicked.

The two women were supposed to meet at a Starbucks. Given how many Starbucks there were in the city, it was a total joke. There was one intersection downtown that had Starbucks on three of its four corners. At least this particular Starbucks was alone at its intersection. Samantha and Lance were outside the coffee shop. There was a chance the killer would see them and recognize them from the museum or outside Winona's house, and they couldn't risk blowing the whole thing.

Two cops in plain clothes were parked inside the coffee shop, having settled in a good half hour before Jill arrived.

Jill was nervous. Samantha didn't have to have special powers to be able to tell that. Her roommate was telegraphing fear in her body language as she walked into the shop.

"This isn't going to work," Samantha hissed to Lance.

"Sure it will," he said back.

She shook her head. The killer was going to be able to tell something was wrong the moment they stepped foot inside the shop. Samantha didn't dare get closer, though, for fear that the killer would sense her and not even get that far. She needed whoever it was to at least get close to Jill before she could easily convince her fellow officers that they had found their man or woman.

You could persuade them.

She rolled her shoulders, trying to ignore the nagging voice inside her head. For three months it had been with her, tempting her, urging her to use her powers. She was doing her best to ignore it, but she wished it would shut up and leave her alone.

"I just want to get on with my life."

"What?" Lance asked, turning to look at her quizzically.

"Nothing," she muttered, mentally upbraiding herself for speaking her thoughts out loud. She was getting sloppy.

"You think the woman in black is going to show?"

"You think the one who tossed Winona's office was the one who killed her?"

"Stands to reason," Lance said.

It did, but there was something bugging Samantha about the whole thing. She couldn't say what it was, but she wasn't completely convinced that the witch who had killed Winona was the same one who had saved her from being shot by her own partner. She felt like she was missing huge pieces of the puzzle, and without them she couldn't even get a proper idea of what kind of puzzle she was working on.

"Hey, you awake?" Lance asked, elbowing her.

She turned to look where he was pointing. A guy in a dark jacket and pants was walking toward the coffee shop, stopping to look over his shoulder every few feet. "You think that's our guy?" she asked. "I thought your money was on the burglar."

"It was, but this changes things. Get ready to move."

"Why? Who is he?"

"Name's Marcos. We had him on a murder charge last year, but the DA couldn't make it stick."

"So?"

"So, he was into black-market antiquities. Stuff that might get the attention of, say, a cultural historian."

"Okay, so it's possible Winona had a run-in with this guy."

"If he takes one more step, I'm moving that from possible to probable," Lance said.

Samantha watched as Marcos walked into the Starbucks. Lance jumped to his feet, pacing closer, and Samantha followed him.

A moment later, the door burst open and Marcos came sprinting out. Two officers were on his heels.

"Police, freeze!" Lance shouted, pulling his gun.

Marcos pulled one of his own and fired at them before taking off up the street. Bystanders scattered, running in every direction. She saw someone fall and couldn't tell whether they'd been shot or just knocked down. The other officers ran to the victim. Lance took off after Marcos and, after a moment, so did Samantha. They went up two blocks, and then Marcos ran into an alley.

Samantha heard more shots fired as she reached the corner, and she dropped down low as she raced in. Her foot kicked a can, and Lance spun around, aiming his gun at her.

"Whoa, whoa!" she shouted.

He scowled and then swung back toward the alley. Marcos was nowhere to be seen. Samantha moved cautiously, making sure to stay behind Lance. She looked up at the sides of the buildings on either side but didn't see any fire escapes that he might have used.

"He's got to be here somewhere. He probably went inside one of these doors," Lance said.

That seemed likely, but Samantha didn't relish the thought of poking her head through the doors just to get it shot at again. Plus, she had gotten close enough to Marcos to sense whether he had any power, and he didn't.

"Look, I'm not sure he's our guy. He's not a wi—" She ground to a halt, cursing herself silently.

"Not a what?" Lance asked.

"Maybe not Winona's killer. If he was, based on this display, wouldn't he have just shot her?"

"He didn't shoot his former partner either. We're just special."

"Not in any way I'd ever want to be special," she retorted, eyeing the door closest to her.

Lance wasn't going to let it go; she could feel it. She hesitated for a moment, tempted to reach out and persuade him to give up the hunt. Now that they knew Marcos was potentially involved, they could get every cop in the city on the hunt. But something still didn't feel right.

"Let's go in," Lance said, moving toward a door on his right.

Samantha reached out and touched the door she was standing in front of. If they were going to do this, they might as well do it right. "No, let's try this one," she said.

Lance turned to look at her. Given his years in the city, she usually let him make those kinds of decisions, so she knew she had his attention now. "Let's just say I got a feeling."

He nodded and moved over next to her. She grabbed the handle, did a silent count, and yanked it open. Lance stormed inside, and she followed moments later. They were in some sort of warehouse. She swept the place with her eyes. Some light came in from filthy windows up on the second floor. There was a catwalk that went around.

"I'll take high ground; you take low," she said, as she

moved toward a narrow metal staircase. She didn't trust Lance to be above her at this point. He was too keyed up. Lack of sleep was combining with his normal aggression to create poor judgment. It didn't help either that he clearly still had a beef with this guy.

The stairs groaned under her weight, betraying any hope she had of stealth. *You could make yourself silent. You could make yourself invisible. Catch a killer and stay safe.*

The voice that was whispering in her mind sounded so logical, so practical. They were both tired. Mistakes could happen; people could get hurt so easily. *Why not use all the tools at your disposal?*

She bit her lip, torn. Then she swiftly made a decision. She'd used magic on this case more than once already and probably would have to a dozen times more before it was over. And this really was more defensive magic than anything else.

She pictured Marcos in her mind, running, hiding. For best results, she should have had a candle or some other object she could have used to symbolize him. Without anything she could use, visualization would have to do. She just hoped it would do the job well enough.

I bind you, Marcos, from seeing me or hearing me until such time I release you.

She felt the energy sweep out of her. Her left hand was wrapped around the banister of the stairs and she could feel the energy rushing along the metal, moving to all parts of the warehouse. If he was inside, it should reach him at some point. She'd just have to go slow and careful for a few moments.

When she finally made it to the top of the stairs, she began to breathe easier. She looked down and could see Lance moving toward the back of the warehouse, weapon constantly moving, like the needle of a compass seeking north.

She looked around at where she was. The catwalk rimmed the building and crossed it twice. Toward the front of the building, it was deeper and there appeared to be an office of some sort. She walked that way, holding her gun at the ready. She had a strong urge to put it away, to use only her magic on him. Marcos had a gun of his own, though, and if she had to kill him, death by bullet was going to be a much easier report than death by head implosion.

She blinked at how bizarre that sounded, even to her. *I really do need to get some sleep too.*

She continued to walk, bolder now. The binding energy she had sent out should have reached Marcos by now.

Finally, she was at the office. An old sign on the door read SHIFT SUPERVISOR. She peered in through the window, which had shards of broken glass still in the sill.

Marcos was crouched down, his hands pressed to his head, rocking back and forth. Guilt, fear? She couldn't quite tell. The signals he was sending out were a mishmash, almost gibberish.

Maybe he's on something.

If he was, she was doubly glad she'd cast the spell. She turned and looked down at the ground floor. Lance was out of sight. Not good. She didn't have time to worry about that, though. Now she just had to time things right.

I'll take his gun away from him before I release him

from the spell. Of course, even that was going to be tricky with the way he had positioned himself. He might not hear the door open because it was being caused by her, but he would most certainly see it open. If he shot wildly at what he thought was air, he still might hit her.

Going through the window was out of the question because of the shards of broken glass. Somewhere in the distance she heard a squeaking sound.

Maybe if I knock the gun out of his hand from here.

That seemed the safest way to do it. She readied herself. A hand descended on her shoulder, and she jerked, startled, and turned with a shout. Thankfully, Marcos didn't hear her.

Lance backpedaled, slamming into the railing of the catwalk. She winced, knowing that Marcos most certainly heard that.

The door flew open and Marcos charged out. Samantha kicked the gun out of his hand, and it went tumbling to the floor below. He turned with a scream, unable to see her.

"Who's there?" he shouted. He tried to run, but he collided with Samantha, and they both toppled to the ground. Her gun went skidding across the catwalk.

"What's happening?" he screamed.

"I release you," Samantha hissed.

She knew what it had to look like to him. One moment he was staring at air, and the next a woman appeared.

He screamed and threw himself backward. His hand came down on Samantha's gun and two shots rang out.

Samantha froze and watched as blood spread across

the front of Marcos's jacket. He too looked down at it and then up at her.

She grabbed her gun and tossed it toward Lance, then eased Marcos back down onto the metal of the catwalk. "Did you kill Winona?"

"Are you an angel?"

"No, but you need to tell me if you killed Winona."

"No."

"Then why were you at the coffee shop?" she asked.

"Someone paid me to go get something from a lady. Cops saw me and I ran."

He started to convulse. He was slipping away, and there was no way for her to save him. "Who? What did they want?"

But it was too late. He was gone.

Lance handed Samantha her gun, and she tucked it back into her waistband. Lance reached down and pulled something turquoise colored out of the pocket of Marcos's pants. A cell.

He looked at it for a moment. "It's got the texts to Jill. This is Winona's phone."

"But he didn't kill Winona. So how did he get her phone?"

"The killer must have given it to him."

Her exhausted mind was working overtime to try to catch up and process everything that had just happened. "He said someone wanted him to get something from the lady."

"It makes sense. If you had killed someone, you'd want to lie low too, hire someone else to get what you needed."

"Yeah, but if the goal is to get the information and you're afraid it might be a trap, why hire somebody the cops are likely to recognize on sight?" she asked.

The answer hit her and drove her to her feet. She could see the same thought come to Lance.

"It's a diversion," he said.

"She wanted us to chase him so she'd have Jill to herself."

She raced toward the stairs. Jill was a sitting duck.

5

Samantha raced down the stairs and outside the building. She headed for the Starbucks, where her roommate was sitting, alone and unprotected.

Idiot! You should have seen this coming.

The two police officers who had been inside the café were dealing with some injured bystanders. Fortunately it didn't look like anything too bad. They all seemed to be in much better shape than Marcos. She kept expecting to feel a surge of energy, proof that another with powers was nearby. There was nothing.

As she ran into the coffee shop, she suddenly saw why. The witch wasn't here because she had called Jill to her instead. Her roommate was gone.

Samantha blinked and then grabbed one of the patrons who was staring through the window at the chaos outside.

"You," she said, shaking his arm.

He jerked and looked up at her. "What?"

"There was a woman sitting in here, brunette, she was at that table," she said, pointing. "Where did she go?"

"I don't know. Her friend came in and then they left together."

"Her friend?"

"Yeah, this smoking-hot chick with blond hair. She was dressed all in black."

"Did you see which way they went?"

"No."

Samantha turned and scanned the other people in the coffee shop. They all had their eyes glued on the events outside. None of them were going to be able to tell her what she needed to know. She walked back to the door and reached out and touched it. She could feel a lingering impression of Jill. Her roommate had been the last person to touch the door.

But beyond that Samantha couldn't feel anything, no emotions. *She probably has her under mind control. That's what I'd do.*

Samantha jerked, angry at the turn of her own thoughts. She walked outside and looked around. They could have walked by all those people in the street and the police officers and no one would have suspected anything amiss if she had done it right.

But why risk it when there are other ways they could have gone?

Samantha turned and began to walk down the street. She reached out, trying to sense her roommate or the witch. There was the faintest impression of them on the sidewalk, almost like a perfume that lingered long after its wearer left the room.

Confident now that she was going in the right direction, Samantha picked up her pace. She moved from a walk to a jog. The impressions became stronger, and she moved faster.

She slowed as she neared a corner and then made a sharp left. There was a park a few blocks up, and she burst into a run, sure that was where the witch was taking Jill. There would be people there, so they wouldn't seem out of place, and it was a good location for her to recharge her batteries quickly by connecting to the energy of the earth. It was easier to gather energy from dirt and rocks and trees than from cement and asphalt.

Samantha's mind raced ahead of her. She could be wrong. The witch might have taken Jill somewhere else entirely. Part of her urged caution, to slow down and follow the trail. Time was her enemy, though. The longer Jill was with the witch, the greater the likelihood that she would lose them, or that if she did find Jill, she would be dead.

She saw the park and put on a fresh burst of speed. She had no idea how she was going to best the witch, or even how she was going to hide the battle from the bystanders in the park. None of that mattered, though, if she didn't get there in time.

A moment later, she was in the park. She didn't even need to look to see if her quarry was there. She could feel the energy rippling through the air, calling to her like a beacon. She slowed slightly, aware that she was drawing unwanted attention. A moment later, though, the energy started to ebb.

No!

She picked up speed again and ran, cutting across the park. She ran until she lost the feeling altogether and then she came to a stop. The witch was faster than she was. She reached out her senses, trying to feel which direction to go next.

Tears of frustration welled in her eyes. If something happened before she could reach them she—

"Samantha? Where are we?"

Samantha spun and stared at the woman sitting on the park bench looking bewildered. It was Jill. Samantha threw her arms around her. "You're okay? You're safe?"

Jill hugged her back. "Yeah, but what's happening? I thought I was in the coffee shop."

Samantha pulled back so she could look Jill in the eyes. She saw no guile there, just honest confusion. Samantha sat down on the bench next to her. "It's a long story."

"Okay."

Samantha took a deep breath. What should she tell Jill? Hypnotism? She might believe it, but then she'd tell the other officers that and things could start to get sticky. Samantha wiped a hand across her forehead. She was sweating profusely. She gazed out over the grass, knowing that the witch's trail was growing colder by the second.

"What is it?"

Samantha sighed. She'd have to let the witch go, for now. She just prayed that when they met next, it would be on her terms. "It's a very . . . complicated story. I need you to trust me for a little while though. I swear I'll tell you the truth."

Maybe. Probably not.

Samantha continued. "But you need to trust me that only you and I can know the truth. When the other police ask why you left the Starbucks, I need you to tell them that you got a call. It was garbled, but it was a woman's voice telling you that because of the shooting you needed to meet me in this park."

I'll pretend one of the patrons—don't know who he was and he's gone now—overheard her say park and that's how I knew to find her here. It could work.

"And what happened when I got here?" Jill asked.

"You sat down and waited and no one talked to you before I got here."

"Okay." Jill looked at her hesitantly, and Samantha could see the uncertainty in her eyes. She knew she was asking the other woman to trust a lot, but there was just enough history between them that she could feel Jill was willing to do it. Jill cleared her throat quietly. "Is that what really happened?"

"Close enough for now. Ready?"

Jill nodded. They stood and headed back to the Starbucks.

When they got there, she noticed that Lance looked more stressed out than she had ever seen him. "Where have you two been?" he exploded.

Jill glanced at Samantha and then parroted what she'd told her to say.

Lance turned to Samantha. "And you didn't see anyone there?"

She shook her head. "I figured once I was there, she probably saw me and there was no use sticking around any longer."

He nodded and turned back to Jill. "Let me see your phone."

As she handed it over, Samantha's heart flew into her throat. How could she have been so stupid to have not thought about this part?

Think! How do you fix this?

Lance tapped the phone and a moment later grumbled, "Unknown number. Great."

Samantha grabbed the phone from him and stared at it. Sure enough, it said Jill had received a call from an unknown number at the right time. She stared at her roommate, struggling to understand. Jill shrugged almost imperceptibly.

Lance looked at the scene on the streets. An ambulance was present now. Two people were being loaded on stretchers. "One grazed by a bullet, one knocked down in the panic and broke an arm," Lance said before she could ask. "Unfortunately, the other officers here were busy with that and missed what was happening with Jill."

Lance's phone rang and he answered it. He took a few steps away. Samantha turned and looked at Jill, still wondering how on earth that missed call had shown up. A minute later, Lance hung up and signaled to her. She gripped Jill's shoulder and then moved over to confer with her partner.

"Well, at least we've got something."

"What?" she asked.

"Robin called. She found one of the letters threatening her mother. I said either you or I would drive down and get it."

"I'll go get the letter from her," Samantha volunteered.

"Are you sure? You don't want to take your room-mate home?"

Samantha hesitated. She couldn't pass up the chance to talk to Robin alone. "Can you do that for me? I just think I need the drive, clear my head a bit."

"Understood. I'll take her home now. I'll arrange for a car to be outside the building for the next couple of days. Given what our killer did today to try to talk to Jill, we can't be too careful."

"Thanks," she said.

She wished she could tell him that their killer might have already gotten whatever she needed from Jill, and if not, a patrol car wouldn't be able to stop her.

She turned. "Jill."

"Yes?"

"Lance is going to take you home. I have to go pick up some evidence. I'll be home as soon as I can. Okay?"

"Okay."

She turned back to Lance. "Now, take her straight home. And don't do anything I wouldn't . . . Just be care-ful, okay?"

He raised an eyebrow, and she glowered at him.

"You've got trust issues," Lance noted.

"You ever stop to think you might be part of those issues?"

He shrugged. "I just call it like I see it. Not my job to diagnose cause. See the shrink for that."

She just shook her head and turned away. She didn't have time to bandy words with him. She needed to get down to Santa Cruz. She was glad she had driven her own car over. She wished she could return Robin's shirt, but it was in the laundry at home. If she stopped to get it, Lance would wonder why she hadn't taken Jill home herself.

She wasn't ready to talk to Robin yet. She still wasn't even sure what she was going to say to her. At least she'd have some time in the car to think about it.

And to wonder about the call on Jill's phone.

Nothing about the day had gone well, and she was beyond exhausted. Yet the two different chases she'd been on had her completely keyed up. She could feel the adrenaline still rushing through her body. When it died down, she was going to crash hard. She would have been happy to let Lance deal with the letter if she hadn't needed to talk to Robin alone.

It sucked trying to do a secret investigation inside a public one. She thought of Ed. At least when everything had gone wrong in Boston, she'd been able to tell him what she was doing and why. She didn't picture herself doing that with Lance.

But she was going to have to come up with a better plan about how to handle the witchy aspects of this case. In some ways, she felt like she was in denial about the whole thing.

She fought the urge to check in with Jada. The coroner would call the moment she had anything, even if it was just speculation. There was nothing she could do right now but try to think and focus on getting back home in one piece. *Today needs to end soon,* she thought, even though she knew it wouldn't.

Samantha didn't know what she'd have done without the GPS device she'd bought for her car before moving to

San Francisco. The sheer number of one-way streets in the city alone were staggering, and fortunately her GPS hadn't sent her down the wrong way yet.

Now it was guiding her back to Robin Lightfoot's house, which she was fairly certain she would have had problems finding without it. At last she was finally parking in front of the girl's house. She just hoped she was catching her at home alone.

When she stepped out of the car, she could feel the slight hum of energy in the air. She was becoming more attuned to the presence of others like her again. When she knocked, Robin opened the door instantly.

"Hi, Robin. Mind if I come in?"

Robin shook her head and stepped aside.

"Is Mrs. Braxton here?" Samantha asked as Robin closed the door behind her.

"No. She went to pick up my great-aunt at the airport. She just left a few minutes ago."

Which meant they had some time to talk. Samantha relaxed slightly.

"Did you find out anything?" Robin asked, her voice tentative.

"Not yet, but we'll let you know as soon as we do," Samantha said.

Robin walked into the family room and sat down on the couch. Samantha took a seat on the chair across from her. Robin pointed to a large envelope on the coffee table. "That's the letter," she said.

Samantha had brought in a pair of gloves with her, and she carefully slid out the letter and read it. It seemed like a pretty straightforward hate letter, spewing vitriol and bile and claiming that Winona had betrayed her cultural heritage. It was unsigned. Hopefully the lab could get something off of it. When she was finished reading it, Samantha returned the letter to the envelope, which she noted was blank.

"Is this what you found it in?" Samantha asked.

Robin nodded.

"Do you know what your mom was working on the last few weeks?"

Robin shook her head, clearly uncomfortable.

"Did you ever hear anyone accuse her of anything? Say she was a traitor or she was violating cultural heritage?"

"Never. I can't even imagine. She's like a crusader for that kind of stuff."

"Where did you find this envelope?"

"It had fallen behind the desk in her office and was wedged between it and the wall. I couldn't focus or go to school. Mrs. Braxton helped me clean up. I told her what we were looking for."

"Well, thank you. This is a great help. I appreciate your doing this."

"I just want you to find whoever did this. Find them and make them pay."

Tears streaked down the girl's face. She quickly dashed them away. Samantha bit her lip, not sure what she could say or do to help.

"Well, that's it. I think I'm going to take a nap before my aunt gets here," Robin said, clearly trying to dismiss her.

It wasn't going to be that easy. There was no telling

when they'd have the chance to talk alone again. "I'm sorry. I have to bring your shirt back later. I came here straight from work."

Robin nodded. "I called him. How come you came and not the guy I called?"

There was fear in her voice, but curiosity as well. She could sense Samantha's power as easily as Samantha could sense hers.

"I'm here because we should talk about your gifts," Samantha said.

Robin dropped her head and squirmed uncomfortably. "I don't want to," she said after a minute.

"It's important. Did your mother know?"

"Yes," Robin whispered.

"But she didn't have them herself?"

Robin shook her head. "My grandfather had them, though. He was a shaman."

"What did your mother think about that?"

Robin sniffed and wiped tears out of her eyes. "She wanted me to study the old religion. She wanted me to be a shaman too."

Silence reigned for a moment while Robin continued to wipe at her eyes.

"And you didn't want to?" Samantha asked, trying her best to be gentle.

"No. I said it was stupid, and we got in a huge fight. She was so mad at me. I told her I was sorry, that I didn't mean it, but she didn't understand. No one I know practices that. Not even her, not really."

"But you knew some people who practiced Wicca?"

Robin nodded. "Mom didn't like me hanging around

with them. She said I was being a traitor to my people, my heritage."

It was so sad. Those who had accused Winona of being a traitor had sent hate mail. And yet Winona had called her daughter the very same word.

"And how did you feel?" Samantha pressed.

Robin shrugged. "It seemed so empty. I mean, they teach us in school that there are no gods and that everything is science and evolution. And the more I thought about it, the more I wondered if I was just a mutation, a stepping stone in evolution."

Samantha's heart ached for the girl. She could hear the sadness, the loneliness in her voice. "Were any of the Wiccans like you?"

"Yeah, one girl. She's a couple of years older than I am. She had power. She said she was going to the circle meetings with the coven, worshipping the goddess, celebrating the moon and the major holidays just to make her family happy but that she'd found something else that fulfilled her."

"What was it?" Samantha asked, trying to keep her voice calm.

"A different coven. They met in secret in the forest. And they all had powers and they could do amazing stuff. And it wasn't about worshipping anything. It was just about empowering us."

Samantha closed her eyes. Witches. Witches had found Robin. Had the same witches killed her mother?

"Did your mother know?"

"Are you kidding? She would have been furious."

"So you had to sneak out to go to these meetings?"

"Yeah," Robin said, coloring at the admission. "I'd go out my bedroom window and walk down the road. Someone would pick me up and drop me off at the same place."

"Do you know the names of the other people in the coven?"

Robin shook her head. "No. Everyone was kind of secretive that way."

Samantha nodded. The darker the magic, the more distrustful coven members became of one another. If Robin was new to the group, it would be quite a while before they trusted her with anything that could reveal them.

"Do you know when the next meeting is?"

"It's supposed to be in a few nights, during the full moon."

"Do you know where they would take you?"

"Yeah. It's this place in the Redwoods. It's called Cathedral Grove, where all the trees grow in a big circle. It's about a twenty-minute drive from here, followed by an hour-long walk."

"Could you show me?"

"Not how to walk in. But there's actually a railroad— it's like a tourist attraction that goes right through that area. It stops at Cathedral Grove so people can get out and take pictures, picnic. My mom's taken me there every summer, so that's how I recognized the spot where we were."

"How do I find this railroad?"

"It's simple. It's called Roaring Camp. It's just up the highway from here."

Samantha nodded, fairly certain she had seen a sign for it somewhere. "It's happening on the next full moon?"

"Yeah, it's in just a couple of days." Robin made a face. "I'm pretty sure there'll be no sneaking out with Aunt Clara around. She has ears like a fox. Plus, I'm not sure I want to keep going anyway. The vibe can get kind of weird there."

If they were practicing the kind of magic Samantha thought they were, "weird" was an understatement.

"If you want . . . help . . . or to talk, I'm here," Samantha said. "I know what it's like having these powers and not knowing what to do with them."

You know what to do with them; you just refuse to acknowledge it, the voice in her head whispered. She struggled to ignore it, but she felt like a hypocrite. She hadn't exactly coped well with her abilities at any point, and she didn't have the foggiest idea how she could help mentor somebody else.

"Thanks, but I'm going to talk to Aunt Clara. I've been thinking about it. I think maybe my mom was right. I think I do want to be a shaman, help people."

Samantha didn't say anything. It was natural that in her grief and feelings of guilt, Robin would make that decision. What would come of that six months or a year or two down the line, only time would tell.

Samantha stood. "I should go. I have a lot to do. Unless you want me to stay until they get back."

"No, it's okay. I'm good," Robin said, standing as well.

"You've got my number. If anything happens or if you need to talk, call."

"I will."

Samantha left, wishing there was something more she could do or say. She prayed that Robin would be okay. She got in the car and drove back down to the highway. It was getting dark and was definitely too late to visit Roaring Camp. She would have to go find this Cathedral Grove in the morning.

Once on the highway, she sighed. It had been a long, crazy day and the lack of sleep was taking its toll.

The phone rang and she answered.

"Hello?"

"You never called back." It was Anthony.

"Right, sorry about that. After the earthquake, things got crazy."

"Oh, *after* the earthquake," he said.

"Okay, and before and during too."

"That sounds better. So what was it like?"

"The craziness?"

"No, the earthquake."

"Weird. Really, really weird. I've felt the ground shake like that before. I've *made* the ground shake like that before. But this made me feel completely out of control and helpless."

"Unless I miss my guess, that's part of the whole point of things like earthquakes and natural disasters," he said with a tiny chuckle.

"Yeah, I guess so."

"You want to tell me what's been going on?" he asked.

She hesitated. She did want to talk it over with someone who would understand, but she really wasn't in the mood to do so right at that moment. "Later," she finally said. "I just need to unwind a bit."

"Later works. I miss you."

Her breath caught in her throat, and for a moment she thought she was going to cry. "I miss you too."

"Since you need to unwind, I'm guessing you don't want to talk about us yet."

"No, sorry."

"That's okay. I believe we've established that we're officially in the boy waits for girl portion of the story."

She couldn't help it; she had to laugh.

"Aha! Victory is mine," he said with mock enthusiasm.

She laughed harder. "I wish you were here," she said before she could think about what she was saying.

"I can be. I can be there in eight hours."

"No. I wouldn't want to put you in danger."

Again, she added silently.

"How do you know I'm not getting into trouble here without you?"

"You're not, are you?"

"No, but I could be."

"Don't tease; it's not funny."

She could hear him sigh. "No, I guess it really isn't, is it?"

"No," Samantha said, "it's not."

A raindrop hit her windshield, followed by another. She looked up. The clouds were low and dark, and she could feel the energy crackling in the air.

"Look, I'm driving and it's starting to rain, so I should go."

"Okay, but pick up the phone once in a while."

"I'll be better," she said.

"Okay."

Silence hung for a moment between them, and she could almost hear him say something, something she certainly wasn't ready to hear. "Okay, bye," she said, and hung up.

Coward, she accused herself.

The skies opened up and water gushed down. She switched the windshield wipers onto high, but they were useless against the sudden onslaught. She slowed down, struggling to see the road ahead of her and praying that no one rear-ended her.

In the dark and the heavy rain, the unfamiliar curves in the narrow road became treacherous. She strained her eyes even as she realized she was gripping the steering wheel overly tight. There were barely any lights on the road, and she didn't see any other cars around. There should have been other cars at this time of the evening, at least she would have thought so. Maybe all the locals had known better than to venture out into a coming storm.

The sky lit up overhead, and she heard the crash of thunder a second later. She slowed down even more, trying not to think about how she was driving through the forest in the only metal target around.

"It's just a storm, Samantha," she whispered to herself. She'd seen plenty.

But something about this one spooked her. Maybe it was the unfamiliar roads or how quickly it had come on. Maybe it was the eerie sensation of being the only person out in it, the isolation of the area that was getting to her.

A bolt of lightning lit up the sky, passing between two clouds. She blinked, momentarily blinded by the brightness. The thunder a moment later was so loud it felt like her breastbone was vibrating. She thought about Robin. She should turn around, go back and make sure the girl was okay.

In the next moment, she rejected that notion. It was just a storm and the girl was inside. She would be fine until her neighbor and great-aunt got there.

Her right front tire skidded unexpectedly on something slippery on the road, and her heart began to pound. Maybe she should pull over and wait for the storm to pass. She slowed down, looking for a place where she could pull off to the side without putting herself in danger of being hit by other cars—if there were any other drivers actually out. There was nothing.

Suddenly a bolt of lightning came down with a crash twenty feet in front of her car, clearly outlining the figure of a woman who was standing immediately in front of it.

Samantha slammed on her brakes, but at the same moment she accidentally sent a burst of energy through the car. The engine died and the car skidded to a halt right in front of the woman.

Samantha stared at her through the windshield. The woman was a couple of years older than her, and her eyes were burning like coals. She was bareheaded and her long raven hair was whipping about her in the wind. She was wearing a short black dress that offered no protection from the storm. But she didn't seem to care. Her head was thrown back as though in ecstasy, as though she were pulling the storm into herself.

She lifted her hands high into the air.

"What are you doing?" Samantha shouted at her through the windshield.

Lightning flashed in the sky.

The woman slammed her hands down onto the hood of Samantha's car. Lightning struck her head, traveled down her arms and into the engine, which began to shower sparks around her.

The car caught on fire, and as Samantha stared in frozen horror, the witch smiled at her through the flames.

6

Samantha's mind raced. She had only moments before her car would explode, killing her. But it was also electrified, and she risked electrocuting herself if she tried to exit. Plus, the witch was waiting for her to try to make a move like that.

The lightning hadn't killed the witch. She'd been able to harness it. *Maybe I can do the same thing with the current in the car.*

The witch was still touching the car and it wasn't harming her. Could it be because she was pushing energy into the car?

Two could play at that game. All Samantha had to do was reverse the flow of the energy and she would gain herself a few seconds. It would be more effective if she was touching part of the metal frame. As long as she wasn't touching the car and the ground outside at the same time, she should be safe.

She reached out and touched a metal part of the door, and she could feel the flow of current through it. She pulled it into herself, gathering power, and then pushed it as hard and as fast as she could back into the door.

The witch went flying through the air and landed several feet away.

Samantha shoved open her door and launched herself out of the car, careful to clear the frame before she hit the ground. A wave of heat hit her, singeing her hair, and she turned to see her car now completely engulfed in flames.

She scuttled away as fast as she could, waiting for it to explode. Then she raised her hand and, without thinking, sent a fireball of her own straight at the witch.

The woman deflected it easily, laughing as she did so. Samantha could hear her laughter even above the sounds of the storm and the roar of the flames.

She's insane.

The witch twisted her hands together suddenly, and a tornado opened up on top of Samantha. The winds felt like a thousand hands trying to tear her apart. She opened her mouth to scream, but the winds snatched her voice from her. She couldn't catch her breath as the twisting winds picked her up and hurled her through the air.

She spun her hands in the opposite direction the witch had, and the churning winds slowed enough to drop her onto the ground with a jolt. She was able to throw herself outside of the tornado. No sooner had she done so than it disappeared.

She turned around and saw the witch stumble, then fall to the ground. Samantha stood, watching, wondering what the witch was going to try next. She stayed that way for several seconds, and Samantha slowly edged closer.

Without warning, the witch leaped to her feet with a shriek and ran into the forest.

The rain stopped instantly, and the storm clouds began to dissipate as quickly as they had formed. Stunned, Samantha walked forward, wondering what had caused the witch to fall to the ground and remain there for so long.

She smelled blood, which made no sense. She hadn't touched the witch. She leaned down and saw that the witch had used blood to spell out a message on the ground.

The last grave.

Samantha stood and very deliberately smeared the blood until it mixed with the water already on the ground. She couldn't have anyone knowing that she had had a confrontation with Winona's killer.

She had no idea what the phrase meant; she just knew that it was one more piece in the whole baffling puzzle. She stood there, thinking hard.

It was a different woman than the one she'd seen early that morning in the forest who had touched Lance's shoulder and kept him from shooting her. How were the two connected? It was possible that they were in the same coven. Which one of them killed Winona?

She waited for several minutes, unwilling to venture into the trees and risk a repeat of the attack from the morning. Sooner or later, the witch would surely come back to finish what she'd started. She couldn't sense her anymore, but that didn't mean she wouldn't come back.

Finally, she let her muscles uncoil. The witch must truly be gone. Samantha took a deep breath.

What do I do now? she thought.

She turned to look at the charred remains of her car. There was nothing she could do to fix it, and she was fairly certain no one else would be able to either. She blinked at it for a moment, trying to force herself to think.

What would a normal person do in this situation?

After another minute's thought, she called her roadside assistance company to send a tow truck. Fortunately, the truck got there within half an hour. The driver stepped out and whistled low as he stared at the car.

"She's fried."

"Yeah."

"Well, I can tow it to a service station for you, but I can tell you right now that it's totaled."

Samantha turned and looked at the charred wreck of her car. "I kind of got that."

"Are you okay? Are you hurt?"

"Shaken, but not broken," she replied grimly.

"All right, well, let's get this over with."

"Do you need my help?" she asked.

"No. Why don't you just climb in the cab? I'll be done here in a minute."

Samantha gratefully got into the truck. She felt like her nerves were completely frayed. She was tired, frightened, and completely bewildered. Nothing was making any sense. Maybe it was because she hadn't had enough sleep. Or maybe she needed to get some distance and perspective on everything. Either way, she felt like it was taking every ounce of strength she had to not totally lose it.

When the driver had finished hooking up her car, he joined her in the cab. Fortunately, he seemed to want to talk even less than she did, so they drove in silence. After about twenty minutes, he turned off the highway into a repair shop that had a gas station next door.

"You going to be okay getting home?" he asked.

"I've got a friend coming to pick me up," she lied.

"Do you need me to wait with you?"

"No, I'll wait inside the gas station. I'll be fine."

"Okay."

He unhooked her car and presented a paper for her to sign. Then he drove off, and she headed to her car. She was grateful that the trunk was one of the only parts of the vehicle that didn't seem to be damaged.

Samantha kept a change of clothes in her trunk for emergencies. It was a habit she had picked up from Ed, who had made the mistake as a rookie cop of going home after a particularly brutal day with blood on his shirt. His wife's terror had quickly given way to anger at him for giving her the scare of her life. Even though Jill was Samantha's first roommate, she had adopted the habit and half a dozen times had been able to change clothes in the middle of the workday without going home. If she'd had her car with them that first time in Santa Cruz, she wouldn't have had to borrow Robin's shirt.

She changed clothes in the gas station restroom and then called a cab to pick her up. There was no way she was having Lance or Jill come out and see her in this state. Sure, she could tell them the car was hit by lightning and caught on fire; it was true enough. She was going to have to tell that story to her insurance company in the morning. The thought of that made her grind her teeth. It seemed ridiculously unfair that she had to deal with such mundane problems when she had supernatural problems on her hands.

The cab arrived, and the driver asked, "Sure you don't want me to take you someplace where you can get a rental car? I know a few places that are open late."

"To be honest, I can't handle dealing with that right now. I'd rather just pay you to drive me home," she said.

"It's your money," he said, shaking his head again.

The drive seemed interminable, and when they finally arrived at her apartment and she had to pay for it, she began to regret her decision not to let him take her to the car rental place. She waved to the two officers in a car outside her building, men she knew by sight but not by name. By the time she staggered upstairs, she wasn't sure if her exhaustion or her hunger was greater.

"I'm home," she called as she walked in, not wanting to startle Jill.

Her roommate was parked on the couch, her face still as expressionless as it had been earlier.

"How are you?" Samantha asked.

Jill didn't answer.

Samantha walked farther into the room and saw that one of the nightly news shows was on television. Normally Jill wasn't one for watching the news. She was far more into history than current events.

"Every channel's talking about the quake. It'll die down in a couple of days," Jill said. She was staring at the television with the slack posture of someone who was doing their best to completely tune out. "Scientists, researchers, psychics, foil hats, they're all out in force today."

Witches too, Samantha thought.

Samantha could tell Jill didn't want to talk about what had happened earlier, and that was fine with her. She walked into the kitchen to make herself a sandwich, listening idly to the television anchor.

It was Samantha's first earthquake, and under normal circumstances she probably would have joined Jill to hear all about it, but now she only half listened as they discussed things like magnitude and epicenter, comparing it to past quakes she knew nothing about.

"I'm here with George Wakefield, a scientist who's made a career out of studying earthquake patterns and trying to create an early-warning system. George, can you tell us a little about what you do?"

"Certainly," a pleasant male voice responded. "For years, scientists have been searching for a way to predict earthquakes. In the past few years, other researchers and I have been studying some fascinating statistics and think we've discovered a crude but effective way of predicting potential earthquakes."

"That sounds intriguing," the anchor enthused. "Can you tells us a little bit about what you've discovered?"

"Certainly. Over the past fifteen years, every significant earthquake has been preceded by a rise in the number of runaway pets."

"Pets? So you're talking cats and dogs here?"

"Yes. We know that animals have senses more acute than ours, and there are numerous documented cases of animals knowing that something is wrong before we humans do."

That's true, Samantha thought. *Just like rats leaving a ship.*

"It's like rats leaving a sinking ship," George continued. Samantha smirked as she piled roast beef high on her sourdough.

"The increased numbers of runaway pets prior to an earthquake are statistically significant and consistent. So, what we're starting to do is monitor reports, trying to locate spikes as soon as they occur. A colleague of mine actually predicted this quake eight hours before it happened."

Samantha carried her sandwich out into the family room. On the television set, she could see George Wakefield. He was in his late forties, with graying hair and intense blue eyes. She lingered for a moment, staring at him. Something about him seemed familiar, like she'd seen him someplace before. She shrugged. San Francisco was a busy city. She could have passed him on the street at some point.

"I've heard weirder things today," Jill said as she flipped channels.

"I've had my share for the day," Samantha said, trying to keep her tone light. "I'm going to try to get some sleep. Wake me if you need me."

"I won't. I'm going to take something to help me sleep. And I got some earplugs I'm going to try."

"Sounds good," Samantha said, wincing at the thought of the earplugs. Well, if it kept Jill from being woken up by Samantha's nightmares, it was a good thing.

Samantha made it into her room and closed the door. She sat down on the bed and for a moment thought about abandoning the sandwich and going straight to sleep. Her stomach growled a protest, though. She hadn't really eaten in twenty-four hours.

She started to wolf down the food, just wanting to get the act of eating over with so she could collapse. Some days were so hard and so long that it made the simple acts feel monumental. Her jaw ached with exhaustion after only a couple of bites. She hurt everywhere, and she struggled just to keep her eyes open. Finally, she dropped the sandwich, only half-eaten, onto the plate on her end table.

She changed into her pajamas, and her mind started to fill with unwelcome thoughts.

Had her captain back in Boston known there were witches in the area when he'd arranged with the captain in San Francisco for her to transfer?

Most people would go a lifetime without ever running into a witch. Why was it she had such terrible luck? Couldn't Winona Lightfoot have been murdered four months earlier, before Samantha got there? Why now?

Why is this happening to me? Haven't I been through enough?

And the full horror of everything came crashing down around her. She fell on her bed, grabbed a pillow, buried her face in it, and began to scream at the top of her lungs. The pain and fear and anger she was experiencing couldn't be expressed through mere tears. As her conscious thoughts were stripped away, all that remained was the unthinking animal self that could still feel great fear and great pain. That was the side that she was connected to as she screamed and beat her fists into her mattress.

And finally the exhaustion won over and she had nothing left in her. She lay still for a moment, panting, drained, in a clouded haze of despair.

And then in her mind she saw the hallway of doors. It

was the place she'd gone before to remember, to find answers about her past that was shrouded in darkness and mystery. She still didn't know why she only remembered bits and pieces of her childhood. She'd had confrontations before with her younger selves at ages five, six, and seven. After those encounters, the memories from those years of her life had come back, a steady stream of information that enlightened and explained but brought no comfort.

Expect for Freaky. She owed it to her five-year-old self for reminding her about the kitten she had created for herself as a playmate and for teaching her how to conjure him again. She brought her hands together, letting the energy vibrate between them until the familiar ball of black fluff took shape. The kitten mewed at her, sounding somewhat cross.

"I'm sorry. It's been a hard day," she whispered to the kitten, who immediately began batting at her fingers.

She rolled over, scooping him up into her arms, focusing on the feeling of his fur against her skin. She closed her eyes and saw again that corridor. The door marked TWELVE, the one the others had warned her she mustn't open, called to her. Light was spilling from under the door into the hallway, causing shadows to shift and slide over one another.

She took deep, calming breaths and forced herself to focus on the memories of her past. She could see herself standing in the corridor. And the three younger versions of herself that she'd already met were staring at her curiously.

"What is it?" she asked.

"You've been gone," Five said.

"We were worried," Six added.

"But glad too," Seven said.

"It's dangerous here," the three of them chorused.

"But I need to understand," she said. "And I don't think I can do that without remembering."

"You don't want to remember," Five said, urgency in her voice.

"I might not want to, but I think I have to. That's the only way to deal with it."

"You're not ready," Seven said.

"Maybe not for Twelve, but I think I can handle her," she said, pointing to the closed door with EIGHT marked on it.

"She's not like us," Six said.

"Why not?"

"She wants to hurt you," Seven said, dropping her voice to a whisper.

Samantha felt the hair rise on the back of her neck.

"Why would she want to hurt me?"

"She doesn't think you've suffered enough," Five said.

Samantha didn't know how to respond. Finally, she found her voice and asked, "Why would she want anyone to suffer? And why would she think that I haven't suffered enough? And why would she want to hurt another version of herself? It makes no sense."

"She's very angry," Seven said.

"It makes her a little crazy," Six said.

"And she doesn't care who she hurts, not even herself. That makes her dangerous," Five added.

"Why?" Samantha asked.

One by one, each of her three younger versions shrugged.

"Then I guess it's up to me to find out, because I'm pretty angry too," Samantha said. She stepped forward and twisted the knob on the door. It opened, and she gave it a good shove.

Out stepped an eight-year-old version of herself. Unlike the others, this girl wore her long red hair in a single braid down the middle of her back. She was dressed all in black and her eyes were glowing red.

Samantha took a step back, stunned by her appearance. The amount of power the child radiated was so much more than the other versions of her did.

"What do you want?" the child demanded.

"I want to know why you're so angry," Samantha whispered.

The child sneered. "Stupid woman. Don't you know the truth can kill you?" The child's hands began to glow red as well, and the more they glowed, the more translucent her skin became, until Samantha could see right through it to the veins beneath. The blood that flowed through them was tinged blue, and she could swear she saw sparks of electricity chasing one another like bolts of lightning running through the girl.

Samantha stepped back and raised her hands defensively.

"I've always heard that the truth can set you free," Samantha said, eyeing the child cautiously.

"Freedom is an illusion! Pain is all that's real."

"I don't believe that," Samantha said.

"Oh no?" The child raised an eyebrow and then lifted her arms. Fire streamed out of her hands, igniting the walls around them. Pain knifed through Samantha's head, searing so intently she screamed and fell to the floor.

The three younger girls raced forward, their hair and clothes on fire, and worked to contain the blaze. They were screaming and crying as loud as she was. She could feel their pain as if it was her own.

Because it is my own. Because they are me and all of this is in my mind. And her eight-year-old self was trying to destroy that very mind.

"You're insane!" she screamed at her.

"You would think so," the girl shouted, making her voice audible over the crackle of the flames.

Samantha could feel parts of her brain dying, nerve clusters shorting out. "You're killing yourself too! How can you do this?"

It went against every law of nature. Her kind had, above all else, an instinct for self-preservation. Because their magic was so directly tied into themselves and the energy they were capable of harnessing and focusing, there were limits as to how much they could do, how much magic they could wield before it became too much and their bodies couldn't, wouldn't give any more.

"You know the thing about magic," child eight said. "It's amazing how much more you can accomplish if you don't care if you live or die."

"What made you like this? Why?" Samantha asked, panting for breath.

Eight lifted her hands and the fire stopped. The other

three little girls retreated, trembling, behind Samantha, their faces covered in soot.

"Because this year I learned the truth."

"And what is the truth?" Samantha asked.

The little girl reached down and grabbed Samantha's hands tight. Pain seared through Samantha as though the child were pouring liquid fire on her. The blazing red eyes seemed to burn brighter. "The only truth there is."

"I don't know what you're talking about."

"Then you're a fool and you're going to suffer."

"But why?" Samantha whimpered, feeling like a child herself, cowering before an angry adult.

"Because you refuse to learn, you refuse to accept, you refuse to believe."

"Believe what?" Samantha screamed.

"Life. Isn't. Fair."

The girl was right, she knew, and Samantha knew it too, and she remembered.

When she was eight, everything had been so confusing. It was the year she had been taken out of school because she had blinded a bully who had knocked her down. She could feel her mother's pride in her, but all her mother expressed was her outrage that she had used her powers publicly. She had remembered that, but not what happened after they got home.

For three hours, her mother had put her under a spell that had made Samantha feel like she was clawing out her own eyes. The pain, the blood, the sudden blindness, and the terror had replayed over and over again until her mother was sure that she'd learned her lesson.

And at the end of it, Samantha had learned more than

just that she shouldn't use her powers publicly. She had learned that she wanted to hurt people, make them feel pain too.

And that year had only gotten worse. Her mother had flown into a rage when she realized that Samantha loved the Christmas tree, which they put up every year so they fit in with everyone else. Samantha had always wished that she could get toys like some of the other kids she had known at school. But that year she didn't even get magic gifts. She had instead seen the tree destroyed before her eyes, along with all of the ornaments, some of which she had made herself. There was never again to be a pretty tree with sparkly lights that made her feel warm inside.

The final blow was when her mother had caught her with Freaky. She'd been forced to banish the kitten, and her mother had made sure that she would never conjure her pet again by blocking the memory of how to do so from her mind. The young witch had been truly, and terribly, alone. And it was that night that she realized life's greatest secret, the one that many knew but few understood.

Life isn't fair.

And as she embraced that knowledge, Samantha cried harder for the loss of a second innocence. The hallway faded from her mind. She found herself in her room at home, and she sobbed until she finally fell asleep, because life truly wasn't fair.

She was standing downtown. She looked up at the buildings around her, and the sun was glinting off the windows.

There were a few trees nearby but no birds chirping in them. The air was still, heavy. It felt ... wrong ... in some way.

She turned and looked at the man standing next to her. George Wakefield, seismologist, earthquake expert.

He turned and looked at her. He was balding, thin hair clinging to the sides of his head. His eyes looked large, enormous behind his glasses. He was mouthing words, but there was no sound accompanying them. She couldn't tell what he was saying to her.

"What?" she asked.

He gave her a strange smile, a smile mixed with sorrow and triumph.

"It's the Big One."

And then the earth was moving beneath her feet. She could hear explosions all around her and realized that water pipes, gas mains, everything was tearing itself apart. Glass shattered above in ten thousand windows and began to rain down on the people below. She reached out to George, to shield him, protect him from what was coming.

But he just took a step back. "You can't save me from this," he said. "At least I know I was right."

And then the earth opened at their feet; a fissure divided them. As the ground continued to shake, it knocked her off her feet. She looked up, on her hands and knees, as utility poles and traffic lights crashed to the ground everywhere. A fire hydrant exploded, and water was gushing. It surrounded George and poured into the fissure in the earth that separated them.

"Run!" she screamed, even as she brought up her hands. She could lift him, throw him, do something, be-

cause she had to. Because she knew what was coming next.

And it happened too fast.

A power line fell, and the cable dropped into the pool of water at George's feet, electrocuting him instantly. It was followed a moment later by a car that was hit by a semi. It flipped end over end and crashed into his charred remains, scattering them to ash.

George Wakefield had predicted the Big One and it had killed him.

Around her people were dying by the thousands. She could feel it, and she screamed at the senselessness, the brutality.

And through the blaring of sirens, the twisting of metal, she could hear laughter. Somewhere, a woman was laughing. She laughed as thousands perished by the moment. She laughed until that was the only sound Samantha could hear. She laughed and laughed. And then she stopped laughing for just a moment and said, "I have what I wanted."

Samantha turned just in time to see a building crashing down on her. She threw out her arms, but her words and her magic failed her. She grabbed for her cross necklace, but it wasn't there. And she knew the building was going to kill her no matter what she did to try to stop it. She fell. The ground was hard beneath her and the first pieces of rubble struck.

Samantha woke with a scream. She was on the floor of her room, tangled in her sheets, and her nightstand had fallen on top of her. It took a moment for her mind to realize that she was alive, safe, and in her bedroom.

"Just a nightmare," she panted.

And at least the sleeping medication Jill had taken and the earplugs must have worked, because her roommate didn't come to check on her.

I should make sure she's okay, Samantha realized as she pushed the end table off of herself and sat up. *I should have talked to her already, but I was just too tired, too strung out.*

She was shaking and sweating. *Just a nightmare*, she repeated. And the memories of it came flooding back over her. They had all the intensity that her memories of the past had when they came to the surface, escaping from the locked corners of her mind. This had been no ordinary dream, she realized in a flash. Just as it had been no nightmare of her past.

It had been a vision of the future.

7

Samantha shuddered. She'd had some visions as a child. She didn't remember what they were, but she could remember that they had happened. This was the first actual vision of the future she'd had in years, though. She sat down on her bed and wrapped her arms around herself as she thought about what it meant.

George Wakefield hadn't looked any older in the vision than he had in the newscast. That would seem to place the vision in the near future rather than the far future. And it was the Big One, the quake that Californians talked about that was coming someday. She'd heard stories about famous quakes in the past and was shocked that none of those were seen as the mythical Big One.

She remembered the feeling during the earthquake, the violence, the loss of control. There was nothing she knew of that could stop it from happening. So, what was the point of the vision? Was she supposed to make sure that both she and George were well out of the city when it hit?

It didn't give her a decent time frame to work with, though. Unless the two of them were going to abandon the city altogether, and possibly even the entire state, there wasn't much that was helpful about it.

She tried to replay the images in her mind. She knew that somehow George had predicted it. Did that mean that his ideas about animals sensing an earthquake coming and leaving the area ahead of time were true?

She leaned down, picked up her clock, and put it back on her end table. It was four in the morning. She hated these middle of the night wake-ups.

She should go check on Jill, make sure she was okay, before trying to go back to sleep. *If I even can get back to sleep.* At the moment, that was a huge question mark.

The day loomed large ahead of her with far too much to do. She exited her room and crossed the hall. She eased Jill's door open just far enough so that she could see her. The other woman was on her bed, sound asleep. Samantha listened to her breathing for a few moments before easing the door closed again.

She hesitated in the hall, trying to decide whether to attempt more sleep or to just stay up. She finally headed for the kitchen. Better to get a head start on the chaos than waste time struggling to get to sleep.

She grabbed a bagel, slathered it with strawberry cream cheese, and ate it. A glass of orange juice washed it all down.

Her insurance company's twenty-four-hour claim service was a pain to deal with, but when she finally hung up she knew she could check that off her list. Fortunately, they were going to reimburse her for getting a rental car while they had her car checked out.

She called for a taxi and took it to a car rental agency near the airport that was open early. She had to practically put a spell on the guy behind the counter in order to convince him that she did not want an upgraded car. She did, however, pay for the GPS service, since she was pretty sure her own GPS was toast.

Installed in her new rental car, which was small and black, Samantha drove to the police station. She had managed to retrieve the letter threatening Winona from the backseat of her car the night before. The envelope was singed, but she hoped that forensics could get something off of the letter anyway. The technician who took it from her gave her a dubious look when she explained what had happened to it.

Then she drove back home. When she got inside the apartment, she was surprised to see that Jill was up. Her roommate looked bleary-eyed.

"Are you okay?" Samantha asked.

"The great thing about sleeping pills is that they make you sleepy. The bad thing is, they make you sleepy."

"Hasn't worn off yet?"

Jill shook her head.

"Why are you up this early?"

"I've got another meeting with one of the professors on campus, and I need to prep for it. Why are you up?"

"Couldn't sleep," Samantha said.

"Tonight you should take some of what I had."

"No, thank you. My dreams are already weird enough without adding medication to the mix."

Jill grimaced. "Amen to that."

Samantha cleared her throat, trying to decide how to bring up the elephant in the room. There was no nice, easy way to go about doing it, though.

"We should talk about everything that happened yesterday," Samantha said.

Jill nodded. "I agree. Not right now, though. I have a feeling it's going to be a very long conversation."

Samantha nodded. She was happy to postpone the inevitable for a while. She stood up, but before she could take a step, the ground seemed to roll under her feet, like a wave heading for shore. She grabbed on to the table and a moment later it had passed.

"What was that?" she asked.

Jill shrugged. "I'd say about three point four."

"What?"

"Aftershock of the earthquake. There were dozens and dozens yesterday, but I felt only one or two of them."

Jill got up and carried her breakfast dishes to the sink. "Well, I've got to go. Professor Hunt is the chair for my dissertation committee, and I want to be ready when I talk to him."

"Thesis," Samantha said.

Jill turned. "Excuse me?"

"You're writing a thesis, not a dissertation, right?"

"Nooo," Jill said, stretching the word out and looking at her like she was crazy.

"You're getting your master's, right?" Samantha asked.

"No. I'm getting my doctorate," Jill corrected, looking

hurt. "Are you really that self-absorbed that you don't even know what it is I'm doing?"

Samantha was taken aback. "I'm sorry. For some reason I thought—"

"Forget it," Jill snapped. "It's been a bad couple of days for both of us. I'll talk to you tonight."

She turned and left the room. Samantha just stared after her. She could have sworn Jill was going for her master's degree. She thought about what the other woman had said. Was it possible Samantha was that self-absorbed that she wasn't paying attention to what was happening around her?

The thought terrified her. For a detective, nothing could be worse. If that was true, Jill had every right to be pissed. In fact, that was the first time Samantha could ever remember seeing her roommate angry. Given all that was going on, she couldn't blame her.

I'd be angry too if I were in her shoes.

Samantha went to her room and fired up her laptop. She spent half an hour online researching George Wakefield and the various theories on earthquake detection and the speculation about the "Big One."

She found contact information for the scientist, determined to call him later in the day and set up an appointment.

Her phone rang.

"Hey, Lance," she said as she answered. "Shoot anybody this morning?"

"Not funny," he growled.

"You're in a mood."

"Captain wants to see us in his office pronto."

"Oh. Okay, meet you there."

She shut down her computer, grabbed her gun, badge, and keys, and headed downstairs.

Once on the street, she stopped and looked around. Her rental car wasn't there. There were half a dozen black cars parked on the block, but all of them were larger and fancier than her car.

Someone did not just steal my rental car.

She walked up and down the block. She remembered parking it on the street. Where? Across the street. There were three cars there, two BMWs and a Mustang, none of which was the car she had rented.

"Everything okay?" one of the officers watching the building called out.

"Just looking for my rental car," she said.

"I think I saw you drive up in the Mustang."

"Thanks," she said, knowing that couldn't be true. She looked down at the keys in her hand. They were the ones the rental car company had handed her. Attached to the fob was a keyless entry. She pressed down on the red alarm button.

And ten feet away, the Mustang's alarm went off. She crossed to it, unlocked it, and put the key in the ignition. The alarm turned off.

"I did not get an upgraded car," she whispered to herself. And yet, when she turned the key, the engine roared to life. She closed the door and then reached for the glove box. Inside was a rental agreement with her name on it for the car she was sitting in.

She slowly put it back where she'd found it and sat there, stomach churning. What was happening? There was no way she could have mistaken this car for what she thought she had. Was someone playing mind games with her? Was she under some kind of spell?

Or am I really losing my mind?

She prayed, harder than she'd prayed in a long time. When she was finished, she sat quietly, reaching out with her mind, searching, feeling. What was truth and what was fiction? She knew witches could impose their will, even on other witches. She herself had made witches see and feel things that weren't real. Had someone been doing something similar to her? And, if so, to what end?

Making her think she had one car when she really had another couldn't serve any possible purpose except to make her question herself. That seemed like such an innocuous thing compared to what they usually did. She was reminded again of the witch in the woods who had threatened her life and then seemingly saved it.

She felt like she was playing in a game she'd never heard of before and no one had bothered explaining the rules to her.

She couldn't sense any foreign energy touching her in any way. She threw up a couple of wards to protect herself from unseen attacks, particularly mental ones. Then, with a sigh, she pulled the car out of its spot and headed for the police station.

Lance was already there and pacing by his desk when she arrived.

"What took you so long?" he asked.

"Car trouble."

He rolled his eyes but didn't comment. Instead he headed straight for the captain's office and she followed.

Captain Sullivan was waiting for them with a less-than-pleased expression. "Shut the door," he instructed.

Samantha did and then she and Lance took their seats.

"What the hell happened?" he demanded.

Samantha exchanged a look with Lance. For once, her partner didn't speak right up. After a moment, Samantha carefully asked, "Sir?"

"Don't pretend that you don't know what I'm talking about."

Who's pretending? Samantha thought, suddenly terrified at the idea that when they did figure out what he was referencing, she might still not know what he was talking about. *Keep it together,* she told herself.

"Okay, let me spell it out for you two. A popular and powerful woman is dead. It's been more than twenty-four hours and you don't even have a suspect. An officer shoots and kills a man yesterday, and I still don't have an incident report on my desk!"

"Sir, I needed to go home afterward and collect myself," Lance said.

"I'm not talking to you, dumbass. I'm talking to your partner."

Samantha started in her chair. "Me?"

"Yes, you. Why the hell didn't you come in and tell me what happened and get started on the freaking paperwork?"

"I was picking up a piece of evidence from the victim's daughter. I handed it over to forensics this morning."

"What time this morning?"

"About six."

"And then what did you do?"

"I went home—"

"Exactly!" Captain Sullivan exploded, rising up out of his chair. "Why wasn't your ass in my office when I got here this morning? Why wasn't any kind of report on my desk?"

She could feel energy surging through her body as he lashed out at her. The urge to kill him where he stood reared up in her, and she wrestled with it, shocked at her own response.

It's not his fault. He doesn't know what you've been trying to deal with, the leads you've been running down.

But no matter what she told herself, the need to act, the need to hurt him, kept growing. Rational thought started to leave, and she panicked as she realized she was losing control of herself.

Kill him for speaking to you that way, the voice inside whispered.

"Answer me, Detective! Why?" he said, slamming his fist down on his desk.

Samantha rose out of her chair and shoved her face in his.

"Because we both needed sleep and we think that catching Winona's killer is a higher priority than explaining why and how another scumbag bought the dust!" Samantha shouted.

Behind her, she could feel Lance grabbing her arm, trying to pull her back.

"I'm this close—" Captain Sullivan said, thumping his index finger in her chest.

Samantha wanted to break that finger. She wanted to break his neck. But from somewhere deep inside, she pulled on strength she didn't know she had, reached out and grabbed his hand, and sent a wave of energy into him.

He blinked and sat down suddenly. "Well, yes, as I was saying . . . What was I saying?"

"You were saying that you understand completely and that we should continue about our jobs," she suggested.

He nodded. "Yes, that was it. Carry on."

Samantha grabbed Lance's shirt and dragged him out of the office.

"How did you do that?" he asked, eyes wide. "You've got some sort of Jedi mind power or something?"

"Never underestimate the power of a really angry woman," she said.

He whistled. "And I thought I had anger-management issues."

"Yeah, you're not the only special one."

"I got that. Listen, why don't you go blow off some steam? Go punch something or whatever it is you need to do."

"I have a lead I want to follow up on."

"Great. Do it. I'll be here filling out forms if you need me. We'll touch base again at the end of the day."

"Agreed."

"Just don't kill anybody, okay? That's *my* thing," he said with a grin.

She just stared at him. *If only you knew*.

Once on the road, Samantha was grateful for the upgraded car. She hit the gas and the roar of speed did a little to help calm her down. First she was losing control over her memories and now over her emotions. It scared her.

And she was using the magic almost uncontrollably. For three months, she'd been fighting it every single day, and now it was like she'd lost the battle, just given up.

It was dangerous and uncalled for. What she'd done to the captain, in front of Lance, had been stupid, childish even. She needed to talk to someone.

She called Anthony.

"Wow, careful. A guy could get used to this," he said.

"I think I'm in trouble," she said.

He was suddenly all business. "What's wrong?" he asked, voice concerned.

She had an insane urge to laugh. What *wasn't* wrong? "I feel like I'm totally losing control."

"With the magic?" he asked.

"Yes. I've been working so hard, trying to put it all behind me again. And now I've come up against a couple of witches, and it's like the floodgates are open. I'm not even trying to solve things without magic. It's almost like"—she hesitated, not wanting to say it out loud, to admit it to either of them—"I've latched onto the witch issue here as an excuse to use the magic in whatever way I want."

"It's possible. I mean, we knew it wasn't going to be easy for you to give it up again. And it sounds like you were doing a pretty good job until provoked."

"I know, but I feel like I can't stop now. I'm doing things . . . I'm not proud of."

"Have you hurt anyone? I mean, anyone you shouldn't have?"

"No."

"Then hold on to that. The Samantha I know is a good person. Trust yourself a little more."

She bit her lip. She wished she could, but she was really starting to wonder, especially given the things that seemed to be slipping her mind, like what color Jill's hair was or what degree she was going for. *Or what kind of car I rented.*

She took deep breaths and focused on the physical sensations she was experiencing, the smell of the car, the feel of the steering wheel.

"Talk to me. What's going on?"

"Thanks. I think I just needed to say some of that out loud. Sometimes it feels like I'm forgetting—I don't know—everything."

"You want to talk about the case?"

"Soon," she promised. "I have to go now, though. Thanks."

She hung up before he could protest.

Deep breaths, she reminded herself. After a few minutes, she began to calm down as she headed out of town.

Samantha headed for the Santa Cruz Mountains. This time her destination was Roaring Camp. She needed to be able to check out the place where the witches were meeting.

By the time she reached her destination, she had calmed down. The captain had had every right to be upset. Everything about this case was emotionally charged. Her old captain would have wanted a same-day report on all those things as well. At least she hadn't killed Captain Sullivan.

He'll live to yell another day.

And now Samantha was free to do what she needed.

The camp was actually located in the town of Felton. Samantha found it with ease and turned in.

As soon as she had parked, she walked to the entrance to the town. She picked up a couple different maps of the area, which she stuffed in her pocket, and perused the information about the place.

Roaring Camp had started off as a settlement formed by Isaac Graham in the 1830s. The authorities had nicknamed it "Roaring Camp" for its wild ways. A few years later, Graham had created a sawmill. The Roaring Camp and Big Trees Narrow Gauge Railroad had been operating since 1963. Two decades later, a train down to the Santa Cruz Beach Boardwalk was added, in celebration of the trains that had done the same thing a century before.

The train wasn't due to leave for an hour, so Samantha walked around, checking out the various other activities, which included gold panning, candle making, and posing for old-time photos. The whole place had a very celebratory air, and she enjoyed watching the families on vacation as they tried to reconcile the 1880s-era lifestyle being depicted with the modern era in which they lived.

As Samantha walked, she was also reaching out slightly with her senses. There were no witches in the little town area, but she was looking for someone who might know something about them.

Witches could leave energy signatures like vibrations behind when they passed through places or touched objects. It could be amplified by a witch on purpose, but most of the time the residual was accidental and faint. Sustained contact with places, objects, and occasionally people could give off vibrations another witch could use to detect and track. Although there were no witches in the area, she was looking for something or someone who had been in recent, sustained contact with a witch.

Inside the General Store she finally found what she was looking for. A guy who looked about twenty-two was stocking shelves, and he gave off some faint vibrations. Samantha walked behind him, brushing ever so slightly against him, and could feel them more strongly. He knew a witch. The question was, did he know he knew one?

Samantha picked up a candle on the shelf nearby, sniffed it, and then put it back. She turned to him. "Excuse me, but I have to take a souvenir back home for my roommate. What would you recommend?"

He smiled. "Candles are always nice. Does she like them?"

"Yeah, but she's a Wiccan and doesn't use them the way other people do."

It wasn't subtle, but hopefully it would get the job done.

"Okay, huh. Then maybe these aren't for her. They're all scented and probably not what she'd use for her rituals, I'm guessing. Although I had a woman in here a couple of months ago buying a bunch of ones with sage in them. She said it was good for cleansing."

He was lying. She could see it in his eyes. He practiced Wicca. It was possible he was a member of the coven that Robin had gone to briefly before being recruited out of it. If so, he'd know the witch who recruited her.

"Yes, it is good for that, but I prefer—um, how's this one?" she asked, quickly picking up a random candle. Then she forced blood to rush to her cheeks so it looked like she was blushing.

He smiled. "Caught you. It's not just your roommate who practices, is it?"

"And here I thought I was being so sly," she said, giggling and flipping her hair. She touched his arm briefly, willing him to see her as his own age.

What she'd said to Anthony in the car was true. It was as though the floodgate had opened and the magic was just becoming easier and easier to use, to rely on.

But lives could be at stake, she argued with herself. *Just like in Salem.*

His smile widened. "That's what you get for trying to play coy."

She sighed dramatically and then stuck out her bottom lip in a mock pout. "I'm just sad because I'm going to be here on the full moon. And I don't have anyone to hold circle with."

His smile faltered slightly. Many Wiccan groups were still very private, and very few would actually welcome a stranger into their midst for a ritual night. And most away from their coven would never dream to ask but would instead arrange to make the ritual required a solitary one.

A few were more open, and she was hoping that in this part of California, where there was already a "love all the people" vibe, there might be a little more flexibility.

"You know," he said, after a minute. "I do know a coven."

"You do?" she asked, radiating as much joy as she could.

He nodded. "We— They didn't use to accept new people that often, but they've been a lot more open lately."

"Looks like I'm not the only one who gave herself away," she teased.

It was his turn to blush. "Well, you know, you have to be careful."

"I understand." She batted her eyelashes at him and took a step closer, violating his personal space. "Anything you could do to help me would be greatly appreciated."

He licked his lips. "I, um, I'll see what I can do."

"Thank you," she said.

"How do I get in touch with you?" he asked.

She reached into his pocket, causing him to jump. She slowly pulled out his phone and then made a show of entering her phone number. Then she handed it back to him. "My name's Sam."

"Sam," he said, "pleased to meet you."

"And what's your name?" she asked.

"Cody."

"Cody," she repeated as she leaned forward, and she could see the pulse quicken in his throat. She kissed him on the cheek, making sure to give a mild electrical current to her lips that would make his skin tingle.

She pulled back slowly. "Merrily met," she said.

He could only stare in return.

"Blessed be," she said as she took a step back.

"Blessed be," he stammered.

She turned and walked away, swaying enough to ensure that he watched her all the way to the door.

Once outside, she dropped the exaggerated walk. She had never been one of those girls who used their sexuality to get what they wanted out of men, and it left a bad taste in her mouth. But just because she didn't play the game didn't mean she didn't know how. She wagered Cody would do everything he could to get her invited to the circle. If the witch Robin had met was keeping up her double life, she would attend her Wicca circle before heading off for the witch one.

She continued to walk around but didn't find anything or anyone else of interest, so she headed over to the train depot. She bought her ticket and boarded the steam train.

A young woman smiled at everyone. "Hi. Welcome to Roaring Camp. The steam train you're riding on is an authentic steam train. Our engine is an actual antique. Today we're going to take you on a round-trip tour of the Big Trees. Some of the redwoods you're going to be seeing are not hundreds, but thousands of years old. I'll be pointing out sights of interest along the way. Now, let's get started."

The train lurched forward, and Samantha settled into her seat. Within moments, they were in the forest and she was able to marvel at the beauty and majesty of the ancient trees. She breathed in deeply of the scented air. Taking the train to her destination was the fastest way to get there. After her other experiences in these mountains, going at night had not been an option, as far as she was concerned. She needed to be able to see what was coming at her.

Her mind wandered as the guide talked on about the beauty around them and the history of the area. The train would frequently slow so she could point things out. Finally the train came to a stop.

"All right. We're going to get off the train here for just a few minutes to see something spectacular called Cathedral Grove. So, if everyone would just follow me," the guide said.

Samantha got off the train with everyone else. Cathedral Grove. That was what she was here to see. She followed the guide and the rest of the passengers, bringing up the rear of the group as they walked toward a perfect circle of trees that was cleared in the middle. The others stopped in the dead center of the clearing. As Samantha lifted her foot to step inside the circle too, a wall of energy slammed into her, throwing her backward.

8

Samantha was thrown back nearly a dozen feet. She landed hard, off-balance, and she flailed for a moment before regaining her balance. None of the others had noticed. They were focused instead on the beauty around them and the singsong voice of the guide.

"This is what is often called a faerie circle," the young woman was saying. "You'll notice that these trees are growing in a perfect circle. What happens is there is a parent tree that would have stood right here in the center of this circle. The redwood would have dropped its seeds around it. The original tree is destroyed by fire or something else, but the seeds grow, ringing the space where the original tree stood."

Samantha could hear people muttering words like "beautiful" and "breathtaking." Someone else said "magical." They had no idea.

"This spot has been used for countless weddings and special events," the guide continued. "I want you to take about ten minutes to look around, take pictures; then we'll head back to the train and continue our tour."

Samantha stepped backward into the forest, careful not to attract attention to herself. Ten minutes later, everyone trekked back to the train. Five minutes after the train headed out, silence reigned in the Redwoods and she turned her attention back to Cathedral Grove.

She walked the outside of the circle slowly, being careful not to trip on roots. The air was very still here and the birds were silent. It felt like the world was hushed, waiting.

Waiting for what?

And then, as she reached out and touched the bark of one of the trees, she felt a jolt rush through her.

Waiting for witches.

There was no doubt in her mind that this was where the coven had brought Robin to perform rituals. The power that was trapped inside the circle was thrumming through the trees. There were dangers associated with using public spaces for rituals, but the witches here seemed to have found a way around it.

As near as Samantha could tell, the normal people had had no problems entering and leaving the circle, and both they and the circle seemed unaffected by the encounter. There were powerful barriers up, though, that kept those with power, like her, out. But those same barriers would be able to let through members of the coven who had erected them.

For a brief moment, she considered going to get Robin but quickly rejected that idea. There was no guarantee that the girl had been embraced as a full coven member with unlimited access. She might need to still be invited or helped inside by one or more of the others. Even if she could gain access, though, Samantha didn't want to endanger the girl.

She walked the outside of the circle twice, testing it for weaknesses, but could find none. Then she walked it a third time, looking for the entry point the coven members would likely use.

Wiccans had strict ways to enter and exit ritual circles. Some witches did the same thing as well, more out of habit or security than anything else. At last she found the entryway between two trees. The energy was slightly different there. It felt like a transition place, like a doorway, part of neither the inside space nor the outside space but the place that connected them both.

Samantha examined it for a moment. She racked her brain, trying to remember if she had ever witnessed a ritual welcoming a new member into the coven she had grown up in. After a few minutes, she gave up. Even if she could remember such an incident, it might not help. The circle here was different from the meeting places her coven had used, and the rituals would likely be different as well.

She sat down, cross-legged, and stared at the circle. She needed to find a way to get inside. It would help her tap into the minds of the witches who held rituals there.

And you can take some of the power for yourself, a voice whispered in her mind.

She gritted her teeth, trying to block that voice. Slowly, she went through everything about magic as it related to circles and their protection she could remember from when she was a kid. She couldn't help but think of all the wards and barriers that were on the house her high priestess had once owned in Salem. She remembered how those barriers had tried to push her out when she was with Ed but how they had let her pass easily with no pushback when she was later with other coven members, pretending to be one of them.

There was something there. Why the one time and not the other? It wasn't just Ed the house had been trying to get rid of that day. She'd heard the voices too, been plagued by her own horrors in that basement. So, why was the second time fine?

Was it possible that some of the wards on the house were taken down before a circle? Or was the difference the fact that she was actually actively using her magic?

Well, she couldn't say that she was avoiding magic the last couple of days, yet the circle still rejected her violently as a stranger.

She could feel the answer shimmering in front of her, and she strained, trying to reach for it. It was no use. The harder she pushed, the farther away it seemed to get.

Her five-year-old self would tell her she was trying too hard.

She closed her eyes, calming herself. She forced each muscle in turn to relax until her breaths were steady and even and her heartbeat slow. She went to the place in her mind where she could talk to her past selves. The three younger girls were peering fearfully out of their doors at Eight, who was having some sort of temper tantrum in the middle of the hallway. She understood and sympathized with the angry little girl.

"Don't open another one," number five warned.

Samantha ignored her and reached for door number nine. She opened it, and out stepped a pale, tired-looking little girl with sad eyes and a resigned expression.

She looked at Samantha. "I know you," she said.

Samantha nodded. "And I'd like to remember you."

The little girl shook her head. "I'm not the one you want. I'm the one who is stuck, trapped between two." She pointed first toward number eight, who stopped screaming and looked up. She pointed next to the door marked with a ten. "I cannot control my rage, nor can I summon my calm. They both come to me, often fighting with each other."

Samantha almost felt like she could relate. But mostly, she was still dealing with the anger more than the calm.

But anger wasn't what she needed right now. She needed calm, self-assurance. So she nodded her thanks to Nine and then she reached out to the door marked with a ten and was surprised she heard no objections from the others.

The door swung open easily, and the girl behind it seemed to float out, feet barely touching the ground, if they were at all. Samantha stared at her, impressed. She looked in her eyes, though, and shuddered. The girl's eyes were dull and lifeless, almost like a doll's eyes. She swiveled her head slowly in Samantha's direction.

"What do you want?"

"To remember and to understand," Samantha said. She could see in her peripheral vision that the other children were staring now, watching the exchange.

"Then first you must move past this," the girl said, gesturing to number eight. "You gain more power when you learn to center and focus, to empty yourself of everything else. All you do is react and respond. You must learn to be, to embrace who you are."

"But how?"

"That is what you must figure out if you wish to progress."

She heard mutterings from the other children, and she could sense their fear and their hesitation. Samantha couldn't help but glance at door number twelve. The door itself now appeared to be glowing. It was practically a translucent red color.

"Don't open that door," Ten cautioned.

So she says the same thing about Twelve that the others do.

She turned back to Ten. "I need to figure out how to enter a circle that I have not been invited to join."

"Everyone with power is connected for good or ill. Their circle is your circle. You must believe this, accept that you belong in it, and the circle will accept you. If you do not believe that you belong, the circle will reject you."

"It can't be that simple."

Ten cocked her head to the side. "Why not?"

"It just . . . can't," Samantha said, at a loss for words.

"When we are little, we understand that all magic is simple."

As if to illustrate, Five conjured Freaky with the flick of her wrists. She was the one who had retaught Samantha how to do that.

"As we grow older, we begin to believe that magic is

difficult, and this belief manifests itself. It becomes difficult when it does not need to be."

Samantha thought of herself. Sometimes magic seemed easy, other times nearly impossible.

"As we mature, we once again must embrace the belief that magic is simple." Ten snapped her fingers, and a wall of flame surrounded her.

Samantha jumped back with a gasp. With another flick of the girl's fingers, the flames disappeared.

"There are only two rules to magic," the girl said, face solemn, still hovering in the air. "Magic is simple. Magic costs. Every action in the universe affects other actions, creatures. Magic drains the energy of the user, weakening them even if only for a moment. There is not an endless supply of energy in your body at any one time. To do great and terrible magic is to risk your own life. But aren't those the stories that get written? The hero risks all and will either save the day or die horribly."

Samantha had experienced firsthand some of the brutal effects of too much magic use on the body. It had nearly killed her more than once. So, what the child said made sense. "Thank you," she said.

"And remember, it's not *their* circle. It's *your* circle."

"I will."

Samantha opened her eyes and stared at the circle in front of her. "It's not theirs; it's mine," she murmured. She needed to believe it, own it.

She pulled off her shoes and socks and set them aside. She needed to feel the ground beneath her feet, be more connected to the place and all that it had witnessed. She reminded herself of what it had felt like to return to her mother's home in Salem after so many years. She relived unpacking her old trunk, taking out the candles, the athame, the cloak and holding these things in her hand.

She still had them. She hadn't known what to do with them and so she had brought them with her. They were buried in a box in her closet. Maybe not getting rid of those things had helped feed the anxiety she'd been feeling for months. But maybe they would ultimately help her save lives.

She stared at the circle. She had powers. She had abilities. She had once been a dark witch. She just had to believe that the barriers placed on the circle would see those things too. They had rejected her earlier because she had powers but did not belong, whereas they had allowed the tourists to pass through them. She couldn't be as the tourists, but she could be, even if only for an hour, like those who had erected those barriers.

"I am Samantha Castor," she said. Castor was the last name she'd been born with, her mother's, but Samantha was the new name she'd taken on when she was adopted. Her full birth name was hateful to her, bespoke horror, and she refused to acknowledge it. She'd avoided using her full name in Salem because if a witch knew your name they had power over you. So she'd blended part of her adopted name with part of her birth name to limit the power that could be wielded over her. Samantha Ryan, the cop, was not a witch. But Samantha Castor had done magic, dark and violent, in Salem, regardless of the reason. The circle would accept her; it must.

"I am a witch descended from generations of witches.

I walk where I will. I do what I wish. I impose my will where I must. You will allow me to pass."

And she stepped forward, believing that the wards would part around her. They did. She kept walking forward, slow, majestic, feeling the earth beneath her toes, until she stood in the center of the circle.

"I am Samantha Castor and you will welcome me."

Her senses flooded with images and feelings. She was connected to the witches who practiced here, who would be here again in two nights. She could feel the essence of their spirits. She closed her eyes and took it all in. As a child, all the rituals she had been a part of had taken place in houses, basements, away from prying eyes. Here, in nature, it felt completely different. The practitioners were pulling on the energies of the earth and not just one another.

She could feel Robin's energy, faintest of all. She could sense the fear and fascination the girl had known while standing in this circle. There were others, their energies darker, more filled with malice. Their hatred practically poisoned the earth. There were two, though, she could feel most strongly. There was something important about them. She pushed, trying to sense.

No! Relax. Magic is simple if you let it be, she reminded herself.

"I am Samantha Castor, and you will show me."

She opened her eyes and she could see images hovering in the air, avatars of the different men and women who shared this circle. Some had hoods that covered their faces; others did not. And two of the faces she could see clearly, she recognized.

There was the witch who had attacked her in her car, her face twisted in a snarl. There was also the witch who had touched Lance in the forest, kept him from shooting her. Her eyes were dark, guarded, keeping her secrets to herself. The eyes of the other witch held a glint of madness that chilled her to the bone. These were the two she had been dealing with, and the circle told her these were the two most important, the two to be reckoned with.

"Now show me what they're doing here," Samantha said.

More pale images flickered, aftereffects like watching home videos projected into the air. They were performing a ritual that was unknown to her. They had a mound of earth in the center of the circle, and as she watched, it seemed to split apart, revealing something buried under the mound.

"What does that mean?"

No answer was forthcoming, but she hadn't really expected one for that. It looked like some form of sympathetic magic, where the witch would use an object to represent something or someone else and then do things to the object in order to cause those things to happen to the person or item they represented. Here the mound and the object beneath it were being acted upon in place of something else, in order to affect something else. As the image shimmered and faded, she noticed a lot of lines covering the ground around the mound. A moment later, the whole image was gone.

Samantha stood inside the circle and half closed her eyes. Feelings washed over her, memories that were not hers but felt no less potent. Terror, blood, greed, hate.

And there was something else, an undercurrent that flowed beneath everything else but that threatened to grab hold of her and drown her.

She delved deeper, sensing, feeling, opening herself up. Something incredibly evil had happened there, something that went far beyond the things she had experienced. She narrowed her eyes to a slit. Suddenly the dirt beneath her turned into a lake of blood. Hands reached up for her; the screams of the dying split the air around her. She could feel the lingering effects of an ancient war that had taken place on that site. It had been a battle between man and monsters, good and evil. There was something familiar about it, haunting.

Cathedral Grove, blessed by some, consecrated and made holy, was cursed and damned by others. The roots of the trees had soaked up blood, so much of it that it had fed them and watered them, making them strong physically and psychically. And there were those who had felt that power and gravitated to it. And some of those had sought to claim the power for themselves.

She could feel through the earth the bones and the ashes of so many, both victims and victors of vicious battles. She felt like she couldn't catch her breath as the bones of hundreds began to whisper to her. The dead remained attached to their remains, their whispers never quite silenced. There was no peace here, not for them and not for her. She clapped her hands over her ears and tried to block out the sounds.

And then ghosts began to rise out of the ground. Most were merely echoes, recorded personalities, and worse, recorded deaths. On the far side of the circle, a three-year-old girl was screaming her head off as a man stabbed her over and over. Samantha shouted at them, but neither specter heard her. They were locked together in their own moment, reliving the horror of it over and over. Even as Samantha watched, the child died again. The man turned, and a knife gripped by an invisible hand slashed him across the throat. He fell to his knees, his blood pouring down into the lake Samantha was standing in.

So many ghosts, many of them playing out the moments of their deaths. It was too much. The pain and fear threatened to sweep Samantha away. Not all of the ghosts were mere recordings, though. Some were much more self-aware.

Such as the young man standing beside her who reached out and brushed icy fingers against her cheek. Samantha jumped backward.

"You don't belong here," he said. His voice held friendly curiosity, but his eyes were filled with a malice that was breathtaking. "You're different. You're—"

"Alive," Samantha said, interrupting.

He smiled, a slow, wicked smile. "I wouldn't call what you do living. More of a kind of surviving, on the edge, the fringe, not of this world, barely even in it."

"What happened here?" Samantha asked, even as she racked her mind to try to remember what she had once been taught about sentient spirits. Something about *not to be trusted* came to mind.

He looked around slowly, meaningfully, gazing at the other spirits. "What hasn't happened here?" he asked.

"What happened to you?"

He gave her that same wicked smile. "I was killed by a woman, a member of my coven. I thought we were making love. She had other plans."

"Sex magic?" Samantha guessed.

"Combined with sacrificial death. Oh, she got a real power upgrade, courtesy of me."

"I'm sorry," Samantha said, not sure what else to say.

The ghost moved closer. "Not your fault."

He was still smiling, and she couldn't help but stare at his lips. They were full. He bit the bottom one gently and the motion intrigued her.

"I could use your help," she said, trying to block out the screaming and the crying of the other spirits around her.

"Whatever you need," he said, his voice slightly huskier.

"There's a coven using this grove now. They're doing bad things," Samantha said.

"Oh, yeah, they are," he said, taking a step closer.

"What can you tell me?" she asked. Maybe she wasn't remembering correctly about spirits. Maybe some of them were trustworthy. After all, what reason did the dead have to lie about anything?

He reached out and took her hand in his. His hand wasn't corporeal. It wasn't really there, but the energy was, and she could feel that. Her hand tingled where he was touching her.

"I can tell you that they've been here a long time. The current high priestess has always been a badass, a power grabber. But something happened about a month ago. Something I've never seen before."

"What was that?" she asked.

"They were doing some sort of ritual. I usually watch. After all, about twenty years ago it was my coven. Most of the old crew are gone now, though. Most are dead; some just left."

"I'm sorry," she murmured. He had such a beautiful voice. It was a shame he had been killed.

"It happens to everyone." He glanced down at their linked hands, and so did she. "In the end, we're all just energy," he said.

He looked up at her, and before she could say anything, he moved in and kissed her. His lips against hers were soft, the energy rippling between them making them feel warm. And she could swear that the longer the kiss lasted, the more real he felt.

He put both his hands behind her head and kissed her more deeply. She could feel him as his energy merged with hers. And then she was kissing him back and she knew she wasn't imagining it; he was real, solid. He slid his arms around her and pulled her tight.

And what had happened to him was so terrible. And everything that had happened to her was a nightmare. And she could never share it with anyone. But she didn't have to lie to him.

"I see you," he whispered. "The *real* you. I understand your pain. I understand your loneliness. I'm so sorry for everything that has happened to you."

"It's not your fault," she said.

"No, but I can help you. I can help share the pain, the burden."

And nothing on earth had ever sounded so good to

her. He was warm and real and he understood, really understood. And she wanted the closeness he was offering. And with every kiss she felt him more. His hands roamed over her body, sending minor jolts of electricity into her, which felt so good.

And then he was lowering her down onto the ground, still kissing her. And when he lay down on top of her, she could feel the weight of him and he didn't just feel real, he *was* real, and he wanted her. And she wanted him.

She opened her eyes. A minute ago, when she had been talking to him, he had been wearing jeans and a polo shirt. And now, now he wasn't wearing anything.

And in that moment, she knew what he was trying to do. She screamed and pushed him with everything she had. He went flying backward and landed halfway across the circle. Suddenly, he was wearing clothes again and all the thoughts that had been flooding her mind were gone. They had never been hers.

"What the hell were you doing?" she screamed.

He stood up and shrugged. "Just because I'm more than just a mindless recording doesn't mean much in the big picture. We all relive our deaths in one way or another. You were about to help me relive mine. And, hey, there's worse deaths to have."

She felt like she was going to be sick.

"Stay away from me."

"Your loss. After twenty years, I've gotten pretty good at this."

And she vowed in that moment that no matter what else happened, she'd find a way to destroy this ghost so he could never do that to anyone else.

"I guess you don't want to know what I saw a month ago."

"I can't trust you."

"Suit yourself. But you might as well trust your own eyes. The echo of it is there. You can see it if you want to."

"Did someone die?"

He laughed. "Not exactly."

"What is that supposed to mean?"

"See for yourself."

He turned and walked away, dissolving back into the ground slowly.

She took a deep breath. She knew that traumatic events could leave images, echoes, in the fabric of a place. Death was the easiest way to cause those echoes evidenced by the ghosts around her, but it wasn't the only trauma that could cause it. The emotional impact was the important part. She was more than convinced that echoes of her haunted at least a dozen places in Salem.

She turned and looked at the ghosts and, one by one, they began to melt back into the earth until only one image was left. She didn't know why she hadn't noticed it earlier. Maybe it was because, of all the things to see inside the circle, at first blush it was one of the most innocuous. A woman with long black hair was standing in the exact center of the circle. She wasn't moving much except to occasionally fall to her knees and then stand back up.

She had her back to Samantha. Samantha walked around her slowly until she could see the woman's face and then she stopped. It was the witch who had summoned the storm and channeled the lightning into her car.

She was standing, eyes closed, chanting. Samantha struggled, but she couldn't hear the words. They must not have been important. As she watched, the woman made a small circle with her right arm. Nothing too special there. Could have been any of a hundred different things she was doing, particularly if she was the high priestess.

Then suddenly the woman's eyes opened wide in panic. The terror in her face was hard for Samantha to look at, but she forced herself to keep watching. And then the witch fell to her knees and her head slumped forward. A moment later, it snapped backward and she stood up. Her face was full of menace. Then a transformation seemed to come over it, and as tears began to stream down her face, Samantha heard her whisper, "The last grave."

9

Samantha shuddered. The image then began to repeat itself. She turned away, unwilling to watch again. What was it she had just witnessed?

With her back to the image, she stared at the trees around her. The guardians of the circle stood, sentinels, beacons. How much had they seen and how much blood they had taken into themselves?

All she knew was that she couldn't stay longer. Neither could she leave this place as she had found it, though.

Take the power, her inner voice urged, and she struggled to ignore it. Is that what had happened to the witch she had just seen? This area was dangerous. There were too many spirits, too much power. She had no idea how to solve those problems, though.

Maybe Anthony would know. He knew more about the occult than she did. His lifelong search for the surviving member of the coven that had killed his mother had helped him amass quite a lot of knowledge on the topic.

Once she got to the car, she should call him, ask him about all that she had seen and heard here.

Except she wouldn't tell him about kissing the ghost. It was a memory she'd like to forget herself as soon as possible. She chastised herself. She should have been able to figure out what he was doing sooner. Then again, as he himself had said, clearly he'd had years to get good at messing with people's heads that way.

There was only one thing she could do. She walked around the internal perimeter of the circle and placed her hand on each tree trunk. She pushed energy from her body into the tree and into the dirt. "I bind this place so that nothing dark may be created here, that no harm may be done." She repeated the actions for each tree.

When she was done, she surveyed her work. The binding spell she had done could be undone, but not before it would cause quite a bit of confusion and mayhem, she hoped.

Finally, she stepped out of the circle of trees. She put her shoes and socks back on. It was a beautiful spot, and it broke her heart that it was being used for dark purposes.

She headed for the train tracks, intent on following them back to Roaring Camp. There was something incredibly peaceful about the forest, and she breathed deeply of the fragrant air. She was going to have to come back at some point in the future to explore the area more.

She pulled out her phone to check the time. She was pleased to see that she had a signal. It was going to be a long walk back. She wanted to take the time to just be still and reflect, but she could already feel the rest of the work she needed to do pressing down on the back of her neck, seeking to crush her. She remembered that she wanted to call George Wakefield, and that was something she could do while she was walking.

She dialed his number and, to her relief, he answered. She hadn't been savoring the thought of trying to leave him a message.

"Hello, Dr. Wakefield. My name is Samantha Cas—er, Ryan. I'm a detective with the San Francisco Police Department."

"Detective, how can I help you?"

"I wanted to discuss with you your theories about earthquake detection."

"I'd be happy to. Forgive me. I'm just surprised that someone from the police department is interested."

"I apologize. I'm not calling officially. This is more of a personal interest."

"Ah, I see. How can I help?"

"Did you really see a significant increase in runaway pets right before the earthquake hit?"

"Yes. It was up fifteen percent in the days before."

"Wow, that is significant."

"Yes, but not nearly as significant as what I've seen since the earthquake."

"And what's that?"

"It's up by sixty percent."

"Sixty percent? Are you sure?"

"The numbers don't lie."

"Is that normal for after an earthquake?"

"Detective, I've got studies that go back twenty-five

years. I've never seen anything like it. Neither has anyone else I've spoken to."

"I'd love to talk to you about this further. Is there a good time we can meet?"

"I'm free tomorrow afternoon. I'll be downtown."

"Great. I'll call you and we'll set something up."

"Okay."

After hanging up with him, she called Jada.

"Hello?"

"Hi, it's Samantha. I'm calling about the Lightfoot case."

"It's about time you or your partner called to check in," the coroner said.

"What do you have?" Samantha asked.

"I can tell you this much. That wood- or stonelike consistency of her skin when we found her?"

"Yeah?"

"It goes straight through."

"What are you saying?"

"I'm saying, I needed to use a bone saw just to get through her skin."

"What could have caused that?" Samantha asked.

"I have no clue. True petrification is when minerals leech into the porous parts of an organism, slowly replacing the original parts. Eventually, the original parts are worn away, and what you have is a combination of minerals like quartz and calcite that end up being an exact model of the original wood or bone."

"I take it that's usually not a quick process."

"As far as I know, there is no flash-freeze version," Jada confirmed. "I'm telling you, though, I'm taking notes. When I'm done writing this baby up, it's going into some science and medical journals."

Crap, Samantha thought. Now she was going to have to deal with that as well. The prospect left her feeling more than a little ill.

"So, anything on possible cause of death other than too many minerals in her diet?" Samantha asked, trying to make light of it so that Jada wouldn't suspect her when the research went missing.

"Nothing, as far as I can tell. This really is fascinating. I've got to hand it to you. You've certainly livened things up around here."

"Oh, goody."

"Look, the second I know anything more, I'll call you."

"I'd appreciate that," Samantha said.

She hung up and could feel her blood pressure skyrocketing. *Focus on the case.*

Winona Lightfoot had been receiving threatening letters and then she showed up dead, basically petrified. The work had to be that of a witch. But why would a witch, or anyone for that matter, want the woman dead? As things stood, it made no sense. She had to stop looking at the witch angle for a minute, because it was clouding her judgment. Instead she needed to take a good, hard look at the victim herself.

She was a bit of a local celebrity, a champion for cultural treasures and a historian. *We need to be talking to her business colleagues and see what she was actively working on.*

That was the only way they were going to make real

progress on this case. Hopefully, her colleagues could shed some more light on Winona's current work. Perhaps some of them had also been contacted by her killer.

The killer was obviously searching for something since Winona's office had been ransacked and Jill, the woman she was supposed to be meeting with a few hours after her death, had been contacted.

I need to get home and talk with Jill. She doesn't remember what happened to her yesterday, but maybe I can help her remember. What is it the killer thought she had?

And what if the person who contacted Jill and the person who ransacked Winona's office were two different people? The circle had shown Samantha the faces of the two witches she'd had confrontations with. Were they working together, divvying up the workload, or working at cross-purposes?

If she could figure out why Winona was killed, everything else would fall into place. The best place to start was with Jill. Even if her roommate was angry with her, she would still want to help catch Winona's killer.

Samantha picked up her pace. She had been so sleep deprived and running around from one thing to the next for the last several hours that she hadn't stopped to think like a detective. That was changing immediately. When Jill got home that evening, they were talking, even if it made both of them squirm.

She was practically jogging beside the train tracks now, trying to remember how far away from Roaring Camp she had to be at that point. She wanted to stop and pull out the map, but that would just waste time. If she stuck to her course, she would get there.

Another five minutes later, she spotted a petrified tree that she recognized from the ride up. The tree was fallen on its side. It looked so lonely and stark, a grim reminder of death. And yet it was preserved instead of falling to ash, as so many other living things did. Just like Winona.

The similarities didn't end there either. The way it was lying reminded her eerily of the way Winona's body had looked when they found her. A very short section of a branch was sticking up from the trunk, reminding her of an arm. A shiver went up her spine as a sudden horrible thought occurred to her. She remembered the face of the witch who had attacked her car, the insanity she'd seen flickering in her eyes. Was it possible this tree had served as some sort of sick inspiration for the murder?

She walked closer, eyes gazing intently at it. Finally she could see the whole thing clearly. She froze. There, burned into the side of the dead tree were three words.

The last grave.

Samantha reached out with a shaking hand and touched the words carved into the wood. Sudden, intense heat and a slight sizzling sound caused her to jerk her hand back. Her fingertips were burnt. Whoever had seared the words into the tree had done so within the last few minutes.

She spun around in a circle. The forest had gone completely silent. No birds or insects made a sound. No animals crunched leaves or rustled in the undergrowth. No wind caused the trees to sigh or creak.

Absolute silence and absolute stillness. And somewhere close by was a witch. She should have seen it coming. She had invaded their territory. And for all she knew, whomever Cody had called to ask about her might have been the one person in his whole Wiccan coven she didn't want him talking to.

Samantha turned, constantly moving, terrified that she would miss seeing the witch when she made her move. And then she stopped, the words of her ten-year-old self ringing in her ears. Fear was not the answer. Calm was. If she could be calm, she would have the ability to focus her energy quickly when and where she needed it. The two witches she had come up against were more powerful than she was. She had to be smarter than they were.

Something touched the back of her shoulder. Samantha spun to face the threat.

There was nothing there.

A whisper, a laugh, came to her.

"Show yourself," she said, licking her lips.

Something tugged on her hair and she twisted around.

Her probing eyes saw only trees.

She thought of the attack outside of Robin's cabin, where the trees themselves had seemed to come alive and tried to kill her. She glanced down at the ground, searching for the movement of roots. All appeared still.

Something shoved her hard, causing her to stagger to catch her footing. She landed on a rock, twisting her ankle. When she turned around, there was still nothing. The witch must have cast a spell to make herself appear invisible.

"Show yourself!" Samantha demanded, trying to throw as much authority into her voice as she could.

That same quiet laugh answered her.

She couldn't trust her eyes, so she had to rely on her other senses. She listened, hoping to hear the crunch of leaves, the rustle of clothes. There was nothing but the steady laughter that sounded like it was coming from right next to her.

A sudden, terrible suspicion dawned on her. She brought her hand to her mouth, covering her lips. For a moment the laughter ceased. She tensed, but a moment later it started back up.

It's not me. I'm not the one laughing.

But it was so close, she should be able to reach out and touch the witch. She stretched out her arms, but her fingers touched only air. The laughter continued as her frustration built.

"Show yourself!" Samantha screamed.

The laughter ceased, and from six inches above her head, she heard someone whisper, "Run!"

It was as though it had been the cue her legs had been waiting for. Before she even knew what she was doing, she was running through the forest as fast as she could.

I should stand and fight. I should find a place to fight. Find the high ground.

But all she could think of was getting away. The witch had been above her that entire time. Samantha didn't know how. Maybe the woman had been hanging from a tree branch like some sort of bat. Her frightened mind conjured much darker images, granted the witch nearly limitless power, but she struggled to bring herself back to calm, to center. Which was nearly impossible when she was running faster than she ever had in her entire life.

Her foot slipped on something, but she grabbed hold of a tree and used it to propel herself onward. Countless small animals ran from her, almost as afraid as she was. A felled tree appeared in her path, and in one move she vaulted it, landing hard on the other side but still on her feet.

And the whole time her mind was screaming at her to stop, but it was as though she was caught in some horrific feedback loop. She was running and she couldn't stop.

She kept going, blood roaring in her ears and lungs gasping for air. She kept running until she knew the witch wasn't anywhere near her. She couldn't sense anyone else anywhere near her. And when she finally screamed at herself to stop, she realized with dread that she couldn't.

The witch did something to me.

She couldn't force herself to slow. Her legs were not hers to command anymore. She had been summoned before, felt compelled to go toward someone and lost control of her body during that experience. But this was being repelled from someone.

How far away does she mean for me to run? Samantha wondered. *Out of the forest? Out of the county?*

And it finally dawned on her as her lungs seared with pain and sweat streamed into her eyes.

She means for me to run until it kills me.

As trees flashed past and the pain built, Samantha could feel her body struggling to heal itself from the muscle fatigue that was tormenting her. Sweat was pouring off of her, drenching her clothes. She was dehydrating, and she could feel muscles in different parts of her body begin to cramp and seize. Her breathing had become ragged, and the deeper she tried to breathe, the less oxygen she seemed to be getting.

She could feel her body starting to shake as more and more muscles cramped. She didn't know how long she'd been running, but the speed had not let up at all.

I'm going to die if I can't make myself stop.

She reached out, praying she still had control over her arms, and grabbed a slender tree as she raced by. The resultant impact caused her shoulder to separate, but she held on long enough to land herself flat on her back.

She popped back up, and her fingers caught at the rough bark, tearing off her fingernails as she tried to hold on. With a wrench, her body freed itself and she was running again, trees rushing by her at blinding speed. Her mind worked frantically, trying to figure out how she could stop what was happening. Even if she had the energy to create some kind of barrier, she was sure her legs would just carry her around it.

She could feel small blood vessels all over her body starting to burst with the force of the blood pumping through them. She stepped down wrong on her left foot and felt the bone crack. She didn't have much time left.

Then she heard the sound of running water. It was coming from in front of her, and a crazy thought took over. Soon a creek was in sight. She raced toward it. Then she was in the water, splashing through.

She bent down and lodged her hand into the crack between two boulders. She cried out in anguish as the bones in her hands and fingers snapped. They held, though, and she fell into the water. Before she could get up, she spun, planting herself facedown in the freezing water. She wedged her other hand underneath some more boulders and held on.

Please, God, let this work, she prayed.

She opened her mouth and sucked the icy water into her lungs. Her entire body spasmed and began to arch and thrash. Terror flooded her, but she kept it up.

The witch had meant her legs to run until she was dead. Maybe she could short-circuit the spell by coming as near to dying as she could.

Her feet kicked wildly, trying again and again to get a purchase on the slippery rocks on the bed of the creek and failing over and over. Her face was downstream from her legs, and after a moment, the water she gulped in was filled with blood from her battered legs.

She continued to convulse as her body fought to live and her legs fought to run. But she forced herself to keep her head under water. Her chest heaved, trying to vomit the water, but there was nowhere for it to go. Finally, darkness began to close around her. Slowly, her legs stopped moving.

I need to move now. Push myself out of the water.

But it sounded like too much effort. Maybe she'd just lie there for a little while, take a nap. She'd feel better after she'd rested.

Her mind drifted down the course of the creek. It

really was beautiful here. She knew she'd been afraid, but she couldn't remember why. That was okay. She didn't want to be afraid anymore. This feeling of lightness was much better.

Snatches of a rhyme she'd sung as a child came back to her.

When witches go to school, little boys cry.

There was more to it; she knew there was. Why could she never remember the last part? She struggled, trying to remember how it went. For some reason, it seemed terribly important that she remember. She had sung it a thousand times, a million even.

The water was getting even colder. Maybe she should move.

Get up!

So very cold, but she couldn't move. And besides, she wanted to remember the rest of the song.

When witches go to school, little boys cry. When witches go to school, bad girls die.

There was more; what was it?

She was colder now, but she wasn't sure she cared. Maybe she'd get up, but she didn't really have to. The creek bottom was pretty comfortable when you got used to it. In fact, she had decided she'd stay. Now, if only she could remember the rest of the song.

When witches go to school, little boys cry. When witches go to school, bad girls die. And—

And what? It was almost there, the last phrase.

And what a bad, bad witch am I.

Pain seared through her, the last of her energy struggling to heal a dead body. All her muscles went completely rigid as electricity arched through them and then hit the water around her. The resultant current jolted her up out of the water just enough for her to cough.

Bloody water streamed out of her mouth before she collapsed back into the creek. Terror returned to her and she thrashed, willing her arms to push her back up out of the water. They wouldn't, but she finally managed to flip over onto her back, her lips barely above the waterline as her head came to rest on a boulder that was only partly submerged.

She hacked again and again as her body expelled the water. Blood vessels all throughout her body began to repair themselves as her body sucked up the energy of the water rushing around it.

She had done it. She had ended the spell. It was moot, though, if she couldn't heal the damage she'd done to her body during drowning. She lay there, too scared to open her eyes, for what seemed like an eternity. The cold water raced around her, making her shiver so hard her teeth chattered together.

She needed to get out of the cold water and into some warm clothes before she went into shock. The January air had been mild today, but the sun was going down and the temperature was rapidly plunging. It was supposed to reach nearly freezing later that night.

Finally, she opened her eyes. She could see slivers of dark sky above her through the trees. Slowly, she sat up, head spinning. She nearly collapsed again, but she managed to stay sitting upright. She reached out with her torn and battered fingers and began to drag herself out of the creek. The pain made her cry, and the tears on her cheeks stung with cold.

"You can do it," she whispered to herself, teeth still chattering.

She dragged herself up and out of the water and collapsed on the ground, sobbing. She lay flat against the earth, wishing she could become part of it. She pulled as much of its energy into herself as she could until she could feel roots in the ground beneath her actually starting to wither and die. They gave their life so that she might live.

It took another half hour before she could stand. The cold was nearly overwhelming her, and she debated ditching her wet clothes. Shock was quickly setting in.

Just walk and you'll warm up, she told herself. She wondered if she should build a small fire but was hesitant to do so. She didn't want anyone seeing the smoke and coming to investigate. She was in no shape to deal with witches or forest rangers.

She put one foot in front of the other, marveling at how much effort a few simple steps took. She promised herself hot cocoa, a hot shower—because she didn't think she could face soaking in a bathtub anytime soon after nearly drowning—and warm, fleecy clothes when she got home. Then she'd crank up the heater and lie on top of the vent in the floor of her room.

And when she made it to her rental car, she would turn up the heat as high as she could. She realized with instant regret that she'd neglected to put a spare set of clothes in the new car. Epic fail.

That was okay. The car would be warm and she could sit and it would be good. She wouldn't even have to drive straight home. She could go to a hotel or even take a nap in the parking lot before she had to drive all the way home.

These sounded like better options to her. Another step. Another. Everything was going to be okay. Soon she'd be warm and safe. She looked up from the ground and looked at the trees around her.

And that was when it hit her.

She was completely lost.

10

"You've got to be kidding me," Samantha whispered, her misery nearly overwhelming her.

Her phone was gone, probably lost to the river. She still had her keys in her pocket, but they would be of no use unless she could find the car. There was no sign of train tracks anywhere. The map she'd shoved into her pocket disintegrated when she tried to pull it out. No one knew she was up here, not even Lance, so help wasn't coming.

What do people do when they're lost? There's something about moss on trees.

She shook her head. Thinking like a regular person was only going to get her in more trouble. She dug her keys out of her pocket, placed them on her palm, and held out her hand. With her free hand, she touched the car key.

"Take me to the lock this key fits."

She felt the energy flow out of her hand, more painful than it normally should have been because of her great exhaustion. She pulled her hand away and the key began to vibrate. It twisted itself around on her palm until it was pointing past her left shoulder.

She turned and began to walk that way. She was so tired that she stumbled every few feet. Finally, she had to put the keys back in her pocket so she had both hands free to help catch herself.

She stopped after five minutes and pulled the keys back out. She was still going in the right direction. She made a micro adjustment and continued on, checking her direction every five minutes. After about half an hour, she came to a stop at a gorge and stared across to the other side.

She wanted to cry but ended up laughing instead, the sound crazy even to her own ears. "The most direct route is not always the best route," she said.

There was a railroad bridge about a hundred feet from where she was. She walked wearily over to it. She gazed across the expanse. She was going to have to walk across.

She bent down and put her hand on the track, feeling for vibrations. The last thing she wanted to do was get halfway across and have a train show up. She couldn't feel anything, so she grimly stepped out on the tracks. She walked slowly and steadily, making sure to pick up her feet so she wouldn't trip.

At last she made it across, and she pulled out her keys again. They pointed straight on, while the railroad tracks curved to the right. She stood there, torn. If she followed where the keys led, she ran the risk of coming across more impassable terrain. On the other hand, she knew the train had made several switchbacks going up the mountain.

She reached up and touched the cross, which was still around her neck. "Which way?" she whispered.

The sun had set and what little light had been left in the sky was fast fading. She knew the railroad tracks might be the longer way to go but that they would get her where she was going and she'd at least be able to see the ground a little more clearly. She shoved her keys back into her pocket, turned. and began walking next to the railroad tracks.

Now that the sun was down, the cold set in with a vengeance, chilling her through and through. She told herself to just keep walking as she rubbed her arms and hands together.

Nearly two hours later, Roaring Camp came into sight and she sobbed in relief. The General Store and the other buildings were closed for the night. It made the area look like a ghost town instead of the vibrant place it had been earlier.

She saw movement out of the corner of her eye and spun, hands lifted, then forced herself to quickly put them down when she realized it was a couple of hikers heading to their car.

She heard a step behind her and she twisted around. Just someone leaving work late, locking up.

The woman looked at her and her eyes widened. "Are you okay? Do you need me to call an ambulance?"

Samantha remembered that her clothes were shredded as well as wet. "I'm fine," she said, trying to make her tone soothing. "But I lost my phone. Is there a pay phone around here?"

The woman pointed.

"Thanks," Samantha said.

"Are you sure you don't need help?"

Samantha took a deep breath. "I'm fine. Forget about it," she said, letting her words wash over the other woman. The woman's eyes unfocused slightly, and then she nodded and headed for the parking lot.

Samantha stumbled toward the pay phone. She had no coins, so she had to call Lance collect. She braced herself for the questioning she was going to get for doing so.

"What happened to you?" he asked.

"It's a very long story. I lost my cell phone."

"Okay. That's going to be an interesting story."

"No, it's really not," she said firmly.

"Okay. So, time to meet?"

"Give me an hour and a half. I'm still in Santa Cruz."

He sighed. "Fine. I'll meet you at Tony's."

Tony's was an Italian restaurant downtown that Lance practically lived at.

"See you there."

She hung up and trudged to her car. Once inside, she cranked up the heater. Her clothes were still sopping wet and it was freezing cold. Now that she was sitting and not moving, the cold began to overtake her and she was shaking like a leaf. She waited a couple of minutes until she got control of herself again. Finally, she pulled out of the parking lot and hit the highway.

The drive home seemed longer than her entire trek through the forest. Maybe it was because she was so exhausted and the heat was making her drowsy. Her body was still struggling to heal, and hunger was the only thing keeping her awake.

At least by the time she parked outside of Tony's her clothes were dry. As she surveyed them, though, she realized they were shredded in several places. She looked like she'd been through a meat grinder.

She bit her lip. If she went home, she'd never be able to make herself leave again. She held her hand up to the heating vent, pulling the energy out of the warm air. She put a glamour on herself so that no one would notice her ripped clothing.

Finally, she got out of the car and staggered into the restaurant, collapsing in a chair across from Lance.

"You've looked better," he noted.

She panicked for a moment, thinking her glamour had failed, and then realized while her clothes should look fine to him, her hair and face were still a mess. *Sloppy. I should have thought about that before I came in here.* It was too late to do anything about it, though.

She grimaced. "I've felt better," she admitted. It was quite possibly the understatement of the century.

"How was your day?" he asked.

"I've had better. My lead didn't pan out," she added hastily, hoping to steer him off that topic. "What about you? Any luck?"

"Struggling to remember a worse day. At least I got the report filed so the captain can get off my back about that."

"Sometimes you've got to thank God for the small miracles," she said.

"We're alive."

"That's not a small miracle," she said with a grunt.

"I was thinking it's time we work on a motive in this case."

"Right there with you."

"Let's start fresh in the morning. I've made a list of friends and colleagues we should go talk to. People don't get murdered for no reason."

"I'm with you. Let's make it happen."

"I don't know why this whole thing has been so screwed up," he said. "It's like it started wrong all the way around. And then the thing with your roommate. It's just been like nothing I've ever experienced before. Maybe it's the quakes. Everyone's rattled."

"I thought Californians didn't get rattled."

"Some do," he said with a shrug. "And there are a bunch who live here who weren't born here."

"Like me."

They were interrupted by the waiter, who brought a giant bowl of spaghetti with meatballs and two plates.

"You'll like their spaghetti," Lance said as the waiter walked away.

She didn't. And she'd told Lance that a dozen times, but it didn't seem to sink in. They loaded it with garlic, which wasn't what she was used to. He loved it and therefore he believed everyone must. At the moment, though, she was too tired to complain.

She shoveled some of the pasta onto her plate and was grateful that it was at least hot. She shoved a spoonful into her mouth and nearly gagged. She looked up at Lance in shock.

"Oh, yeah, I had them add extra garlic today. I know how much you like it."

She managed to swallow her bite and then she grabbed for her water. She drank half the glass and then looked up at him.

"I'm going to kill you."

"Nah, you love me. We both know it."

She considered her options. At the moment, killing Lance seemed like an excellent idea. Productive even.

She felt a flash of heat through her body and realized with a start that the thought of killing someone was actually exciting her. That realization flooded her with horror. She reached up and gripped her cross, trying to ground herself. What was wrong with her? Had all the attacks brought this on?

She took several deep breaths and struggled to banish the dark thoughts that were threatening to consume her. *Focus. Choose something you can control to focus on.*

Slowly, she raised a shaking hand, signaling to the waiter, who scurried over.

"Actually, I'd like chicken fettuccine Alfredo, hold the garlic."

He nodded and headed for the kitchen.

"What are you doing?" Lance asked incredulously.

"Saving your life."

He smiled. "You crack me up, Ryan."

You wouldn't say that if you knew I wasn't joking, she thought. She gripped the edge of the table with her free hand as she struggled to bring herself under control. She could feel the wood giving way beneath her fingers, heating up and warping.

Ten minutes later, when the waiter returned with her food and set it down in front of her, she finally let go of the table. She glanced down at the wood and could see indentations from her fingers. She hadn't left her fingerprints on the table so much as in it.

She picked up her napkin and wiped her forehead. From freezing to boiling. She was going to get sick if she wasn't careful. At the moment, though, something so mundane as a cold seemed the least of her worries.

Lance was still talking, and she struggled to figure out what about. It had to have something to do with the case they were working. But she didn't want to talk about it. She didn't want to talk about anything. She had nearly died a few hours before. And as far as her body was concerned, she *had* died.

"You bored, Ryan?" Lance asked suddenly, his voice seeming unnaturally loud to her.

She shook her head. "I don't feel so good. I think I'm coming down with something."

He made a show of moving his food farther away from her. "Well, keep it to yourself, whatever it is."

She couldn't think of anything sarcastic to say in return. She was beginning to sweat. She really was too exhausted. She shouldn't be here. She shouldn't have cast the glamour on her clothes.

Her legs were beginning to shake.

I'm still in shock.

She felt the glamour starting to slip. She didn't have enough energy to take care of her body and keep the glamour up. She dropped her knife on the floor on purpose. She bent over to pick it up, blood rushing to her brain as she did so.

She pressed her fingers to the wood floor and pulled

for all she was worth. Energy from everyone in the room flowed into her, bolstering her. She had to force herself to let go as her body eagerly drank up what she was feeding it.

She sat up slowly.

Lance looked slightly dazed.

"You okay?" she asked.

"It's been a rough couple of days. I guess it's all sort of catching up to me."

"Let's finish eating so we can get out of here. I for one need to sleep for about a week," she said.

"Good idea."

They ate the rest of their meal quickly. Lance paid without a word about her fettuccine and they got up and left the restaurant. She could see other people around the restaurant looking tired. That was her doing, but it couldn't be helped.

Outside in the parking lot, Lance breathed in deeply of the cold air and it seemed to revive him a bit. "Walk with me for a minute," he said. "There's something I want to show you."

She wanted nothing more than to refuse, but she didn't want to arouse his suspicions. They walked two blocks in silence, and she looked around, wondering what it was he wanted to talk about, to show her.

"You know, Lance, is this going to take much longer? I'm really beat," she finally said.

"Take a look around," he said, slowing to a stop.

"I have been," she said, wondering what was going on in his head.

"You notice anything weird around here lately?"

Samantha glanced at him, wondering if this was some kind of trap. If he could prove his partner was crazy, he could get her transferred or suspended. She hadn't known him long enough to be sure just exactly what he was capable of.

"Define weird," she said, keeping her tone carefully neutral.

"I haven't seen a homeless person in two days."

"You know, you're right," she said. It was surprising. The city's homeless were usually everywhere. She remembered how surprised she'd been the night of the murder not to find any of them in the area.

She looked around. "Usually there's half a dozen guys on the street at this hour."

"At least. They've been gone so long, even the urine smell is fading."

He was right. It was something she'd trained herself to ignore, but things had definitely changed.

"Has the department been cracking down lately?" she asked. "Is there a new shelter open that serves better food?"

He shook his head. "Not that I've heard. Even if the department were cracking down, it wouldn't be this effective. And we'd have heard about any new shelters."

"Where do you think they've all gone?"

"I don't know. But that's the seventh missing dog poster I've seen in two blocks," he said, pointing to a flyer on a utility pole.

"And the third moving van," Samantha said, pointing across the street.

"You ever get the feeling there's something someone's not telling us? Maybe there's something they know that we don't?"

She shrugged, not trusting herself to answer that question.

"I'm not wrong here, am I?" he asked.

There was an edge to his voice, a pleading.

She nodded toward the woman directing the movers. "Isn't that the famous palm reader from the pier?"

"It looks like her. Why?"

Samantha glanced at him. "Just wait here a minute for me," she said. She dropped her voice and pushed a little bit of persuasion into her words, not enough to over-power him, but more than enough to make her feel guilty about it.

She made it across the street, dodging a couple of cars.

The woman turned to watch her. Her long gray hair hung in a single braid down her back. Her face was heav-ily lined, but she had the eyes of a much younger woman.

"You should arrest yourself for jaywalking, Detec-tive," the woman drawled as Samantha stopped in front of her.

"Who was walking?" Samantha retorted. "And how did you know I was a detective?"

"I've seen you around. Something I can do for you?"

"Yes. A friend of mine is a fan of yours and wanted to know why you're leaving and where you're planning on setting up shop?"

The woman chuckled. "I seriously doubt any friend of *yours* is interested in me."

"Just because I'm a detective—"

"It isn't that, witchy."

"Excuse me?" Samantha asked, forcing herself to stand her ground and not take a step away from the older woman.

"Just 'cuz I don't have the power doesn't mean I can't sense it."

There was no use denying it, Samantha realized quickly, so she dropped the pretense. "Why are you leaving?"

"Same reason so many others are."

"And exactly what is that?" Samantha asked, struggling to keep her growing irritation out of her voice.

"Problem with your kind is you aren't good with telling the future."

"And you are?"

"Better than you, it would seem. I've at least got the good sense to get out of here."

"But why? What's coming?" Samantha asked, feeling fear prick her scalp even as she voiced the question.

"I don't know. But it's time to go before it gets here. I can feel that in here," she said, patting her chest. "When something deep inside tells you to run, you usually don't have time to stop and ask why. Now, if you'll excuse me, dear, I have to go."

Samantha sighed and headed back across the street.

"Everything okay?" Lance asked.

"Yup. She's definitely headed out of town, though."

"What were we talking about?" Lance asked.

"All the people leaving the city."

"Oh, yeah. Weird, don't you think?"

"Yes, I think so."

"Yeah. Okay, I've got to go get some rest so we can try

to tackle this thing fresh," he said, rubbing his eyes. "I parked on the next street over."

"All right. See you in the morning."

He turned and walked away. Samantha squared her shoulders and headed back to her car. She puzzled over what they had been talking about as she drove.

Samantha made it back home and noticed that there was a moving van parked in front of the building next door.

"Careful! Okay, tilt it toward me."

She looked up and saw a man and a woman trying to get a couch down the stairs. The man's hands looked like they were slipping. Samantha moved quickly and grabbed one end of the couch, bolstering it up before he could lose control.

"Thanks," he grunted.

"You're welcome."

Together the three of them got the couch the rest of the way down the stairs and up into the moving van. As soon as they'd put it down, the man extended his hand. She shook it.

"Thanks for the assist. Sorry that we're leaving before we had a chance to really get acquainted."

"Where are you guys headed?" Samantha asked.

"A church in Texas called two days ago looking for a new pastor, and here we are heading out," the woman said with a smile.

"It was the funniest thing too. We've been here six years. Love the church, love the parishioners. About a week ago, though, it hit both of us at the same time. It was time to go. And the Lord provided an opportunity.

Just like he sent you to save me from killing myself just now," he said.

"What kind of church?" Samantha asked.

"Evangelical," the couple answered in unison before bursting into laughter.

Samantha nodded. "And about a week ago you both just decided it was time to move on?"

The wife's face clouded over slightly. "It was the oddest thing. We used to love it here, but it's, I don't know, different somehow." She shook her head. "And now we're off. A new adventure."

"Well, good luck to you both," Samantha said, before climbing down out of the van.

"Thanks. Same to you!" he answered.

Lance was right. People were leaving the city. But it wasn't everyone. It was those who had a slightly different view of things than the rest of them. Many of the city's homeless, through drink or mental illness, had always been a bit off. The woman who claimed to be psychic. The Wiccan coven she had met in the park. Now evangelical Christians who were sensitive to the interactions of the supernatural in their lives.

And if she was being honest with herself, she'd been feeling the urge to leave as well. At first she'd thought it was because she wanted to get away from the witch activity that seemed to be surrounding this case. Now she wasn't so sure. Were all these people picking up on some kind of early-warning system? She couldn't help but think about George Wakefield and what he'd said about animals fleeing their homes before earthquakes. Samantha didn't have to be a witch to know that dogs and cats were sensitive to things, people, and events that most humans weren't. She thought of all the lost-dog fliers. And from where she was standing, she could see one for a lost cat.

And she knew, deep in her gut, that her fears were true.

Something was coming.

She managed to get upstairs. Helping with the couch had drained a lot of her borrowed energy. She really was in need of a week's worth of sleep. She made it inside her apartment and felt herself relax. Jill was sitting on the couch watching television. She glanced up at Samantha but didn't say anything.

They needed to talk, but Samantha didn't have it in her to talk tonight. She kicked off her shoes and hung her keys on the hook beside the front door. She heaved a sigh of relief. She was home. Safe.

She turned to head toward her bedroom and Jill screamed.

"What?" Samantha asked, spinning to look at her roommate.

Jill was pointing at her, eyes wide.

Samantha glanced down and saw that the glamour had failed. Her torn, dirty clothes were showing in all their glory.

"I'm okay," she hastened to assure the other woman. "It was a rough day, but I'm fine."

Jill shook her head violently from side to side.

Samantha took a step forward, and Jill scooted farther away from her on the couch.

"Jill, it's me, Samantha. What's wrong?"

"You, you're wrong," Jill said.

Warning bells went off in Samantha's head. "Wh-what do you mean by that?" she asked, trying to keep her voice from shaking.

"I saw . . . I saw . . ." Jill said, sounding like she was babbling.

"What did you see?" Samantha asked, feeling her voice drop to a lower register as she tried to soothe Jill.

"Your clothes. One moment they were fine and the next moment they were shredded, bloody. In the blink of an eye, just like it was magic."

Samantha squeezed her eyes shut, cursing herself for being so careless.

"How is that possible?" she heard Jill ask.

Samantha opened her eyes and met her roommate's stare. "You got it right, Jill. It *is* magic."

And Jill began screaming again.

11

"Quiet!" Samantha shouted.

It had the desired result. Jill stopped screaming. A moment later, though, Samantha realized it wasn't of her own will. Jill's mouth was still open, but no sound was coming out.

Samantha wanted to collapse. It was all too much. She wasn't prepared to deal with any of this. And now that she had inadvertently muted Jill, there was no way out of this but a full explanation.

"I'm going to go get changed and then we're going to talk," Samantha said. "Do you understand?"

Jill nodded, mouth still open, eyes wide in terror.

"Please don't scream," Samantha said. She released Jill's voice, and the tail end of the scream echoed out before Jill snapped her mouth shut, staring warily at Samantha.

Samantha turned and headed toward her bedroom. Nothing about the day was going well; that was clear. She changed into her warmest, fleeciest pair of sweats.

The shower would have to wait, as desperate as she was for it. She headed out to the kitchen, determined that she'd at least have cocoa. She made them each a cup and brought Jill's to her, hoping it would work as a peace offering.

Jill took the mug, staring at it as though it might be poisoned. She set it on the coffee table.

"Jill, it's time we talk," Samantha said, sinking down on the far end of the couch.

Jill looked at her and nodded slowly. She turned off the television and drew her feet up under her on the couch.

"Let's deal with what you just saw a bit later. I wanted to talk about what happened when we tried to capture the person who'd been texting you."

"This is about how I ended up in the park yesterday with no memory of how I got there?"

"Yes. Now, we've been friends for years, right?"

Jill nodded.

"What I'm going to say is going to sound a bit crazy and so I need you to just trust me and keep this between us."

"I'll do my best," Jill said.

It was more than Samantha had hoped for.

"I believe that the person who lured you out of the coffee shop and into the park was using a form of mind control on you."

"You mean like hypnosis?" Jill asked, her brow furrowing.

"Yes, something just like that," Samantha said, struggling with not wanting to tell her the whole truth. "I believe that she might have gotten some piece of information or something from you before I could find you."

"Is that what you were doing just now, some kind of mind control?"

"I said I want to talk about that later. I want to just focus on yesterday at the moment."

Samantha felt like a coward, but she knew that once Jill heard the word "witch," the chances of her becoming hysterical and completely uncooperative were high. She needed to get what information she could out of her before that happened.

"Okay. You know I've been racking my brain and I still can't figure out what Winona's killer would want from me."

"Me either. But the killer knows."

Samantha took a sip of her hot cocoa. Jill's still sat untouched.

"And you think that if they hypnotized me, which would explain my moving a few blocks and having no memory of it, that they might have said something to me or asked me something while I was in that state?" Jill asked.

"Exactly."

"And you're going to ask me to undergo hypnosis to see if you can retrieve that memory, aren't you?"

Samantha nodded, keeping her eyes glued to Jill's face.

"And just who do you propose that I go to in order to have this done?"

"Actually, I know how to do it, if you'll let me."

"Somehow, I'm not surprised," Jill said, her face expressionless and her tone neutral.

Samantha stared at her, struggling to figure out what that was supposed to mean. She reached out slightly, trying to sense what Jill was feeling, but there was such a mixture of colliding emotions and thoughts that it was impossible to pick out a dominant one.

"So, will you let me try?" Samantha asked.

Just do it. You don't need her permission or cooperation. You can wipe her memory of it afterward. The voice in her head was louder than usual, and she struggled to silence it.

Jill cleared her throat. "You know, once, in college, when you and I were studying at my apartment, you looked at my smoke detector and told me I should make sure it was working. That was all. There was something odd about the way you said it, though. When you left, I checked it out and it was dead. I put fresh batteries in it. Two nights later, it went off. There was a gas leak in the oven. It saved my life. You saved my life."

"You never told me," Samantha said, staring at her in surprise.

Jill shook her head. "People ... some people, they would always say that there was something weird about you. I told them they were crazy. Then, when that happened, I knew you had saved my life somehow. But I didn't want to know how."

Samantha didn't know what to say. In truth, she didn't even recall telling Jill to check her smoke alarm. Was it possible that all those years she'd lived with the nightmares, she'd also been having the dreams, the premonitions that she had thought were relatively new things the last few months?

"I can understand not wanting to know," Samantha said, hoping that it would be her out.

Jill took a deep breath. "That was then. I was young. I hadn't seen much of the world. I'll let you do what you want to, look for the memory, but only if you agree to tell me the truth. The *actual* truth."

Samantha sat quietly and finally nodded. "Okay. Let's get this done, and then I'll tell you everything."

"No. First you tell me everything," Jill said, folding her arms across her chest defensively.

"Okay," Samantha said. She wasn't happy, but she didn't see any way around it if she wanted Jill's help. She continued to struggle to silence the inner voice that insisted she didn't need Jill's cooperation.

She cradled her mug of cocoa, focusing on the sensations of warmth in her hands. It was a trick her adoptive father had taught her. When faced with intense stress and anxiety, focus on small physical sensations that you could quantify and fixate on. The mug was smooth and warm. She could smell the cocoa, and it smelled like the holidays to her, probably because it had a touch of peppermint in it.

"So, I was raised in a coven."

"Wiccans? Pagans?" Jill asked interestedly.

Samantha grimaced. Jill was, after all, an anthropologist. This part probably would be interesting to her.

"Neither. It was a dark coven based on power and greed, not any discernible faith. They ... we ... were witches."

Jill raised an eyebrow. "You know, historically speaking—"

Samantha cut her off. "*Real* witches, with real powers, who did very, very bad things."

Jill nodded slowly. "I'm listening."

"When I was twelve, the coven attempted to raise a demon. Everyone was slaughtered except for me."

She paused, waiting to see Jill's reactions. It was telling to her how carefully her roommate chose her next words. "Many cultures believe in the demonic and have rituals for either expelling or summoning those types of entities. Some of these ceremonies involve inviting the entity to embody one member, who then purports to speak for it. Other ceremonies make use of certain types of hallucinogens."

"Jill, I'm going to have to stop you right there. We need to be on the same page here, talking about the same thing. Now, you told me what happened with the smoke alarm, and you know what you saw when I came in the house."

Doubt crossed Jill's face. Samantha could tell by looking in her eyes that the scientist had already begun to question the evidence of her own eyes, started cataloging possible explanations for what she had seen.

"You used the word 'magic' earlier," Samantha continued.

"I probably should have said illusion," Jill answered. "But yes, some sort of magic trick."

"It was no trick."

Jill smiled. "Don't be silly. Of course it was. Nothing else makes sense."

Samantha raised her hand and Jill's cup of hot cocoa slid across the coffee table to her.

Jill jumped with a small cry and then settled back in her seat, shaking her head. "You almost got me with that one. I've seen magicians do stuff like that. There's got to be a wire or a magnet or something."

Samantha groaned. She was too tired to spend all night playing games, trying to make her roommate believe what she clearly didn't want to believe. "Jill, didn't you tell me you had a dog when you were a kid?"

"Yes, why?"

"Can you picture her in your mind for me? Picture her when she was a puppy."

"Okay. Now what?"

"Now just watch."

Samantha focused on Jill. She reached out and touched her hand and immediately she could see the dog. It was a tiny puppy, a cocker spaniel–poodle mix. Samantha pulled her hand from Jill's.

"Watch closely," she said.

She put her hands close together and energy began to form between them. Samantha held the image of Jill's puppy in her mind, and slowly it began to form. She was tired, so it took a while. She also wanted her to be perfect, and she didn't have the connection with the puppy that she did with Freaky.

Moments later she was finished, and the small ball of fur landed on the couch. It looked up at her, panting, and then bounded over and landed on Jill's lap.

Her shock was plain to read on her face. Samantha felt herself tense, waiting for the reaction to the dog.

As the dog began to lick Jill's nose, her face crumpled and she was laughing and crying all at once and hugging the tiny creature. Samantha smiled. She knew what it was like to be reunited with a pet from childhood. Before she even realized what she was doing, she had conjured Freaky.

The little black kitten stared at the puppy with wide-eyed fascination. He stalked slowly across the couch on tiny, silent paws. Samantha reached out and scooped him up. "You can play with Roxy later," she whispered.

The kitten twisted in her arms, paws reaching out and waving in the air in the direction of the puppy. Samantha laughed, surprised by just how much her little companion wanted to play with the puppy.

After a couple of minutes, Jill looked up and noticed Freaky. "Who's he?" she asked, wiping the tears from her eyes.

"He was the kitten I had as a child."

"Can I keep her?" Jill asked, hugging the puppy.

Samantha bit her lip, suddenly regretting her choice. How to explain to her roommate that Roxy wasn't a real, living, breathing dog but merely an energy creation? "It's complicated. We can talk about it later, but she can stay for now," Samantha said.

Jill nodded.

Samantha cleared her throat. "So, as I was saying—"

"You're a witch," Jill interrupted.

"Yeah. No. I was. It's complicated."

"I can imagine. And it's all real?"

Samantha nodded.

"And whoever came to talk to me yesterday was a witch too?"

"I'm afraid so."

"How does it work exactly? How do you get your abilities?"

"We're born with them. We can sense the flow of currents, energy, magnetism, things like that. And we learn to manipulate them. It can get complicated, but that's the nutshell version."

"That's a lot of responsibility," Jill noted.

"Yeah. Well, some don't take it as seriously as they should."

"So, everyone with the power is a witch?" Jill asked, scratching Roxy behind the ears.

"Hardly. People with the power belong to different creeds, faiths, and walks of life. Only those with a true lust for power are drawn to the darkness."

"Isn't that true of so many things?"

Her statement took Samantha aback. She had never really thought of that, but once Jill had said it, she had to admit the truth of it. "I guess so."

Jill nodded. "So, go on."

"I was adopted by a very kind couple, and I gave up my past completely, the magic, everything I owned, even my memories."

"Wow, that's intense," Jill said.

"It wasn't easy, but it was necessary."

"It's very unusual that someone can give up their history that completely. Usually they keep something, even if it's just a reminder."

"I didn't want any reminders," Samantha said, reflexively touching the cross around her neck.

"What happened?"

"A few months ago, a dark coven started sacrificing

girls. I was a detective with the Boston PD. My captain knew of my past and asked me to go undercover to stop the killings. I finally agreed. It was bad, even worse than I had thought it would be. When it was all over, I was once more the last witch standing. But I couldn't go back to my old life."

Samantha could hear the stress in her voice. She didn't want to tell Jill about the accusations and betrayals. "My captain helped arrange for me to transfer out here. New job. New city. New everything."

"Old Samantha," Jill said softly.

Her words pierced Samantha's heart, wounding deeply. "Yes," she admitted. That was certainly something she didn't want to discuss further, though. "I've been here three months and now I'm investigating a homicide that has witchcraft written all over it."

Jill leaned forward. "Really? Winona? What was it?"

Samantha shook her head. "Not able to really discuss that yet."

Jill leaned back, clearly disappointed. "I still don't get what her killer wanted with me," she said.

"That's what I want to figure out. Are you ready to help me?"

Jill nodded hesitantly. "What will it involve?"

"You know how you pictured Roxy and I was able to create her?" Samantha said.

The puppy was now curled up in Jill's lap. Her ears twitched at the mention of her name, but she didn't move otherwise. Freaky was attacking the arm of the sofa, and Samantha lifted a hand to dispel the energy but quickly thought better of it. She didn't want to have to explain how all that worked and how it was going to pertain to Roxy until she'd gotten what she needed to out of Jill.

"But I don't remember what happened," Jill protested.

"You don't have to. The information's there; your mind still recorded the events. You just have been denied access to those memories. If you think about sitting in the coffee shop and then sitting on that park bench, I can establish a connection and try to find those memories."

"You make it sound like you're going to be walking around in my head."

Samantha smiled grimly. "It's an easy metaphor to understand."

"Will I have to remember?"

Samantha made note of the other woman's word choice. Jill didn't want to remember.

"Hopefully not. I'll do what I can. And I'll leave the memories intact so that someday, if you want to, you can possibly access them."

Jill shuddered. "Who would want to remember something like that?"

"It's not always a matter of *want*," Samantha snapped, upbraiding herself for her instant defensive reaction.

"Let's do this before I change my mind," Jill said. She took a shaky breath. "What do you need me to do again?"

"Just think about being in the coffee shop and then being on the park bench."

"Is it going to hurt?"

"No. It will be like when I got the image of Roxy from your mind just a few minutes ago."

She reached over and took Jill's hand. She could feel her roommate's pulse pounding in her wrist, the blood thrumming through her fingers. She was far too upset for this to go well for either of them.

"Just breathe in and out slowly, deeply," Samantha said, dropping her voice lower and allowing her words to wash persuasively over Jill. The change was almost instantaneous as the other's pulse slowed and her muscles relaxed.

"Good. Just keep doing that; you're doing great," Samantha said. "Just relax. If you want to fall asleep, that's fine."

She gave her words the force of suggestion. After a few moments, Jill's head tilted back against the couch. Her eyes closed and her breathing became shallow and regular.

Samantha already had the trail of the memories she was looking for. Jill had been thinking hard about sitting in that coffee shop. She had been nervous, apprehensive, jumping at every little sound, staring at her phone every five seconds, and studying everyone in the store very, very carefully. All of Jill's senses had been on overdrive. Samantha could hear the chatter of patrons around Jill, smell the coffee fragrance heavy in the air, taste the bitterness of the coffee Jill herself was drinking. Samantha saw the moment when the memories skipped and felt Jill's bewilderment as she came to on the park bench staring up at Samantha. She saw herself through her roommate's eyes. Jill's perceptions of her made Samantha look slightly taller, more in command than she knew she had been at that moment. Jill trusted her, respected her, even when given reason not to. All of that Samantha could feel.

It was unnerving to see herself through another's eyes. It was something she'd done only a handful of times before. It was odd how the picture she could see was not the one she saw when standing before the mirror. To Jill, Samantha even looked younger.

She could feel Jill trying to take it all in, looking around the park, smelling the fresh-cut grass and trees. There were birds in the trees, but she was only dimly aware of their singing. Jill had felt like she was coming out of a fog or from under a trance.

And knowing the exact moment her memories jumped helped Samantha to track down the missing information. Jill's memories of the coffee shop ceased as the door opened and she looked up. A quick impression, a woman, not old, but not too young. Samantha couldn't see the woman's face or hair color, but she did feel a sensation of sudden warmth, what Jill had experienced the moment the witch hijacked her brain.

Samantha worked through Jill's mind, trying to access the information that the witch had tried so hard to hide. At long last she found what she was searching for and, with a small cry of triumph, she pushed and Jill's memories came into focus.

She watched as the witch walked through the door. It was the younger, blond one. She walked up to Jill's table, smiling, but Jill's will was already subjugated to her.

She's powerful to have done it from so far away, unless she had some other way to connect to her, Samantha thought.

The witch was smiling, but it didn't reach her eyes, which were instead cold, calculating. The witch reached out and Jill stood, taking her hand. Outside there was screaming, gunfire. Everyone rushed to the windows to see what was happening. No one paid attention to Jill and the witch as they walked out of the store.

They made it all the way to the park and sat on the bench before the witch began to talk.

"Jill, I need to know if Winona spoke to you at all about mountains and caves and things buried under or inside of them."

"No," Jill responded, feeling sleepy and not sure why the woman was asking.

"It's important, Jill. You must think. Did she give you any maps, books?"

"No, she gave me nothing. We only just spoke."

"Did she mention any of these things to you?"

Samantha could feel Jill struggling, trying to think, wanting to answer the woman, to please her. "No. Nothing. And we didn't talk about mountains or caves. We talked about the mission era and the effect of the Spanish settlements on the native populations."

"It's important that you tell me, Jill, who Winona would have spoken to about mountains."

"Drake Everwood. He graduated last semester. He studied spirits of the mountains. Winona helped him with his dissertation. I was jealous. I think he picked a better topic than I did. Spanish settlement on native inhabitants has been done so many times."

"Excellent. You have done very well, Jill."

"Thank you."

"You are not going to remember speaking to me at all. You will forget this conversation and have no memory of how you got here. Do you understand?"

"Of course I do."

The witch turned, looking away from Jill, surveying the park as though she was looking for someone or something. A frown creased her brow. Samantha could almost feel the energy that was rippling through her hands as the witch lifted them. She had long, slender fingers, and blue light arched at the tips.

What was the witch waiting for? Samantha wondered. From what she had heard, it sounded like she had asked Jill all she had wanted to. Why hang around longer at the park, just begging to be caught?

"Jill, you must wait here until someone comes for you. Do you understand?"

"Yes," Jill said.

"If I have need of you, I will call to you."

Call to you. The words sent an icy chill down Samantha's spine. Not *call you,* which implied the use of a phone. *Call to you.* She still had a grip on Jill's mind, waiting in case she should need to summon her.

Samantha was about to pull back, disengage from the memory, when something stopped her. The witch still hadn't left. Samantha wanted to see which way she went when she left the park. She waited, viewing the memories all the way through. Jill had been so completely under the witch's spell that her mind hadn't even questioned what was happening, none of it.

The witch made a movement as though she were going to leave. Then she twisted on the bench and grabbed the sides of Jill's head. Samantha flinched as she saw a close-up of the witch's face, filling her field of vision.

The witch put her face right up next to Jill's. She stared intently into her eyes and then she smiled.

"Samantha, this message is just for you."

Samantha jerked back, nearly dropping Jill's hand. She pulled herself quickly back together and maintained connection with Jill's memory of the event.

"You have not listened to me when I warned you that you need to leave. I respect your persistence, but, honey, even the craziest Castor witches knew when to cut and run."

Samantha gritted her teeth. The witch knew her true family name, the last name she had abandoned years before but used again briefly in Salem. Words had power and none more than names.

"So, listen carefully, Samantha. It's time you and I meet face-to-face. We need to have a little chat. I'll meet you the night before the full moon. I'll see you at two a.m. at the carousel at Santa Cruz Beach Boardwalk. Don't make me come and find you. Nobody's going to like that. And, Samantha, come alone. I can't be responsible for what will happen if you bring others into this. We just need to talk girl to girl. Or rather, witch to witch."

Samantha could feel herself shaking with rage. The witch had used her roommate as an answering service. It was a violation of Jill's privacy and her own.

"So, see you there. And in the meantime, try not to get yourself killed."

The witch winked as she pulled away. Samantha half expected her to blow a kiss, but she didn't. Instead, she got up and walked away, but was quickly outside of Jill's field of vision. And it was less than a minute later before Samantha showed up. She practically wept with the frustration of it. She had been so close to the other witch.

And she would be close to her again soon enough. She would have to carefully prepare for their meeting. She was just so grateful she had some time to do so. She was also incredibly grateful for one other thing. The witch had put so much energy and thought into the message she left her that she'd left a tiny piece of herself in there too. And now Samantha had a bit of power over her as well. Because now she knew the witch's name was Trina.

12

There was nothing else to see of Jill's encounter with Trina. Samantha pulled out of her roommate's mind and sat quietly for a few minutes while Jill continued to sleep. She had gotten more than just a name and the invitation from the encounter, though. She'd also gotten the next possible target of the coven: Drake Everwood.

Samantha couldn't help but wonder what the coven was looking for and how something tied in with mountains and caves was worth killing Winona for. And if Winona had given the information freely to Drake, why withhold it from the coven when they came asking about it?

Unless they didn't ask at all.

Samantha glanced at the clock in the kitchen. It was nearly ten and she was exhausted. She was in no shape to do any more police work that night, and if she did run across Trina or any of the other coven members, she'd be worse than helpless in a fight.

I risk my life by going to see him now.

She closed her eyes and sighed. She risked Drake's life by waiting until the morning.

She opened her eyes and stared at her roommate, who was still peacefully sleeping.

"Jill, wake up."

Jill opened her eyes and looked at her. "Is everything okay?"

"I need you to tell me where I can find Drake Everwood."

A little over an hour later, Samantha was knocking on the office door of Dr. Everwood at California State University, East Bay. His roommate had kindly informed her that he was working late after the night class that he had taught.

"Come in."

She started to open the door, but it stopped after only a few inches. A large box was blocking the way.

"You manage to get through the door, you can come in," a voice said.

Samantha rolled her eyes and shoved against the door, hard. It budged only a little bit. She gritted her teeth, not sure what exactly Dr. Everwood was playing at.

She stomped her foot on the ground and the box flew back nearly a foot. She opened the door all the way and walked in.

She saw a guy with dark curly hair bent over a pile of papers, red pen in hand and a scowl on his face.

"Congratulations. Stupid question deterrent. You must have a real pressing question that you didn't give up and save it for tomorrow." He slashed through something on the paper he was studying with the pen. "Really, these concepts aren't that difficult."

"Excuse me?" she asked.

He looked up. "Oh! Sorry. I assumed you were one of my students. And, well, clearly you're not. I think I'd remember you. You know, with the red hair and all."

"Okay," she said. "Let me help you out here. I'm Detective Ryan with the San Francisco Police Department."

She showed him her badge.

He flushed. "Okay, clearly not a student. What can I help you with?"

"I'm looking for some papers—"

"Are you kidding me?" he interrupted. "Campus police got the SFPD involved? What a huge waste of the tax payers' money. Well, and your time, of course. I'm sorry that they called you out here. I mean, if you can actually help that would be fantastic, but I wouldn't think this would even be in your jurisdiction. I mean, this is Cal State Hayward after all. Sorry, East Bay. I'll never get used to that. Most of my family went here. I was on campus a lot as a kid. Back when it was called Hayward, you know, not East Bay. Which is ridiculous, right? They don't call Cal State Fullerton Cal State Orange County. They call it after the city it's in. And, well, this is Hayward. I'm sorry. Should we get started? I've got a list of things around here somewhere."

He plunged his hands into a massive, teetering stack of papers on his desk.

"Hold on," she said. "You need to let someone else get a word in edgewise."

"Hmm? Oh, yes, sorry. What?"

"I have no idea what you're talking about."

"Sorry. Are you new to the area?"

"I meant about the papers," she said with a grimace.

"Oh! Sorry. Yes, last night someone broke into my office. It was so weird. I'm usually here at night. It's peaceful. I can get a lot done. I was here last night. I stepped away for a minute. It was to get a soda or something. I think that was it," he said, sounding suddenly vague and unsure of himself. He shook his head and waved his hands. "That's not important. What is important is that when I got back, someone had trashed my office and taken some things."

She looked around at the piles of papers stacked haphazardly everywhere, including a set teetering dangerously on top of a filing cabinet that had half its drawers open. Several crumpled pieces of paper ringed the trash can.

"So, that explains the condition of your office."

"No, I cleaned up all that mess after the campus police left." He looked around and then nodded. "Yeah, everything's in its place now."

She snapped her mouth shut.

"Yeah. Now, here's that list of things they stole," he said, handing her a piece of paper.

She scanned it briefly. There were three things on the list. "Bound copy of your dissertation, file with source material for your dissertation labeled 'Source Material Diss.,' and a model of the Santa Cruz Mountains made out of clay."

"My girlfriend made that model for me. She's a sculptor. And the dissertation? I had it published. I don't know why someone would steal my copy. I mean, I know students can get kind of stalkerish sometimes, but please."

"These were the only things that were taken?"

"Yes. I can't say that definitively, of course, since I haven't gone through every single piece of paper in the filing cabinet yet. But test keys, grade books, nothing like that was missing."

"I don't think one of your students did this," Samantha said.

He slammed his fist down on the desk. "It was a present for my birthday. There are no take-backs!"

"You think you're girlfriend took these things," Samantha said, struggling to read between the lines.

"Well, ex-girlfriend, actually. She wanted that model back and I wouldn't give it to her. I didn't ask for her birthday present back."

"What's her name?"

"Jess Simpson. Jessica. Yeah, I was dating Jessica Simpson. That was always a funny gag. No relation to the famous one, of course, but you know, I didn't always tell people that. She's a Buddhist. But let me tell you, when she wants something, she is so not Zen."

"Can you describe her for me?"

"Five feet, brunette, green eyes, hands usually covered in some sort of clay or paint."

His description didn't match any of the people she had seen in the images of the coven at Cathedral Grove.

"Do you have any proof she did it?"

"No, but who else would want that stuff? It had to be her, just trying to piss me off."

Samantha walked forward and put her hand on the one bare patch of desk she could find. The lingering energy impression was still there. It had been Trina who had taken those things. And given Drake's confusion over why he had stepped out of his office, she was willing to bet Trina had done the same thing to him that she'd done to Jill.

"Okay, Jess didn't do this. I need to talk to you more about what happened."

"She didn't do this? Are you sure?" he asked.

"I'm sure. Now, let's go back over everything."

He nodded.

"Now, close your eyes and tell me exactly what happened last night."

"Why do you want me to close my eyes?"

"Because I don't want you to be processing images from the office as it is right now. I want you to focus on capturing a clear picture of how it was last night," she said.

"Okay. You're the detective."

He closed his eyes. "Okay, I was working late,"

She reached out and touched his hand. "Sleep."

His head slumped forward on his chest. She kept hold of his hand and watched his memories from the night before.

She saw Trina enter his office much the same way she had. Trina was questioning him about the papers Winona had given him.

He was telling her he had forgotten to return them but that they were in his filing cabinet. He got them for her. When she asked him if that was all, he told her he'd given Winona back a very old map she had loaned him but he had a copy of it printed in his dissertation. He then said he'd used the model to help him with some of the research. At the end of the interrogation, Trina had told him that he wouldn't remember the encounter and had sent him off to the vending machine and told him not to come back for five minutes.

She could feel Drake's confusion as he stood, staring at the vending machine, not really wanting anything but not sure why he wasn't just going back to his office. Finally, when five minutes were over, he returned and was shocked to find his office had been trashed. Samantha wouldn't have believed it, but the memories she saw showed her how much worse the office had looked than it did now.

That was it. No hidden messages for her.

"Wake," she said. She pulled back her hand as his head lifted.

He opened his eyes. "And like I said, that was it."

"Thank you. You've been very helpful," Samantha said as she headed for the door.

"Call me when you find my stuff, okay?"

"Dr. Everwood, I'm not here about your missing papers. I'm a homicide detective. I'm investigating Winona Lightfoot's murder. Thank you for your time."

"Wait!"

She turned back to him and lifted an eyebrow.

"This is about Winona?"

"Yes."

"I am so sorry. You must think me an idiot," he said.

"No, I don't."

"Please, sit. I'll help you in any way I can."

"You've already hel—"

He shook his head impatiently. "No, I haven't even gotten a chance to tell you about the phone call she made to me the day before she died."

Samantha sat down. She was shocked. She had been so focused on following the witch angle of the case that once again she had ignored something that a homicide detective should never ignore. She should have told him why she was there and questioned him to see if he knew anything about why someone would want Winona dead. After all, she and Lance had a list of people they were supposed to follow up with in the morning, hoping to answer that very question.

"I'm sorry. Please, tell me what happened."

"She called. I could tell she was excited, but she had a weird edge to her voice too, like it was more than just excited, somehow. She said she had found something out about the Santa Cruz Mountains; tracked down a story her grandfather used to tell her about a spirit in the mountain. She specialized in the mission-era time period, but she knew a lot about precontact civilization, lore, stuff like that. She wanted to know if I had heard anything about an ancient battle that took place there. She knew that I'd done my dissertation on mountain spirits."

"And had you heard of anything like that?"

"Not there. There's a ton of stories about Mount Shasta, but that's part of the Cascade Mountains, way north of us. Even some crazy stories about Mount Diablo here in this area, but it's not part of the Santa Cruz Mountains either."

"Did she say anything else?"

"Yeah. She said if a woman with long black hair came

to me and asked about it, I should claim ignorance and let Winona know. I figured it was a rival researcher." He stopped, and realization lit up his eyes. "You don't think the person she was talking about was the one who killed her, do you?"

Samantha was almost certain. "We can't rule anything out at this point. Can you think of anything else?"

"No, it was a brief conversation. I was running to class. I felt terrible when I heard what happened."

Samantha pulled a business card out of her pocket. "If you think of anything else, please contact me immediately."

"I will," he said, taking the card from her.

"You don't have an extra copy of your dissertation here, do you?"

"No. I can get you a copy, though, if you think it would be helpful."

"Please do. I'll be in touch."

She stood and so did he. "I'm sorry I wasn't more help."

She forced herself to smile at him. "You did just fine. Let me know if you think of anything else."

Samantha left the office and quickly made her way down to the ground floor. The building seemed to be empty except for Drake. She hesitated, not liking the fact that he was alone there at this time of night.

There was nothing she could do for him, though, short of escorting him home or trying to set up some magical barriers. But with her living more than an hour away, if someone attacked those barriers she would never get there in time to help save him.

She hesitated at the exit to the building. Trina had gotten what she wanted from him and had left him unharmed, just like Jill. Why then had she or one of the other witches killed Winona?

She still felt like she was playing catch-up and more and more pieces were being constantly added to the board. Soon, she'd lose sight of the bigger picture altogether.

She made it to her car without encountering anyone. It seemed there were very few people on campus this late at night so early into the semester. The drive home seemed to take less time and she wasn't sure why. When she got in, Jill had already gone to bed.

Samantha headed to her room, kicked off her shoes, and fell face-first into a pillow.

The morning came far too early and Samantha struggled to stay awake as she tried to eat a bowl of cereal. She was almost finished when the phone rang. It was Lance.

"What do you want, Lance?" she asked, barely suppressing a yawn.

"My partner. You seen her lately?"

"I'll be downstairs in a minute."

"Too long. I'll come up and get you."

He hung up, and she briefly thought about face-planting in her Frosted Flakes.

Jill walked into the kitchen, humming lightly to herself. Samantha eyed her warily. "How are you this morning?"

Jill shrugged. "Still a little weirded out and a lot curious. We have a lot more to talk about."

"Oh, joy. Listen, Lance is coming up here. Remember that we need to keep this between us."

"I know."

There was a knock on the door, and before Samantha could stand up, Jill had bounded over to open it.

Lance stepped inside, closed the door, and then swept Jill up in his arms and kissed her while she squealed in delight.

Samantha just sat, staring, in shock.

"Did you miss me?" Lance asked.

"Every minute," Jill said breathlessly.

"What the hell is going on?" Samantha asked. "I thought you two couldn't stand each other."

"Shut up," Lance growled.

Jill just laughed. "I know. It's going to take a bit to get used to."

Samantha felt like she'd missed something. Jill and Lance barely knew each other. And even though he'd driven her home the day before, the reaction was far too intense even if they had made some sort of connection in those few minutes.

"It's not anywhere near April Fools' Day," she said.

Jill looked at her like she was crazy. "What on earth are you talking about? You know that Lance and I have been dating for the last couple of months."

Samantha didn't know any such thing. What was happening to her? The hair color, the car, those could be explained away if she tried hard enough. But this? Impossible. Either someone was messing with her, or she was truly losing it.

"Samantha, what's wrong?" Jill asked.

"I think I've got a headache," Samantha said. She stood and took her bowl to the sink. She downed some aspirin and prayed that her head would clear soon. She had a sneaking suspicion it was going to be a long day, though. Thanks to the scheduled meeting with Trina, it was going to be an even longer night.

She grabbed her badge and gun from the bedroom. When she returned, she tried to ignore the lovesick look that Jill and Lance were sharing.

"Let's get out of here," she said.

A minute later, when they were in the car, Lance punched her in the shoulder.

"What was that for?"

"Not cool back there," he said.

"Are you kidding me?"

"You know I don't like reminding Jill that I didn't like her at first. It's embarrassing, and she gives me crap about it. Don't do that to me."

"Who are you and what have you done with my partner?" she asked.

"Very funny."

But Samantha wasn't joking. For the rest of the drive, she stared at Lance out of the corner of her eye. He and Jill had never told her they were together. Lance had pretended to barely know her the other day. What was happening? Lance even seemed different, nicer somehow.

Because he's a man in love, she realized. *When did that happen? Has the whole world gone mad?*

They parked at the university. As they got out of the car, Samantha looked around. "Who are we here to see?"

"Marcus Rogers. Head librarian and on-again off-again boyfriend to our deceased."

Once inside the library, an assistant led them to Marcus's office. He was a thin man with graying hair and thick glasses perched on top of his nose. As she shook his hand, Samantha pushed her way into his mind and in one glance saw what she wanted to know. He had no idea what Winona had been mixed up with that got her killed.

Unfortunately, there was no way she could tell Lance that. She needed to find some other way to make use of this trip.

"Did Winona have an office here?" she asked after the introductions were made.

"Ah, no. She did a lot of lecturing here, but was not an employee of the university. She did, however, like to use conference room two here in the library a lot. She'd spend hours on end working in there."

"Thank you." She turned and looked at Lance. "I'm going to go take a look around. You got this?"

"Yeah," he said.

"Great."

She exited the office and quickly found the conference room in question. Fortunately, it was empty. She walked in and closed the door. She stood in the room for a moment, quietly, trying to pick up on any sensations that were overwhelming.

Unfortunately, she couldn't sense the presence of any witches, which meant none had been there—at least, not recently. She ran her hands over the table and sat in every chair. There was nothing she could pick up on, though.

Finally, she left the room and walked out into the stacks. She found a section on local history. Drake had said Winona had found something that verified a story her grandfather had told her. It was possible one of these books held a clue to what Winona was working on. But there were hundreds of books, and it would take dozens of cops days and days to go through them all. And given that she couldn't tell them what to look for or even why she knew they held something important, it would be a useless effort.

I have to know what she found out. She could feel the desperation that had been building in her since they had found Winona's body. She felt that time was running out somehow. She felt guilty for how she had pushed her way into the librarian's mind a few minutes before, but really, what choice did she have? It wasn't like she could ask everyone they interrogated if they knew why witches would want Winona dead.

She dropped her hands to her side. "I summon the book that can help me," she whispered. She felt her fingertips begin to tingle with energy. She lifted her arms so that her hands were touching the bookshelves that faced each other. She walked down the aisle, trailing her fingers along the spines of the books in the fourth row. She reached the end of the row and had found nothing. She turned and repeated it, one row higher.

There were better ways to do this, but she didn't have

access to any of her tools at the moment. Plus, the last thing she needed was for a book to actually fly into her hand as someone walked by. This way she only risked looking strange.

On her third pass, the fingers on her left hand received a shock of electricity as she touched one of the books. She stopped and grabbed the book. *Santa Cruz Then and Now*. It was old, and when she opened it she realized it was written in the 1940s.

She tucked the book under her arm and headed back toward the office, where Lance would probably be finishing up with Marcus.

She popped in just as Lance was standing to go. He handed Marcus a card, and as she did the same, she remembered that she had to get a replacement cell phone for the one lost to the water. She was about to tell him that she needed to borrow the book, but stopped. If it really held useful information, the fewer people who knew she had it, the better.

She managed to get it out of the building without anyone seeing and without setting off the alarm.

"Any luck in there?" she asked as she slid it underneath her seat in Lance's car.

"No. You?"

"Didn't find anything or anyone interesting," she fibbed. "But I do need to get a new cell phone."

"What happened to yours?"

"I lost it."

"You lost it?"

"Yeah. And if you bring it up again, I'll have a good long talk with Jill tonight about you."

He swore under his breath, and she turned toward the window so he wouldn't see her smile.

After she got a replacement phone, they followed up on a couple more leads, both of them dead ends as well. They went to grab lunch, and at the diner Samantha excused herself. She called George Wakefield and set up a three o'clock meeting with him.

She had just sat back down at the table when the whole building jolted hard. It lasted less time than it took for her to think about standing up.

"I hate those," she said between clenched teeth when the aftershock was over. "How much longer are they going to happen?"

Lance shrugged. "Can't be many more left."

The waiter brought their food, and they ate in silence. Lance refrained from making any jokes or saying something snarky to the waiter, which she counted as a miracle. When the guy brought around slices of fresh apple pie, Lance began to talk.

"Most murders are committed by someone the victim knows."

"Yes, that's true," Samantha said, digging into her own piece of pie.

"Family, boyfriend, colleagues, everyone seemed to like the woman."

"Someone didn't."

"Yeah, but who? I don't buy that this is random. It's not like she was mugged on the streets or dragged down a dark alley. Whoever killed her had to have followed her into the museum. She still had all her valuables, and there were no signs of sexual assault. That rules out random."

"But it doesn't necessarily point at family and friends."

"Unless we've got a serial killer on our hands, I think it does. And I don't know about you, but I haven't seen any other petrified bodies showing up. And I still hate that Jada can't give us a clue what could have caused that."

"Maybe it was spontaneous."

He gave her a sideways glance. "Like human combustion? I don't think so. No, someone killed her. We find out who and I'm sure we'll figure out how. Personally, I think it sounds like some kind of science experiment gone wrong."

"Maybe she owed somebody money," Samantha said.

"Her financials came back clean. I can't see a motive or a suspect from where I'm sitting. Can you?"

Samantha shook her head. It felt terrible deceiving him, but what else could she do? It had been bad enough telling Jill her secret. She had no intention of adding Lance to that special little club.

"I'm telling you, there's something we're missing."

She glanced at her phone. She needed to get ready for her meeting with George, but she didn't necessarily want to share that with Lance.

"Well, I know I'll be missing a dentist appointment if I'm not careful. Can you drop me home after this?"

"Seriously, can't you reschedule?" he asked, looking at her incredulously.

"Sure. You look into a magic ball and tell me what day

we're not going to be working a case, and I'll reschedule."

"Fine."

They finished, and a short while later, he dropped her off.

Samantha walked upstairs and into the apartment.

"How's it going?" she heard Jill ask.

"Okay."

Samantha stopped in her tracks as Jill walked into the room.

"What are you staring at?" Jill asked.

"Your hair. It's got purple streaks in it."

"And?" Jill asked. "Your point being?"

"When did you dye it?"

"This morning."

Samantha sagged against the door in relief. She wasn't going crazy.

"I was starting to get sick of the green streaks, so I figured today to change them to purple. You like?"

And just like that, everything came crashing back around her. Jill was staring at her, waiting for an answer.

"It's better than green," Samantha forced herself to whisper.

"I'll take the W."

"W?"

"Yeah, as in Win. Are you okay?"

"Just tired."

Samantha headed for the bathroom to splash cold water on her face. What happened when people with powers went crazy? Was this what it was like? Did they start seeing things, misremembering things? Had the strain gotten to be too much?

Get a grip. Someone is just messing with you. That's all that's happening here. But deep down she wasn't so sure that was what was happening. She thought of all the corridors in her mind, all the repressed memories she'd been letting out these last few months. Could the fact that she was regaining lost memories be screwing up other parts of her brain? Was it all too much too fast? She really wished her parents weren't on a cruise. She didn't like the idea of trying to explain this all to her adoptive father, but as a psychologist, he might have some insight.

And just the right set of papers to have me committed if I am cracking up.

She changed her blouse and then headed back out to her car. She tried to shake off the sensations that were assailing her. She felt like she was going crazy, and it was starting to spook her a bit.

Before she realized what she was doing, she found herself dialing Anthony. He was quick to answer, and the warmth in his voice made her blush.

"How can I help you?" he asked after a minute.

"I just need to talk, I guess. I feel like I'm going insane."

"What's wrong?"

She explained to him in detail how things seemed to keep changing, like Jill's hair color and relationship status.

"It's possible you're just overly stressed, focused on other things," he suggested.

"Or I'm cracking up."

He paused. "You know, I knew a Wiccan once who was very sensitive to things around him. He didn't have powers like you, but he once told me that there were times he could swear he was shifting into other realities."

"Other realities?" Samantha asked, fighting to keep the skepticism from her voice.

"Yeah. It's like for every choice we make, there's a universe where we made the opposite choice."

"Multiverse theory? I heard about it once."

"Exactly. Well, this guy I knew swore that from time to time it was almost like something happened and he felt like somehow he'd shifted into one of those other universes. It was as though time had changed on him, and something he remembered clearly had no longer happened in our reality."

"I've never heard of magic doing anything like that," Samantha said, still dubious. It seemed more likely that someone had put some kind of curse on her to make her forget or misremember things.

"And just how much do you actually remember about the magic you learned as a kid?" he asked, failing to hide a note of sarcasm.

A lot more than I used to, she wanted to tell him. But she couldn't. She wasn't ready to share the memories that were coming back with anyone yet, least of all Anthony. His mother had been murdered by the coven she grew up in, and Samantha had a secret fear that one day she would get back a memory of seeing his mother die.

The murder of his mother was the reason Anthony had sworn as a kid to hunt down the surviving witch from the coven who had done it. When he had realized Samantha was that survivor, he had tried to kill her. It made their relationship that much more complicated. Still, as long as she had no active memories of his mother, it made her feel a little bit better.

Maybe I wasn't even there when she died, she told herself.

"Even if it was possible, that requires insane amounts of energy, and for what purpose would you even do something like that?" she asked.

"I can think of one or two reasons to change the past, or at least try to move into a timeline where it hadn't happened the way you remembered it," he said darkly.

She grimaced. "Point taken."

She was getting close to her destination and so she reluctantly ended the call.

She found a parking space downtown, which was nothing short of a miracle. She walked two blocks to the spot where George Wakefield had suggested they meet. He was already there, and when she arrived, he smiled pleasantly and introduced himself.

As she was shaking his hand, though, she was overwhelmed by a sudden sensation of danger. Something was terribly wrong. She looked around quickly, expecting to see a witch coming after them.

There were just business people and tourists walking by, though.

"Are you okay?" he asked.

Am I okay? I don't know. People have been asking me that a lot lately. She felt the urge to laugh but was pretty convinced that was one step further down the path of crazy.

"Yeah, sorry. I'm—"

She turned to look at him and stopped short. The clothes that he was wearing, the buildings outlined behind him. Everything about the scene was eerily familiar, and a moment later she realized why.

Everything was as she had seen it in her vision. The Big One was about to hit and thousands of people, including them, were about to die.

13

"We have to get out of here!" Samantha screamed.

"What? What on earth are you talking about?" George asked.

"The earthquake, the Big One, it's going to happen right now. Everyone's going to die!"

There was a beat as he blinked at her in astonishment. Then anger filled his eyes. "If this is your idea of a joke, I'm afraid it's not funny. I'm afraid you won't find it funny either when I report you to the authorities. I believe impersonating a police officer is against the law."

Samantha pulled out her badge and shoved it in his face. "I am a police officer. Now, let's go!"

She grabbed his arm and began to pull. He resisted, and she looked him in the eyes and commanded, "Follow me!"

And then they were running, practically knocking down people in their path. Her mind was racing. Where should they go? Everywhere around them were tall buildings waiting to fall. The city itself was built on a landfill, and the cement beneath their feet could open up at any moment and swallow them.

"Where are we going?" she heard George shout.

"Somewhere safe."

"And where on earth do you think that is?"

His question brought her up short. She spun to face him. "The water. If we can get to the water and get out on it, in a boat maybe, we'll be safe."

"I can't run that far," he said.

She looked at him and realized he was wheezing, panting from the exertion.

"We have no time. We have to try."

And then she heard a groaning sound that seemed to come from deep within the earth. A moment later, she fell as the ground began to shake. She screamed and reached out toward George. Between them a crack appeared in the cement.

And then it all stopped.

She lay still for a moment and then got up shakily.

"Not exactly the big one I was expecting," George said wryly.

"I don't understand," Samantha whispered. "It was just like I saw it, but then . . ." She reached up and her hand closed around the cross necklace. It was still there. In her vision it had been gone. But in her vision, George had been wearing the same clothes as he was now and some of the passersby had looked the same as well.

"Maybe you should tell me exactly why you wanted to talk to me," George said.

She nodded. "It's going to sound crazy."

He lifted an eyebrow. "My dear, crazy is my stock and trade. How about we go get a cup of coffee?"

"But what if another one hits? Maybe I'm just early."

"Tell you what. Why don't we drive down and get that cup of coffee at Fisherman's Wharf. Fewer big buildings, okay?"

Samantha nodded.

His car was parked closer, and so she let him drive. She was too rattled anyway. San Francisco, with its plethora of one-way streets, crazy locals, and lost tourists, was just a bit too much for her to handle at the moment.

They ended up getting clam chowder in sourdough bread bowls at a little restaurant. Samantha always thought that particular meal was one of the most fundamental building blocks of San Francisco cuisine and culture. She could barely taste it, though, as she sat there with George and wondered why they were both still alive.

She finally broke down and told him she'd had a dream, unwilling to use the word vision. She explained how vivid it had been and how when she'd met him, it had all come rushing back to her.

"You are not the only one who dreams such things. You would be surprised. Sometimes they can turn out to be prophetic, though often not exactly how we pictured them. For example, had you not made us start to run, we would have been standing in the exact spot you dreamed during an earthquake. That much of your dream would have been true. It just wasn't the Big One it was in your dream."

We were lucky. The words kept ringing over and over in her mind.

"Why do you stay?" she asked.

"Why would I go?" he asked.

"If you really believe that there is a Big One and that it's coming someday, why would you stay here?"

He smiled gently. "Because it is my home. I love it here. And not even I can yet say when that quake will hit. Maybe not even in our lifetimes. And besides, where would I go? The thought of tornadoes, now, that terrifies me."

"I guess there's something anywhere you go," she said at last.

"It's the great leveling of the playing field. Hawaii is beautiful, but every few years a hurricane causes massive destruction. That keeps many people from moving there. I think it's easiest to cope with the disasters and problems that you were raised with. I think of an earthquake as just part of life, whereas to you it is something to be dreaded."

"You're a very smart man," she said. "But there are things I grew up with that still terrify me."

He shrugged. "That I cannot help you with. I can, though, bring you some of the data I promised." He pulled a large envelope out of his overcoat and handed it to her. "I hope it helps."

"I'm sure it will. Thanks. So, this sudden increase in runaway pets . . . Do you think it is indicative that another large earthquake is likely to hit?"

He shrugged. "If the numbers were smaller, I'd be more likely to think so. But these numbers are so staggeringly high, I'm not sure what to think. It makes me wonder if somewhere someone is blowing a giant dog whistle, or if the cats have discovered that the mice one county over taste better."

"But if you had to guess?"

He sighed. "If I had to guess, I'd say something significant is happening or about to happen. And if I were a gambling man, I'd think this a perfect time to move to Las Vegas and place a wager or two when I got there."

He glanced at his watch. "I should be taking you back to your car. I'm sorry, I did not plan this out well."

"I didn't help much with that," she admitted.

They drove back in silence. When he dropped her at her car, she thanked him.

"You know, call me if you have any more of those dreams." His face turned sad. "I had a friend who used to dream of earthquakes too. Sadly, she has passed."

"I'm sorry to hear that," Samantha said.

He nodded. "Winona was a good woman, and I will miss her."

Samantha froze, halfway out of her seat. "Winona?"

He nodded.

"Winona Lightfoot?"

"Yes, you know her?"

Samantha sucked in her breath. "I'm one of the detectives working on finding her killer."

"Anything I can do to help, please let me know," he said.

Samantha sat back down. "You say she dreamed of earthquakes too?"

"Yes. We talked several times over the years. But over the last month, she had dreams nearly every night. They terrified her."

Samantha felt her mouth go dry. "Was she dreaming of the Big One, like me?"

"I don't know, but I do know that in her dreams, the epicenter was nowhere near the city."

"It was in Santa Cruz, wasn't it?"

He looked surprised. "Yes. How did you know?"

"Lucky guess," she whispered. "Did she tell you anything else about the dreams?"

"No."

"Was that unusual?"

"As a matter of fact, it was. Before, when Winona would dream about an earthquake, she would tell me everything. She even would fax me pictures she drew of buildings or things she saw, just in case it would ever be of use. With these, though, she just told me she had them and that they centered on Santa Cruz. She would never say anything else."

"Maybe she didn't remember the dreams very well; that happens."

He shook his head. "I could tell when she called the first time that something about the dream was really upsetting her. But when I asked her what it was, she refused to say, wouldn't even acknowledge that she was upset about anything. And then afterward she'd just call to say she'd had the same dream and about what time it had been when she had it. There were never any details, no sketches."

"Maybe there was something she didn't want you to know."

"I don't know. It could have been something deeply personal to her."

"Thanks for your time. I'll call if I need anything else."

As Samantha got into her own car, she wrapped her shaking hands around the steering wheel. Why did everything connect to Santa Cruz? She thought of the ritual she had seen the witches performing, the one with the large dirt mound and the lines on the ground. Trina had been looking for information about something to do with the mountains.

Were they trying to shake something loose? Expose something? She felt like the answers were there, just outside of her grasp. She was getting closer, though. And when she met with Trina in a few hours, she planned on getting the answers out of her, no matter what it took.

She drove back home and jumped on her computer to do a little research about the place where she would be meeting with Trina. When she was done, she forced herself to lie down and try to get a few hours' sleep before the work ahead. Her mind kept racing, though, and she relived both the dream and the reality of the earthquake over and over. Why had they been different?

Why were so many things different from what she thought they should be or even remembered them being? After a while, Jill knocked softly on her door. She was going out to dinner with Lance.

"I'm going to catch up on my sleep. I'll see you in the morning," Samantha said.

Hopefully, Jill would take that to heart and not try to wake Samantha when she got home. She wouldn't be there.

When she realized that sleep just was not going to come, Samantha got up and started reading the book she had gotten from the library. Given her recent experiences with questioning the right people about the wrong things, she didn't want to miss anything. Something in the book was vitally important, but she didn't want to make assumptions about what it was. So she started reading at the beginning.

It began talking about the development of Santa Cruz from a mission to a full-fledged town and seaside resort community. There didn't seem to be anything in that section that would be of interest, but she kept reading.

When it was finally time to leave the house, she slid the book under her mattress. It wouldn't survive more than a cursory inspection of her room, but she did put a glamour on the bed to cause people to want to avoid it. It wasn't much, but there wasn't much she'd be able to do to stop a really powerful, really determined witch from finding whatever she wanted to in her room.

She dressed all in black for the meeting. She wore flat black, no gloss on any of her clothes, including the button on her pants, which was fabric covered instead. It would help her fade into the shadows, keep people's eyes off of her. She stuffed her badge in her pocket. She debated taking her gun and finally decided she should. She could tuck it into the back of her waistband and put her shirt over it so it wouldn't attract attention.

Finally, she got into the car and checked her gas levels. The long drives back and forth were becoming frustrating, but at least she was going late enough that there were fewer cars on the roads than there had been earlier. Still, she was scheduled to arrive plenty early. She needed to do some reconnaissance of the spot, given that she'd never been there and the area would be home turf for Trina.

As she drove, she thought about calling Anthony but decided against it. She needed to be focused and calm when she met Trina, and if there were two words that she couldn't connect to her discussions with Anthony, it was those two.

Even the thought of him made her pulse skitter a little bit. She mentally slapped herself. There would be time later to think about guys.

If she wasn't dead, that was.

The drive seemed to take even longer than usual, and she was relieved when she finally made it. She parked in one of the parking lots and put a glamour on the car so that no one would pay any attention to it. The last thing she needed was a nosy security guard sniffing around it while she was busy dealing with Trina.

She settled back in her seat and tried to center herself as she prepared to wait. *Trina, what is it you hope to accomplish tonight?* she couldn't help but wonder as she fingered her cross.

Santa Cruz Beach Boardwalk was famous the world over for its rides and attractions steps away from a fabulous California beach. In January, the park was only partially operational on weekdays, with the game arcades and the bowling lanes open but none of the rides. By midnight the entire place was shut down. Samantha had been there for two hours, watching the last stragglers leave and memorizing the routes and schedules of the security guards patrolling the place. The bitter cold ensured that no one was lingering on the beach.

It was half past one when Samantha headed to the carousel, where she had been told to meet Trina. She moved silently, keeping to the shadows and staying close to the buildings. She walked slowly, her senses attune to everything around her. She didn't know what Trina wanted, but she was sure that her well-being was not the other witch's top priority.

She passed the Giant Dipper, the famous roller coaster's track hulking in the darkness next to her. She'd been on one roller coaster in her life, when she was fourteen. It was with a group of others from her church. She remembered the experience in vivid detail. It had helped to underscore for her just how different she was from everybody else and how little she had in common with the kids her age.

The others had laughed and screamed and exited the ride with adrenaline rushes. She had been bored. The motions of the vehicle were entirely predictable, and the gravitational and centrifugal forces it exerted on her body paled in comparison to other things she had experienced. Standing there staring at all the others laughing and screaming as they relived their experiences with one another, she had never felt more alone in her life.

It was the day she had given up trying to fit in and had opted instead for being left alone by her peers. The first real friendship she'd had was with Ed, her former partner. She still missed him.

"No time to get sentimental, Samantha," she told herself.

She kept walking and passed the Haunted Castle, a spooky ride. She knew that a little farther up the boardwalk was the Fright Walk, a walk-through haunted-house type attraction. She shook her head. One of the memories she had recovered from her seven-year-old self had involved a haunted-house-like experience set up by members of her coven. It was used as a teaching tool, a training ground. Young witches were sent through with instructions that they must only react to things that were real threats. Things that were fake must be ignored at all costs.

Samantha remembered being frightened and knowing that terrible things waited, lurking in the darkness just beyond the door, ready to kill her. She had also known that the punishment for failure would be severe. So into the darkness she had gone. Inside she had encountered ghosts, both real and created special effects, real witches and costumed witches, things with eyes that glowed red in the dark and skeletons that would spring out of nowhere. She had hesitated before each new nightmare, wanting to be sure it was a real threat and not a staged one.

At the end, she had been scolded for hesitating more than once, but she had passed the test because she hadn't used her powers on anything that didn't merit them. Too bad she hadn't shown the same restraint a year later, when she'd blinded the school bully.

She kept walking and came to the carousel, a genuine antique with beautiful hand-carved horses. The creatures stood frozen, still, eyes and mouths gaping open as lights glinted off them, making them seem almost alive. She was early. She got up on the platform and began to walk among them, trailing a hand along their smooth sides, feeling the wood and the years of joy that had been captured in the creatures.

She kept moving forward. Ahead of her, a particularly striking white horse drew her attention. The creature's head was down, neck arched as though it were fighting the pull of an invisible rider on the reins. She moved forward, eyes fixed on it.

And then at last her fingers touched it, and she jumped back with a startled cry. The wood of that particular horse felt more like the petrified flesh of Winona Lightfoot. She reached out and touched it again and there, deep down, she felt the echo of life. This was not a horse carved out of wood. This was a horse who had been turned to wood.

She ran her hands over the creature, feeling, listening, trying to understand what had happened. *Why would someone do this to any living creature, particularly a horse?*

"It's faster than carving one," a voice whispered behind her.

Samantha twisted around, lifting her hands defensively. So intent had she been on the horse that she hadn't noticed the approach of the witch who had summoned her.

Trina was standing there, her blond hair back in a ponytail. She too was dressed all in black. She crossed her arms and gazed defiantly at Samantha, as though daring her to strike first.

Slowly Samantha lowered her hands. She let them hang loosely at her sides, though, ready to move at a moment's notice.

"Trina," she acknowledged.

"Samantha."

"Well, you called this meeting. What do you want?"

"To warn you to back off."

Samantha raised an eyebrow. "Or what, you'll try to kill me again?"

"That wasn't me. I saved your life, remember? Kept your partner from shooting you."

"Why did you do that?"

"Let's call it professional courtesy."

"I'm not a witch," Samantha snapped, although the denial sounded hollow even to her own ears.

"I didn't say you were."

There was something Trina wasn't telling her. She could see it in the other woman's eyes, feel her hesitation. The circle had named her as one of the two most powerful witches in the coven. What was it, exactly, that she was afraid of? And if she hadn't been trying to kill her that night, had everything been the doing of the black-haired witch, high priestess of the coven?

"What is it you aren't telling me?"

Trina looked away. "Randy was . . . a colleague."

Samantha gaped at her. Randy Turner had been an undercover FBI agent who had gotten killed in the final showdown in Salem. They hadn't realized until the end that they were fighting on the same side, and he had given his life to help her defeat Abigail, the resurrected high priestess of her old coven, and destroy the new coven that had been operating in Salem and had dared to bring back the dead. Randy had warned her that Salem was one of just many front lines in an ongoing battle and that he was not the only one fighting it.

She stared at Trina, understanding at last the other's reluctance to come right out and say anything. "So, you and Randy worked together?"

"Sometimes we were even partnered up. Not this time though. He went there and I came here. I was about to join him because things out here were relatively harmless . . . by comparison."

"But then he got killed."

Trina nodded. "And things changed here."

"What happened?" Samantha asked.

"I still haven't figured out what the catalyst was, but things took a turn for the darker . . . *much* darker. Active recruiting increased. Spellcasting became much more ambitious. And then a few weeks back, something happened to Giselle."

"Giselle?"

"The one who's been trying to kill you."

"Long black hair, likes to channel lightning?"

"That would be the one. She got a power boost the likes of which I've never seen before. It was uncanny. And then we started doing the rituals to cause the quakes."

"You guys are causing them?"

Trina nodded. "I've done what I can to minimize them, soften the impact. But the coven is definitely behind it."

"But why?"

"I don't know. Giselle's been keeping her own counsel on that. There's something about them, though, that's different. These are not just your standard earth-quakes."

"What are they?"

"Not a clue. I just know that things seem different after each one. I can't explain it. I'm still trying to figure out what she possibly hopes to accomplish."

"Mass destruction via natural disaster?"

"No, that's what I thought at first, but then I realized she didn't seem to care about that. There's something else she's after."

"Does anyone else in the coven know what's going on?" Samantha asked.

"I can't tell for sure. I have my suspicions, but no con-firmation as of yet."

"I guess the question is, what could she really hope to gain from causing earthquakes if not destruction?"

"Well, I told you it's not a natural disaster kind of thing she's after. She seems very focused on one specific thing. I just don't know what it is. All I know is that it has something to do with the mountains around here."

"Are there a lot of local legends about these moun-tains, something that might give you a clue?"

"No. I mean, the entire area is a convergence of ener-gies, so magic done here tends to be more powerful. There's one of those mystery spots, you know, where gravity seems to work slightly differently, but as a coven we've never been there. I mean, I can't figure what she's after. If we were talking some of the mountains farther north—like Mount Shasta, which has been a hotbed of weirdness for decades—then, yeah, sure, we would have somewhere to start. But whatever it is, it's situated right around here."

"Winona Lightfoot must have held some key to the puzzle. Why else kill her?"

"Not a clue. That wasn't your everyday killing either. You don't see petrification every day, no offense to the horse," Trina said, reaching out to touch the animal's flanks. "It takes an insane amount of energy."

"Well, Giselle has got to be one of the most powerful witches I've ever encountered."

"But she wasn't, not until recently. The whole thing makes no sense."

Samantha flexed her fingers, the knuckles cracking. "Maybe it's time you bring me inside. I've got some experience with this sort of thing. And two heads are better than one. Why don't you recruit me? I can help you if I'm on the inside."

"No, it's too dangerous. Someone wants you dead."

"I think it's your high priestess."

"She's not my high priestess," Trina snapped, glancing over her shoulder.

Guess I'm not the only sensitive one who's hiding behind semantics, Samantha realized.

"At any rate, I don't think it has anything to do with her. I don't think she even knows who you are. I can't explain it exactly, but I get the impression that it's someone else who wants you dead and Giselle's somehow pledged to do it. So, got any enemies who want to see you in the grave?"

"All my enemies are dead," Samantha said.

"Yeah, that's what I heard."

"There has to be some way we can work together."

Trina shook her head. "I've been doing this job for a lot of years now, and partnering with someone who isn't undercover never works."

"Then why are we here?" Samantha asked.

"So you know not to try to investigate me or arrest me or kill me or whatever it was you were thinking. I'm giving you a heads-up. When and if this all comes to a showdown, we both need to know we're on the same team."

"If I'd known who Randy was, it might have made all of the difference," Samantha said bitterly. The man had died in her arms.

"Maybe, but maybe not. When things go really bad in a coven, it gets messy. Lots of people die. But then, I don't need to tell you that." Trina half turned, surveying the area behind her before she turned back.

"I'm not going to back off on the investigation," Samantha said.

"I wouldn't ask you to," Trina said. "Matter of fact, with people busy looking at you, no one's paying the slightest bit of attention to what I do or do not do. Having you running around out there causing chaos and making things difficult for the coven is actually a huge help to me. But I have to warn you, I'm not going to be there to protect you all the time."

"Thanks for the heads-up," Samantha said, struggling to keep the sarcasm out of her voice.

"Yeah, no problem," Trina said as she twisted her head around again.

"What do you keep looking at?" Samantha asked.

"Nothing, I guess. I just keep feeling like we're being watched."

"Maybe you're just paranoid," Samantha said, though a shiver crawled its way up her spine and she found herself glancing around, probing the shadows with her eyes. "Did one of the shadows move?" She blinked hard, straining.

"Maybe. That's what this line of work will do to you," Trina said. She paused. "You know what? I'm out of here." The witch turned and started walking away quickly.

Samantha glanced around once more. She took a step forward, and the carousel horse she was standing next to swiveled its head and bit her arm. Samantha shouted, and out of the corner of her eye, she saw Trina take off at a dead run.

14

Samantha turned to the horse. Its eyes were now glowing red. It shook itself, and wood turned to flesh. She could feel its teeth champing down hard, breaking bone and tearing sinew.

She yanked her arm free and turned to run. The animal kicked her hard in the ribs and sent her flying into the horse behind. She smacked her head on the pole and struggled to retain consciousness.

She pushed herself to her feet, knowing if she couldn't stand she was dead. She took a step and then the entire carousel lurched as it began to turn. In the dim light, the horses rising up and down looked demonic, their eyes glowing red, their teeth baring at her.

It's not real, she told herself. But she wasn't so sure as the creatures writhed, struggling to reach her, held in position by the poles that anchored them to the floor. Their screams of rage and fear pierced the night, drowning out the tinny sounds of the music that had begun playing. She was trapped in the inner ring.

She made a dash for it and grunted as hooves kicked her. She felt teeth snapping at the nape of her neck and then the scream of frustration from the horse as it was lifted up and away from her. She jumped off the carousel, landing hard on the ground.

She heard laughter as she staggered to her feet. A fireball left her fingertips, smashing into the side of the building next door.

Steady, she told herself. She hadn't even intended to conjure the fire. She had to calm herself down before she accidentally set the entire place ablaze.

"Looks like someone doesn't have as much control as she should," a familiar voice taunted.

Samantha stepped into the open, away from the distraction of the carousel, and braced herself.

"Who was your little friend? Didn't want to stick around for all the fun, huh? Oh, well, at least you and I can play."

"If you want to fight, come out here and face me," Samantha shouted.

"You want to stand and fight instead of run and hide. Are you sure?"

"I'm positive," Samantha said, raising her chin. She refused to let the witch hear in her voice the fear she felt in her heart.

"Your choice. But one way or another, you're going to die tonight."

"Is that right?" Samantha asked, searching the shadows.

"Yes," a different voice answered from behind her.

Samantha jumped to the side as an athame cut through

the air where she'd been standing. She spun around and came face-to-face with an older man, his lips twisted in a snarl, his eyes glowing a hellish yellow color.

Samantha sent a pulse of energy toward him, and he flew backward, crashing into a trash can. Giselle stepped out from the shadows nearby, her face twisted like an insane comedy mask.

She was outnumbered. Samantha turned and ran.

"Knew you'd run!" she heard Giselle cackle behind her.

A bolt of lightning hit the ground a foot in front of her, causing her to shy to the side. Another hit and another.

She's herding me, sending me in the direction she wants me to go, Samantha realized.

Stand and fight, a voice seemed to hiss in her ear.

Another lightning bolt whizzed by, and Samantha spun and planted her feet. She sent a shower of fireballs at Giselle and the other witch. Unbelievably, Giselle caught them and began to juggle them, laughing as she came closer.

"Fire only burns if you let it," she taunted.

"What do you want from me?" Samantha screamed.

"Not me, dear. Her. She wants you dead," the male witch said.

Samantha didn't know if he was talking about Giselle or if he was referencing the fact that someone else wanted her dead, just as Trina had suggested.

Giselle lobbed the fireballs high into the air and let them rain down on her as she laughed. In a moment, her hair and clothes were on fire. Samantha could see smoke rising from her skin, but the witch either didn't notice or didn't care.

Giselle lunged forward suddenly, reaching for Samantha. Samantha jumped out of the way, the heat from the fire singeing her eyebrows.

"You're insane!"

"It has been said," Giselle chuckled, still smiling even though her hair was a halo of fire now.

The two witches approached and Samantha backpedaled, furiously trying to think of what she could do. It felt like every bit of magic she had ever known was leaving her.

Behind Giselle she could see the carousel. The petrified horse was still struggling, and suddenly he bounded off the whirling platform. He turned and galloped over to them, eyes blazing with red fire.

Samantha reached out toward the animal and grabbed what little of a mind there was left. She made a twisting motion with her hand, followed by several quick flicks of her fingers.

Before they knew what hit them, the horse had kicked both Giselle and the other witch hard enough to break bones and send them flying.

Giselle landed on her back. The horse charged her again and reared up, preparing to plunge its front legs down on her. With a cry of rage, Giselle slammed her hand into the ground. The horse became an inanimate thing once more, perched precariously on its two hind legs.

Samantha turned and ran. She ducked into the arcade, looking for a place to hide. Before she could move farther into the building, though, all the games came to life. Sirens and sound effects of every kind blared forth. The cacophony of noise startled her, and she clapped her hands over her ears.

There was nowhere she was going to be able to hide from the two witches, she realized. She was going to have to fight her way out of there.

You can do this. Magic is simple, she tried to remind herself. She turned. Giselle and the man were standing just inside the door.

"She's going to free it, and there's nothing anyone can do to stop her!" Giselle shrieked, making herself heard even above all the noise.

"Who are you talking about? What's she going to free?" Samantha demanded.

"It doesn't matter. You won't live to see it."

The windows and glass screens around her exploded inward.

"What are you doing?" the man shouted as he tried to shield himself from the flying missiles. As glass shredded her clothes and cut through her skin, Samantha fell. Everything went black.

She was trapped in her own mind. She could see the hallway of doors and several of her younger selves staring at her with frightened faces. The ten-year-old version was standing over her, shaking her head and looking thoroughly disgusted. "What is the use of us teaching you if you refuse to learn?"

"She's stronger than I am," Samantha gasped.

"No, but she risks more and with reason. The one who controls does not care if the vessel perishes."

"What does that mean?" Samantha asked. "What are you talking about?"

"You have eyes to see. Why do you not use them? Magic is simple. Magic costs."

"I have nothing left to give," Samantha sobbed.

"That's where you are wrong," Ten said with a sigh. "But you refuse to use your gifts, your knowledge. You refuse to do what must be done."

"I'm doing my best."

"Maybe. But you're not doing *our* best. That's why I'm going to help you."

"What are you going to do?"

Ten shook her head and turned to the door marked with an eleven. She reached out and opened the door, and a slightly older version of herself stepped out. Her eleven-year-old self didn't smile, didn't blink. She carried an athame in her right hand and it was dripping with blood.

And Samantha didn't want to know what or who that blood belonged to. She felt her stomach twist, and she began to convulse. Fear and revulsion filled her, and she struggled to wake up, to leave the hall of doorways. But Ten grabbed her arm, gripping it tight.

"You're not going back out there," Ten said. "She is."

And Eleven vanished in front of her eyes. Samantha felt sick and dizzy. She screamed, but Ten just kept holding her in a viselike grip.

"She can do what must be done even if you are not ready to," Ten said.

"What's happening? Where is she? What's she doing?"

"Your job," Ten said.

Samantha screamed, kicking out at Ten, but she couldn't shake the girl's grip on her.

Wake up! Wake up! Wake up! she commanded herself, but it was to no avail.

She stared up at the ceiling and realized that it was translucent. She could see lights through it, flashing and exploding. Her mind at work. Her mind controlled by a self other than her. An impact tremor made the ground beneath her shudder.

"What's happening?" she screamed, but none of the children would answer her. Instead they all stood, listening, watching something she could not see.

She kicked and screamed, but it was no use. And through it all, she felt sick to the depths of her soul. It wasn't right. Terrible things were happening, she knew. She could feel them even if she couldn't articulate exactly what they were.

And then suddenly Eleven reappeared. There was even more blood dripping from her athame, and her dress had splatters of blood on it as well.

"What did you do?" Samantha whispered.

"Don't you mean 'what did *we* do'?" Eleven asked.

"No. No! I'm not you. I didn't do whatever you just did."

"You'll have a hard time proving that to anyone, including yourself," Ten said.

"We warned you," Five said.

"We tried to stop you," Six added.

"You've gone too far," Seven accused.

"What's happening?" Samantha demanded.

And then Samantha was opening her eyes. It was still night outside. She could see the moon from where she was lying. The witches were gone. She couldn't feel their presence anymore.

She blinked slowly as she sat up. She could hear the crunching of glass all around her, and her hands where they pressed against the ground were being gouged by a dozen tiny shards. She struggled to her feet, broken glass falling to the ground around her. She cautiously shook out her clothes.

She could feel dozens of pieces of glass embedded in her skin. She passed her hands slowly over each arm, willing the glass to the surface. She stepped forward, more glass crunching under her feet.

She should get out of there. With the witches gone, she was free to leave. She walked half a dozen more steps and then stopped abruptly as she saw a figure slumped on the ground to her right.

Her heart began to pound. She crept forward cautiously, wondering if a poor security guard had gotten caught in the crossfire. At last she could clearly see the body, and her heart stopped for a moment.

It was the second witch who had been stalking her. The man lay dead, eyes frozen in a blank look of terror. There was blood everywhere, and it took her a moment to realize that the man's chest looked like it had exploded outward. His intestines were all around him on the floor. Someone had literally caused his internal organs to explode out of his body.

No, not someone, me. *I did this,* she realized. And there, on the wall behind the body was the proof. She had burned her coven's symbol into the wall above the body.

I am as God. That was what the ancient lettering meant.

She fell to her knees and vomited. This had been Eleven's doing, and it was all her fault. She should have listened to the younger girls. They had warned her not to open more doors. But she had ignored them and had let the monsters walk free, and one of them had taken over her mind, done all this carnage while she was unconscious.

She forced herself to get up. She had to see if she had killed Giselle as well. If she had, maybe all of this could be over.

They both deserve to die, a voice inside her head whispered. *It's no different from the witches you killed in Salem. You have to take care of this coven like you took care of that one.*

She had no proof that the entire coven was engaged in whatever evil Giselle was doing, at least of their own knowledge and free will. There had been one murder, not several with the promise of more. It wasn't like Salem.

But they're causing the earthquakes and risking the lives of countless people in doing so, she argued with herself.

She hunted for a few minutes but couldn't find another body. Giselle must have escaped.

She returned to the first body. She very carefully scorched the wall to obliterate her coven's symbol. Finished, she headed for the parking lot, determined to get out of there as fast as she could.

Once on the road, the full impact of what had happened hit her and she shivered with anguish. There was still glass in her legs and torso. She even felt a few pieces in her face. She didn't take the time to stop and remove them. She just wanted to get home as fast as she could so she could get into a hot shower and try to wash off the horrors of the night.

She reached for her phone. She wanted to talk to Anthony, needed to talk to him. He would understand. He would help her. Her hand froze, though, before she could call him.

Her eleven-year-old self had had blood on her athame when she first came out of her door. Given what she had accomplished while in control of Samantha's body, she was now convinced it had been human blood. Had her eleven-year-old self been involved with the human sacrifices her old coven had performed?

A sob escaped her. Was it possible in some cruel trick of fate that she might even be the witch who killed Anthony's mother?

She started screaming at the top of her lungs and punching the steering wheel. It couldn't be true. It mustn't be true. But even if she hadn't done it, she'd clearly been capable of it. She'd probably been there when it happened.

She could feel memories beginning to wake in her mind, crowding forward. "No!" she screamed, rejecting them. She didn't want to know. She didn't want to remember. For her own sanity, she couldn't.

"Anthony, I'm so sorry," she heard herself sobbing over and over.

She couldn't talk to him. Not until she could do it without fear and guilt. If she had killed his mother, she'd never be able to look him in the eye again.

Tears came, and she let them fall freely even though they partly blinded her. She didn't care. Part of her struggled with the belief that if she got killed on the windy road she had to drive, she deserved it for everything she had done.

With my luck, I'd be fine and whoever was in the other car would be hurt, she finally thought. With that thought foremost in her mind, she wiped her eyes and forced herself to slow down. She had no control of the past, but she could control the here and now.

When she finally made it back into the city, she breathed a sigh of relief. Minutes later, she exited the freeway. She was ten minutes to home.

Her phone rang. Given the time of night, she was sure it had to be Anthony. She couldn't answer, but she checked anyway. It wasn't Anthony. It was Robin.

"Hello?"

"Samantha? There was an intruder in my house." Robin's voice was fearful.

"Hang up and call nine-one-one," she said.

"I can't. I'm scared. He was . . . like us."

"He's gone now? You're sure?"

"Yes."

"Is your aunt there?"

"No. She left to pick up some of her prescriptions at the pharmacy hours ago, and she hasn't come back. She's not answering her phone."

"Do you know how to make a protection spell?"

"I—I don't know."

Samantha pulled a U and headed for the freeway. "Listen, I'm on my way right now, but it's going to take a while to get there."

"Please hurry," Robin whimpered.

"I'll be there as fast as I can. If he comes back, I want you to make a circle on the ground around yourself and stay inside it no matter what happens. You have to make the circle with your blood, and it has to be complete, no gaps. If you do that, nothing outside the circle can touch you. Do you understand me?"

"Yes, I'll do that, but please come."

"I will. I promise. Keep your phone on you and call me if anything else happens."

Samantha hung up and pounded her steering wheel in frustration. If only Robin had called while she was still down there. There was nothing that could be done about that, though.

She briefly thought about pulling her police light out from underneath her seat. But driving with it on for that far would attract attention, and if any other officers wanted to assist her then she was stuck explaining why she hadn't just sent local cops to Robin's house.

She needed to get there a lot faster than the speed limit would allow. In her heart she knew there was only one solution. Keeping her left hand on the wheel, she reached down with her right and unclipped her detective's shield from her belt. She held it up. She could feel the power building up in her body, electrifying, exhilarating. A bit of sympathetic magic was what was needed here, and the badge would have to do as a symbol of police officers. Normally, this kind of magic was done with candles or dolls, but in a pinch, you could make a lot of things work.

"I name thee every police officer between me and Robin's house," she said, feeling energy flowing from her fingers into the badge.

"You will not see this car and you will not see me."

She placed the badge in the glove compartment, where it would be in the dark and out of her line of sight.

She wrapped both hands around the wheel as she took the ramp onto the freeway. She was intensely grateful that it was late and there was little traffic to worry about. Bay Area traffic during the busy hours of the day could easily double and sometimes even triple a person's drive time.

As soon as she had merged onto the freeway, she slid over to the left-hand lane and then floored it.

The car leaped forward with a surge of power. Adrenaline began to pump through her as the speedometer climbed above one hundred. Cars in front of her scattered without her even having to flash her high beams at them. The rush she was getting from the speed was incredible, but fear was riding alongside as well. It was taking all of her concentration to make sure that she didn't hit any bad patches of road that could cause her problems.

She turned on her high beams, needing to see farther down the road because of the speed at which she was traveling. In the headlights a minute later, she saw the bumper of a police cruiser. She came screaming up behind him and then had to change lanes to pass him.

As she flashed by, neither officer in the car even glanced her way. A few seconds later and she was in front of them. She checked her rearview mirror, where the car was rapidly becoming a dot.

Her magic had worked. Satisfaction flooded her at the realization.

Don't be too proud of yourself, she cautioned.

There was a loud bang as the car jerked hard. She gritted her teeth as she struggled to regain control. A moment later the car straightened out. She'd hit a pothole. Samantha realized she was lucky to have kept control of the car. She was also lucky she hadn't taken out the tires or the rims, from the feel of things.

Steady; focus.

At last the cities fell behind and she hit the road curving through the mountains. She took one curve, and the car began to fishtail wildly. As soon as she had straightened out again, she cut her speed. She would be no help to Robin if she was splattered along the highway.

At last she came to the turnoff, and she wound upward until she arrived at the house. She parked, opened the door, and as she stepped out of the car, a wave of wrongness hit her. The hair all over her body stood on end.

She raced up to the front door. It was locked. "Robin!" she called, pounding on the door.

There was no answer.

Samantha grabbed the doorknob again and willed it to open. The door flew open, and she leaped inside as it slammed shut again behind her.

"Robin!"

She didn't see her in the kitchen and she made her way toward the back of the house.

"Robin! Where are you?"

As she came into sight of Winona's office, Samantha froze.

Robin was standing just inside the room, her back to Samantha, facing the window. Her back was straight and stiff, her arms were bent, her hands out of Samantha's line of sight. The girl was barefoot.

"Robin?" Samantha called as she moved closer.

Robin didn't move, staying perfectly still as though she were a statue.

And a horrible thought occurred to Samantha. Maybe the girl had been killed and petrified just like her mother.

She walked closer, scanning the area for signs of anyone else. There was no one, just the girl standing with her back to her.

"Robin?" Samantha asked as she reached her. She placed her hand on the girl's shoulder, and Robin jerked, then turned around. Her eyes were wide, her pupils dilated. Her face looked slack.

"Robin, what's the matter?"

Fire exploded in Samantha's body. She looked down and saw a knife protruding from her stomach. Blood was starting to gush, coating Samantha's shirt, the knife, and Robin's hand where it gripped the hilt.

15

Samantha fell backward, slamming to the floor with enough force to jar every bone in her body. Robin staggered but kept her feet, still holding the knife. Samantha pressed a shaking hand to the bloody wound in her abdomen.

I'm dying, killed by a child I'm supposed to be helping, she realized. Around her everything became clearer. Colors looked sharper, brighter. Her vision telescoped, and she could see the tiny imperfections in the wood grain of the floor. She could hear the blood pumping out of her body, smell its metallic tang in the air.

She was going to die if she couldn't start knitting her body together immediately. But she could see Robin getting ready to attack again.

Need to form the circle. So much blood.

There was more than enough blood to form the circle, but her muscles were seizing up. She touched her stomach with her hand and then began to smear the blood on the wood.

Robin bent over her, and she kicked out at the girl,

catching her in the knee. Robin staggered backward before falling.

Samantha struggled to move, to sit up, so she could stretch and complete the circle, but her body wouldn't respond. She tried to reach out with her mind, will the blood to run in a circle around her, but her thoughts were scattering, fading into oblivion.

I need help. God, save me! she prayed.

And in the next breath, she knew what to do. She brought her hands close together, and a moment later Freaky appeared. The kitten gazed at her with wide eyes.

"Circle of blood," she whispered.

The kitten rolled from her chest onto her stomach, coating its black fur with her blood. Then it jumped off and onto the floor and began to drag itself around her, wiping her blood onto the ground.

She couldn't keep her eyes open anymore. She didn't know if Freaky would be able to finish the circle before Robin stabbed her again. If she didn't focus and start to heal herself, though, it would be a moot question.

Everything seemed to go black for a moment. Then, slowly, she could feel warmth spreading throughout her body, burning like fire as it reached her stomach. She could feel the wood floor beneath her. The wood had once been a living thing, and some of the energy was still trapped in the lumber. She pulled it into herself. She could feel blood vessels begin to mend.

A sandpaper tongue licked her cheek. Freaky.

A moment later, she felt the air shimmer around her. Robin had tried to attack the circle, but the circle held. Freaky had protected her.

Muscle began to knit itself back together, pain knifing through her as it did so. She screamed in agony as toxins raced through her system. She rolled onto her side so that she could vomit.

Outside the circle, Robin kept attacking again and again like a mindless automaton. The circle did its job, holding true. Freaky scampered up onto her head and sat perched there. She could hear him hissing, and tiny claws pricked her scalp.

She finally was able to open her eyes again. Where everything had been so sharp and clear before, now it was hazy, her vision obscured by her own pain and exhaustion as she worked to heal herself. Robin was throwing herself at the energy barrier. Each time she did so, Freaky hissed.

Samantha struggled to keep her eyes open.

"Robin, you've got to stop," she whispered.

It was pointless. The girl had been mesmerized. It was no mean feat for one witch to do that to another with power. It usually required elaborate preparations and was always best done when hair or blood of the victim was used in the spell. Samantha wouldn't be able to break that mesmerism until she could exit the circle.

Samantha's wounds were continuing to heal, but not nearly fast enough. And then memories of what had been done to her and the others a few months before in a Salem graveyard came flooding back to her.

The circle kept others out, but it did not have to keep her in. She moved her hand slowly, hoping that Robin wouldn't notice. She put her index finger just over the side of the circle and pressed it to the ground.

The wooden floors had given all the energy they

could, but the girl who was standing on them had not. Robin was barefoot, making it that much easier. Samantha pulled energy as hard as she could, sucking it out of Robin, through the floor, and into herself.

It worked, and Samantha pulled the energy as hard as she could, her damaged body starving for it.

Robin yelped and tried to jump back, but Samantha was in control now. She pulled with everything she had, and the increased energy sent her healing abilities into overdrive. Moments later, she was sitting up even as Robin tumbled to the ground.

I have to release her or I will kill her.

Samantha forced herself to let go and yanked her hand safely back inside the circle. Robin was on the floor next to her, just outside the circle, head twisted her direction, rage burning in her eyes.

"It's going to be okay," Samantha heard herself saying, even though she knew the girl was in no position to be able to hear it.

"I'm going to kill you," Robin whispered.

"Not today."

Freaky was still standing guard, hissing at Robin. He had hopped down off of Samantha's head, and he was bouncing around the circle, his back arched high.

Samantha sat up slowly. She wasn't finished healing, but neither was she on the verge of death anymore. Robin's eyes were glazing over. The spell was losing its potency, its hold on her diminishing. Still, it would be a few hours before it was gone completely.

Samantha coiled all her muscles. Robin still held the athame, and she was going to have to move swiftly to free the girl before she could attack again. Robin closed her eyes, her breathing labored.

Samantha lunged and slammed her hands onto either side of Robin's head. She sent waves of electricity flooding through. "Burn out the thoughts that are not hers," Samantha commanded.

Robin screamed and began to thrash. Samantha threw her body over the girl, pinning her to the ground.

Seconds later, it was over. Robin ceased to struggle and after a moment asked, "What's going on?"

Samantha pulled away warily, watching the hand that held the knife. Robin didn't make a move to lift it, though. That was an excellent sign.

"Did I try to kill you?" Robin wailed suddenly, her voice cracking with stress.

"It wasn't you. You were ... possessed," Samantha said. It wasn't an accurate description of what had been done to her, but it explained the important part simply enough. "You weren't in control of yourself. Someone else was."

"I'm so sorry," Robin sobbed. "I don't know what happened."

"It's not your fault. Everything is okay now."

Samantha stood up gingerly and stared down at her bloody shirt in distress. "Except for my shirt. It's not okay. I'm afraid I'm going to have to borrow another T-shirt."

"Okay."

Samantha moved into the kitchen and peeled off her shirt. She grimaced at it. No salvaging this one either. After a minute, Robin joined her, bringing with her a plastic bag and a purple T-shirt. Samantha dumped the dead shirt in the bag and closed it up tight.

"I can put it out in the trash," Robin said.

"No, that's okay. I'll get rid of it," Samantha said. The last thing she needed was for whoever had done this to Robin to get ahold of her blood.

She used some paper towels to wash up, dumping them in the bag as well. Her pants she was just going to have to deal with when she got home. Fortunately, there didn't seem to be too much blood on them.

"Exciting end to an awful day," she said grimly.

"I'm so sorry," Robin said, repeating herself.

"It's not your fault. Do you hear me?"

Robin nodded glumly.

Samantha put on the T-shirt and pulled her hair back. Blood was drying in it, and she wrinkled her nose in distaste.

"What's wrong?"

"You know, I made it years on the force without being shot or stabbed. It seems like those days are gone forever, and I miss them."

Robin turned red and bit her lip.

"What?"

"I used to wish I had a more exciting life. I used to dream about it."

Samantha sighed. "Be careful what you wish for. It's a lesson everyone needs to learn, but especially people like us."

"Maybe I'll become a cop. Help people like you do."

"There are a lot safer and saner ways that you can help people," Samantha said. "But you can help me right now."

"Anything. What can I do?"

"Did your mom ever tell you stories about the mountains? Or maybe your grandfather told you a story?"

"My grandfather told me a lot of stories. I don't remember most of them. Mom, I don't know. I can't think."

"Take your time and try. It's important or I wouldn't be asking," Samantha said.

"What kind of story?" Robin asked.

"A story about something hidden in or under the mountains around here."

"Nothing like that that I can think of. But Mom was kind of funny that way. She collected stories of our culture and that of other tribes, local histories, all that kind of stuff. She liked facts, though, not what she considered fantasy. She never told me any of the really colorful stories. I only heard those from Grandfather."

"And yet she knew that the supernatural existed and wanted you to be a shaman. That is odd."

"Sometimes I think she just wanted my life to be more normal, you know? I think it was hard for her sometimes, growing up as Grandfather's daughter and not having powers of her own."

"Your mom was a complex woman."

"I think I'm only beginning to figure out the half of it," Robin said.

A phone rang and Robin answered it. After a minute she hung up. "That's my aunt. She's been stuck waiting for a tow truck for hours. She finally got one. She said she should be here in about twenty minutes."

"Then we'd better get this place cleaned up," Samantha said.

She turned toward the other room and then stopped with a gasp. Her blood on the floor still formed a circle, but that wasn't all. There, on the floor, spelled out in her blood, was a familiar phrase.

The last grave.

Samantha stared at the words in blood. How had they gotten there? She and Robin were alone in the house. At least, she thought they were.

"Who did this?" she whispered.

Robin looked down at the message. "I think you did. When I was possessed by whatever that was, I could still see and remember. And I remember watching you write it while I tried to kill you."

"It can't be," Samantha whispered. She couldn't have written it. She would have known. And why would she have written it?

A chill seemed to pass through her as she stared at the words. "I couldn't have done this," she whispered.

And yet doubt assailed her. There had been that one moment, she thought it was only a moment, when she had blacked out before her body had started healing and Freaky had licked her. Had she been out long enough that she could have done this?

She knelt down slowly, mouth dry, heart hammering painfully in her chest. She stretched out her hand and then pulled back. She heard a whimper escape her. She didn't want to know. Because if she had done this, what else might she have done?

"I have to know," she whispered, trying to convince herself.

She reached out and touched one of the bloody letters. And she saw herself, lying in the circle dead. No! Not dead, but dying. And Freaky was crawling over her and Robin was attacking the circle.

Samantha watched herself as she moved her finger and began to write.

"No!" she screamed, yanking her hand back and throwing herself halfway across the room.

"I'm sorry," Robin said. "Should I not have told you?"

Samantha looked up at the girl and had an insane urge to laugh. Fear rippled through her. Had one of her younger selves done this? Had the witch found a way to control her as well? Either possibility was terrifying. "No, it's good you told me. It's important," Samantha said.

She grabbed some paper towels and mopped up the blood, adding the used towels to her bag. She turned and saw tiny red paw prints weaving through the house toward the front door.

Freaky. She hadn't dispelled his energy and he was still covered in her blood. She groaned and began mopping up after the kitten. When she finally found him, he was staring at her from a perch on the coffee table. He trilled at her for a moment, and then she scattered the energy. She wiped up the remaining blood and returned to the kitchen.

She grabbed the bag and deposited it in the trunk of her car, then went back inside. "I'll stay until your aunt arrives," Samantha said.

"Okay."

Another thought occurred to her. "Did your mother

ever talk to you about her dreams, particularly ones dealing with earthquakes?"

"No," Robin said. "I didn't know she had them too."

"You dream about earthquakes?" Samantha asked.

"A few times in the past, but a lot lately. I keep having this recurring dream that I'm standing near the entrance to a cave. There's someone else with me, but I can't see her face. I don't know who she is. In my dream I know her, but you know how that goes."

"Yeah. What happens?"

"We're standing in front of this cave and there's an earthquake. I can hear rock, like, breaking apart or something, like an avalanche. The cave entrance gets a little wider, like there's a crack in the rocks around it. Red light comes out of it. Then the girl with me disappears and I wake up."

"Disappears how? Does she fall into the cave or leave?"

"No, just like vanishes—there, then gone."

"Did you tell your mom about these dreams?"

"Yeah. She always wanted me to tell her my weird dreams. She said it helped cleanse you by getting it out of your head and into the world."

"Did you ever notice if there were earthquakes that occurred shortly after you had the dreams?"

"To be honest, I don't know. I kind of tried to adopt Mom's philosophy, not think about it once I talked about it."

Samantha had a suspicion that Winona hadn't been telling George Wakefield about her own earthquake dreams but instead had been telling him her daughter's. If that was true, then why had she not shared the details of the later dreams with him? Was it because the symbolism meant something very specific to her, something that connected with the research she had been doing about the legend her father had told her as a child?

Samantha thought about trying to take a look at Robin's memories of the dream, but she was hesitant to mess around with the girl's mind given what she had just gone through. It could be traumatic for both of them.

A truck pulled up outside, and a minute later, an older woman came inside. She had a pleasant face with a few similarities to Robin. She was carrying an oversized purse and was wearing a look of dismay.

Robin went to hug her. "I was worried about you," she said.

"I was worried about me too," the older woman admitted.

"Auntie, this is Detective Samantha Ryan. I called her when you didn't come home."

"And you rushed over. That was nice of you," the older woman said, studying her from behind her glasses.

"I was happy to do it. I just got here a couple of minutes ago. We were getting ready to go out and look for you."

"I've had the most unbelievable night," the older woman said. "The car broke down on the highway, and there was no cell service. It took forever to flag someone down, and then I had to wait hours for the tow truck."

"I'm sorry you've had such a rough time of it," Samantha said. She was willing to lay odds that there had been some magic at work there. Clearly Giselle or one of the other witches had wanted to get Robin alone for a while. But why? Was it just to try to have her kill Samantha? Or would that have been the icing on the cake?

The lady waved her hands. "I'm sorry to worry anybody. Now look, it's morning already and I haven't been to bed yet."

. "Do you want me to cook you some breakfast?" Robin asked.

"No, child, I think I'm just going to go to bed. Detective, it was nice meeting you."

Samantha shook her hand and took the opportunity to check to see if the woman's memories of the night had been altered. They hadn't, she was relieved to discover.

"Well, Robin, walk me out?" Samantha asked.

"Sure."

They walked outside, past the car the tow truck had dropped. Fortunately, he hadn't blocked in Samantha. She turned and looked at Robin. "Be careful. Now that you've seen a protection circle, be sure to form one of your own if you suspect anyone is near."

"I will."

Samantha reached out and touched her shoulder. "It's not your fault. I just want you to be safe."

Robin nodded.

Samantha again fought the urge to take a peek at her memories. At this point, she was likely to see the image of Robin stabbing her before she could stop herself. Traumatic memories jumped to the surface oftentimes, especially with the very young. She was sure she didn't want to see the images of herself being stabbed. Also, she didn't want to risk damaging Robin's mind by being the second person to mess with it in such a short time.

"I have to get some sleep and do some work, but I'm going to be out again later today to check on you."

"I'm sorry you have to keep driving all this way."

"It's okay. I don't mind," Samantha lied. "I just want you to be safe, and I want to catch whoever is behind all this. If you remember anything else about the mountains or your earthquake dreams, give me a call."

Robin nodded.

Samantha stared at the girl in her rearview mirror as she left a minute later. She couldn't help but feel that Robin was alone even though her aunt was there. It was too easy to isolate the girl, use her. For now, though, Samantha didn't know what else she could do for her.

She cranked the music loud once she hit the highway. The last thing she wanted at the moment was to be alone with her own thoughts or risk falling asleep at the wheel. There was too much at stake. She couldn't lose it now.

When she finally made it home, she was relieved to see that Jill had already left for the morning. She called Lance, trying to forestall him showing up.

"What's up?" he asked.

"I just got home. Robin Lightfoot called because she thought an intruder was snooping around her house. I ended up going down there for a while. Still no luck on turning up anything from her mom's papers."

"Was there an intruder?"

"Hard to say. I lectured her about calling nine-one-one next time."

"Good."

"I'm going to crash. I'll call you when I wake up in a few hours."

"Okay. I got a couple more leads. You want me to run them down?"

"Yes, please," she answered, knowing that he likely had nothing that would be of interest to her.

She hung up with him and went back down to her car. She retrieved the bag of bloody towels and her shirt and headed to the basement of the building, where she knew there was an ancient furnace that supplied all the apartments with heat. Five minutes later, her bag and its contents were nothing but ash.

She made it back upstairs and into the bathroom, where she stripped out of her clothes and got into the shower. She cranked up the hot water as high as it would go and let it pummel her body. She closed her eyes as she let the water run all over her head and face.

So much blood and gore needed to be washed off. She wished it was just as easy to wash off the stains and blood that tainted her mind as it was the external ones. She stayed in the shower long after the water had turned cold, scrubbing her skin and hair as well as she could.

When she finally stepped out, she dumped her pants in the sink to soak out the blood, put the T-shirt in the washer, and headed for her bedroom. Dressed in pajamas, she sat down on her bed and stared at the clock. She was exhausted, but her mind was racing and she didn't know if she'd be able to get to sleep.

"Sleep," she said, in her deepest, most persuasive voice. Then she sighed because, as usual, she couldn't influence herself that way.

"Because that would be too easy," she said with a sigh.

She pulled the book out from underneath her mattress and started to read from where she had left off. Within three minutes, her eyes were crossing and her muscles spasming. She still knew that if she tried to lie down, though, sleep wouldn't come.

She put her hands together and conjured Freaky. Petting the kitten always helped to relax her. She was relieved to see that he was clean, without a sign of her blood on him. She didn't want to imagine what giving an energy kitten a bath would have looked like.

The small kitten snuggled onto her lap, stretched, and promptly fell asleep.

"Traitor," she whispered, as she stroked his head. "You're supposed to keep me company because I can't sleep."

He either didn't hear or didn't care. A minute later, he was snoring. She rolled her eyes and picked the book back up.

Somewhere in here is a clue I need to help all of this make sense, she thought. *I just have to find it.*

She just wished she weren't too tired to read it. Once she got some sleep and woke up, she was going to be back on the clock dealing with Lance and Robin and whatever else the day decided to dump on her.

"There's got to be an easier way to do this," she groaned.

And then she thought of the lectures given by her younger selves. Maybe there was an easier way to do it.

"Magic is simple. I'm making this too complicated."

She put the book on the bed and passed her hand over it. "Show me what Winona Lightfoot found."

The book cover opened and the pages began to fan her as they flipped rapidly. They stopped abruptly, and she stared at the heading at the top of the page.

Hell Hole Cave.

16

Samantha stared at the words. Hell Hole Cave. Robin had said her dreams about the earthquake had taken place at the entrance to a cave. There was a rough drawing of the cave entrance, which was very narrow. She stared at it intently. There was something familiar and frightening about it.

Why should such a thing scare me? she wondered.

Maybe it was because she was so tired and so overwrought. The suggestion of caves and mountains and earthquakes coupled with the name Hell Hole was clearly playing havoc with her imagination.

Get a grip, Samantha.

She picked up the book and stared at the page.

The Hell Hole Cave located in the Santa Cruz Mountains on Gray Whale Ranch is one of the most dangerous caves of the three hundred miles of caverns lying beneath California. The depth of this cave has never been adequately measured. Entrance to the cave is gained through a small opening in the side of the mountain. It is a tight fit, and only the slimmest and hardiest of souls should dare venture there. The cave has a successive series of narrow passageways and open caverns and several steep drops. One of the large caverns in the mountain is known as the Hall of Faces, where people leave sculptures in the clay walls. Other sections of the cave are rich in minerals such as quartz.

Perhaps the most intriguing part about the cave, though, are the historical references to it. Some Indian legends suggest that the faces depicted in the Hall of Faces are not carved by visitors, but are actually the only surviving remains of a small tribe that took refuge in the caves during a war between two larger tribes. Another legend has it that there is pirate gold buried in one of the lower chambers. Most mysterious of all is the rumor that ancient peoples trapped a demonlike monster inside this mountain and left only a series of narrow openings as a way for one person once a year on the anniversary of the entrapment to make their way down and check that the creature was still captive.

The only reason we know of this last rumor is that a Franciscan friar at Mission Santa Cruz in 1792 made a note in a record that a young male had been brought to the mission and treated for extreme injuries incurred while checking up on the condition of the beast under the mountain. Based on what the young man said, the friar was the first to refer to the cave as the cave into hell. He also noted that the young man was out of his mind with a fever, ranting, and had sustained deep puncture wounds to the abdomen. Despite their best efforts, they were unable to save him.

A week later, a large earthquake caused some rock slides in the mountains. When the friar finally went to check on the man's story, he discovered the cave exactly where the man had told him, but could not pass as far into it as the man described, possibly because of collapsing walls.

Samantha put down the book. Her pulse was racing. Drake had been studying spirits of the mountain, Winona had discovered this book, which reinforced a story her shaman father had told her. Trina had told her the witches were causing the earthquakes in an effort to look for something. Robin had been having recurring nightmares about an earthquake happening while she was standing at the entrance to a cave.

What if Giselle is attempting to free the monster buried under the mountain?

Everything was starting to make sense, fall into place. The witches wanted to know what Winona knew about the legend. The ritual she had seen the afterimage of in Cathedral Grove had involved a mountain with lines on the ground. She was guessing they were fault lines and that they were working to crack open a portion of the mountain in order to release the monster or to enable someone to get inside and get close to it.

But how would they know which area to try to widen? If the caverns truly went on for miles underground in many directions, how could they be certain that they were striking in the right place?

She was sure that this was what Giselle was trying to accomplish, but she felt like there was still a piece to the puzzle that she didn't have. What would make her think she could target the area well enough to accomplish her goals? Moving a ton of rock debris was a challenging task for any coven, but without precise directions, it would prove fairly impossible.

"What am I missing, Freaky?"

The kitten just continued to snore softly.

Samantha closed the book and put it on her end table. She turned off the light and picked up Freaky, who mewed plaintively. She lay down and put the kitten back down next to her. He snuggled into her side as she closed her eyes and prayed that sleep would come. She was going to need to be as rested as possible if she was going to stop the coven from unleashing a demon.

She was standing on a steep hillside, staring at the opening of a cave. There was a metal grate across the top part, leaving only a small entrance.

"Do you think we'll fit in there?"

She turned to the speaker. It was Robin, who was staring at the cave with a look of dread on her face.

"I think we have to. So, we'll do what we must," Samantha told her.

"I'm afraid."

"Everyone's afraid. It's okay to be afraid. It's what you do about it that's important."

"I don't want to go in there."

Neither did Samantha. There was something ominous about the entrance. Even the air itself felt somehow wrong here. She hunched her shoulders, trying to fend off the feelings of darkness and doom that seemed to be creeping up on her, as stealthy as shadows, as inevitable as night.

"We have to go in. We have to find out if it's really there."

"But what if—"

The earth began to shake, and Samantha could feel herself shaking apart with it. She was standing there with the girl one moment, and the next moment she was gone. Samantha was somewhere else entirely. It was dark where she was.

Where am I? When am I?

The earth continued to move, and around her she could hear things buckling and groaning beneath the strain. And then rocks began to rain down on her head.

Samantha woke with a shout and sat straight up. Her bed was shaking, sliding across the floor. The book and lamp both fell off her end table and the picture of her parents flew off the wall and hit the ground, the glass shattering into a hundred pieces.

Freaky was clawing his way up her body, eyes wide in terror. She grabbed him and leaped from the bed, sliding across the floor in her socks and slamming into the door. She cursed as she tried to wrench it open and then she sat, huddled with the kitten in the doorway as the house seemed to shake itself apart around her.

I don't want to die. Not here, not like this. The thoughts flashed through her mind. Freaky had dug all of his claws into her arms and was holding on for dear life. Apparently, he wasn't ready to die yet either.

The door to Jill's bedroom flew open, slamming into the wall with a thud so loud they both jumped. Samantha wondered how much longer it could possibly last and whether they should try to make it outside or stay right where they were.

At last the shaking came to an end. They sat there for what seemed an eternity, both waiting, both afraid to leave the doorway for fear it would start back up again. Slowly Freaky retracted his claws.

"I think that was even bigger than the first one," Samantha told the little kitten. Freaky didn't seem to disagree. Slowly she stood up and moved back over to the bed. She dropped Freaky on the floor before she shoved her bed back in place. She picked up the book and the lamp, then headed out to the kitchen to get a broom and dustpan to take care of the broken glass.

Once that was finished, she sat back down on the bed. The dream she'd been having before the earthquake hit came back to her, rattling her more than the quake had. She realized she knew exactly who the other woman in Robin's dream was. It was her, because she had dreamed the same dream. And even she didn't know where she had disappeared to.

She forced herself to take deep, calming breaths. Freaky was burrowing under the blankets, and she reached out and petted his tail absently. Then she stood up and walked out to the family room, where she turned on the television.

There was a news update about the earthquake and she

listened. ". . . another earthquake along the San Andreas fault line. Because this quake was bigger than the one from a couple of days ago, this one is now being classified as the main earthquake and the others as foreshocks."

She was right. This one had been stronger than the first one.

"For more updates on this and the unfolding story of the murder at Santa Cruz Beach Boardwalk, tune into the news tonight at six."

Samantha turned off the television. She shouldn't have been surprised that the Boardwalk scene was making news. She wondered how on earth the local police down there were going to spin everything, particularly the carousel horse who had left his post.

She turned to head back to her bedroom and jumped when she saw Roxy come padding down the hall. She had forgotten that the energy puppy was still around. She really was going to have to figure out what to do about Jill and the dog.

She changed into clean clothes and then sat down at her computer. She searched online for more information about the Hell Hole Cave. She found a few pictures of it, mostly of the entrance and a few from inside the cave itself. There were several short write-ups by people who had actually been inside. She discovered that in the room of clay faces there was also a guestbook that people signed. That was a cute touch.

More information than that was sparse, though, and there was nothing about the ancient legend. She did find information on some of the other more famous caves in Santa Cruz that were home to distinct animal species and were favorite haunts of students. She read about the clean-up efforts for one of the caves. Winona's name was mentioned in relationship to it. Apparently, she had been one of the more outspoken proponents for maintaining the cave in its natural state and keeping revelers out. Finally, she found a Web site that actually gave coordinates for the cave.

There seemed to be nothing else online about the cave. She finally gave up.

She went into the kitchen, made herself a quick sandwich, and called Lance. It went straight to voice mail.

"Hi. Finally awake and trying to play catch-up. Checking in to see where you are and what I can do to help."

She hung up and quickly ate her sandwich. She kept expecting to receive a call back and was surprised ten minutes later when he still hadn't returned the call. She finally tried calling again, but it still went to voice mail.

"Now I know why Ed always got so frustrated when I had my phone off," she told Freaky and Roxy, who were both regarding her with enormous eyes.

"Are you two going to play nice if I leave you alone?" Samantha asked.

They just blinked at her.

She finished getting ready to go and then headed downstairs to her car. She slid behind the wheel and contemplated her next move. She didn't want to waste time waiting for Lance to call her back. She finally decided to go down and check out the Hell Hole Cave. After that, she could check in on Robin like she'd promised she would. It had only been a few hours, but the girl had to be completely traumatized from earlier.

She pulled a piece of paper with the location of the Hell Hole Cave out of her pocket and punched the information into her GPS. She needed to go see this place for herself.

It was two hours later that Samantha was standing in front of the entrance to the cave. It looked as it had in her dreams. It was in the side of the mountain, which was green and lush. The top half of the entrance was covered by a grate, leaving only a narrow slit at the bottom. A person would have to back into it to get inside. She thought of some of the pictures she'd seen online. Half the people shimmied through on their backs and half on their stomachs. She didn't care to go in there at all. She shuddered just thinking about it.

The air was cold and crisp, but that didn't account for the chill that seemed to be settling into her bones. There was something deeply unnatural about the place. Samantha bent down and slowly, hesitantly, moved her hand toward the rock wall just inside the cave entrance. She hesitated. It should be cool, but it was radiating enough heat that she could feel it even before she touched it. The hair on the back of her neck stood on end.

What would she see if she connected with the stone? Would it be the creature purportedly trapped inside or the effect of spells being cast by witches? She held her breath and put her hand on the stone.

It was hot, but she didn't see either of the things she expected. She saw herself, crawling into the hole, going deeper and deeper. She saw herself barely avoiding being bitten by a black widow dangling from the ceiling.

She saw herself skidding down a deep incline and then losing her footing and falling headlong into the darkness.

She screamed and jerked her hand away. "This is not the future. I am not going in there," she vowed.

But in her heart she knew that wasn't true. If all fingers pointed to this place, sooner or later she was going to have to go inside. Her mouth felt dry and her stomach queasy. She wiped her hot, sweaty palms on her pants. She backed away slowly, not wanting to take her eyes off the cave. It was almost like she feared that if she turned her back on it, something would reach out to suck her inside.

It was ridiculous, but the fear that was pumping through her system couldn't be denied. She stared hard at the metal grate that partially barred the entrance. She wondered who had put it there and why. Why not cover the complete entrance? She had read that there were several tight squeezes once inside. Maybe to prevent more explorers from getting stuck, they had positioned the grate in such a way to restrict access to only those skinny enough to get through the tight spaces inside. Maybe the grate had originally covered the entire cave entrance and determined adventure seekers had gotten rid of half of it.

As she stared, the grate suddenly seemed to be brighter, shinier. There was less grime covering it, and it was more easily recognizable as metal. She blinked, wondering what was causing the illusion. She glanced up at the sky, but the clouds were obscuring the sun. She stepped forward hesitantly and touched the metal, trusting her other senses. It felt clean.

"What is happening here?" she wondered out loud.

It could be a glamour spell, but for what possible reason? It made no sense. A glamour spell would be more likely used to obscure the cave entrance altogether. The clouds overhead began to darken, and a light drizzle of rain started. She gazed around apprehensively.

The last time she had been in these mountains, the rain had been accompanied by thunder, lightning, and a witch bent on killing her. She turned and began the hike back to where she'd left her car.

She turned for a last look back at the cave. Through the thin veil of rain, she could barely even see the barrier anymore. It certainly wasn't shining like it had been a minute before.

She turned, hunching her shoulders up against the cold, and walked. Around her, the trees seemed to be whispering to one another. It was just the wind blowing through them, but after her experience the other night, she'd never look at trees the same way again.

A high-pitched scream caused her to whip around quickly. It had come from the direction of the cave. Was someone trapped in there? She stood, hesitating. She didn't want to get near the thing again, but if there was an innocent hiker trapped, she should help. A second scream drove her forward until she dropped on her knees in front of the cave entrance.

"Hello!" she shouted. "Can you hear me?"

There was no answer. "Hello?" she called again.

It might not have even been coming from the cave. The mountains were loaded with trails. Someone could have slipped and fallen on one of them. She put her hand inside the mouth of the cave and touched the stone. It was considerably cooler than it had been when she touched it before. As she pulled out her hand, she noticed something else that was different. The barrier that was blocking the top portion of the entrance was no longer made of metal. It was wood, old and faded. The word DANGER had been scrawled across it.

She touched the sign. It felt old even. Her confusion mounted. Something was happening here, changing this place, in ways that she couldn't explain.

She thought about the scream she'd heard. Was it real, from a living, breathing person, or some sort of ghost or echo from the past?

Magic is simple.

She placed both hands on the rock just inside the cave and felt the buildup of energy in her body. "If there is a living human down there, this energy will go to them. If there is no living human down there, it will come back to me."

She pushed the energy into the rock and then waited. A minute passed, two. She knew the caves were supposed to be extensive, but a person shouldn't be able to reach that far into them. *Maybe there is someone down there, trapped. God, please, I don't want to have to go down there.*

And then she felt a surge of energy hit her fingertips and pass into her body. Her energy had come back. "Nothing living down there, at least not human," she whispered.

She stood shakily to her feet, relief flooding her. But the cave mouth just gaped at her, as though it were laughing. She could almost hear it whisper, *Another day.*

Not if I can help it, she vowed.

The rain had ceased. It was just a cloud burst apparently. She felt her spirits lighten slightly as she hurried away from the cave. She couldn't help but feel that she'd dodged a bullet. However it had happened, she was truly grateful.

Samantha returned to her car and breathed a sigh of relief when she hit the road. She hadn't liked what she'd felt at the cave, and she just wanted to put as much distance between it and herself as she could.

Her mind churned as she drove, conjuring up all sorts of gruesome images for her to ponder. Finally she came to the turnoff, and a minute later she was parked outside of Robin's house.

There was no sign of the car her aunt had been driving the night before. Hopefully, that meant the problem had fixed itself. She sat for a moment, trying to compose herself. She didn't want to alarm Robin. The poor girl had been through enough already.

Samantha got out of the car, remembering that she had forgotten Robin's T-shirt in the clothes dryer. *Oh well. I'm sure I'm going to be out here fifty more times this week,* she thought drily.

Robin was outside, picking some herbs from the garden along the side of the house. She seemed none the worse for wear and very focused on what she was doing.

She looked up as Samantha approached.

"How are you today?" Samantha asked. "Feeling better than last night? I know I certainly am."

"Who are you?" Robin asked, fear flashing across her face.

"What do you mean?" Samantha asked, taken aback.

"You . . . you're like me."

"Yes, we've been through this," Samantha said.

Robin dropped the flowers and backed toward the house. "What do you want?"

"Robin, is something wrong?"

She could see the girl's eyes. Unlike the night before, they looked normal. But what was this if not some sort of spell? Could the girl's mind have finally shut the door on the traumatic events of the past few days, similar to what Samantha had done with most of her childhood?

"Stay away from me!"

Robin turned and ran up the steps to the house and inside, slamming the door behind her.

Samantha stood for a moment, wondering what had just happened. If Robin had gone into denial, they were going to have to work this out together. Personally, she would like nothing better than to get in her car and get out of there, forget she knew of Robin or had ever seen her mother's petrified body. For the first time since the whole nightmare had started, she let herself think about just leaving. She might not be able to go back home to Boston, but there were plenty of other cities out there. Let the rest of the police department deal with this mess.

As much as Samantha wanted to, though, she couldn't just leave the girl alone, not with witches out there intent on using her. They had killed Robin's mother, and Samantha knew that Giselle would have no problem doing the same to Robin if it suited her purposes. Samantha took a step toward the house, and the door opened and a woman came out onto the porch.

"You're not wanted here. Get off my property," the woman said. Her eyes blazed with anger, and her posture was mildly threatening. That wasn't what shocked Samantha, though. What shocked her was who it was she was staring at.

The woman standing on the porch glaring at her was a very alive Winona Lightfoot.

17

"What are you doing alive?" Samantha burst out. Even to her it sounded like the worst question in the entire world.

Winona cocked her head to the side. "Are you the one who's been sending me those letters?"

"Winona Lightfoot?" Samantha asked, trying to recover. It had to be a trap, an imposter. It wouldn't be the first time a witch had killed someone and taken their place. She thought of Salem. She refused to be fooled by that trick again.

"Who wants to know?" the woman demanded, hands on her hips, anger sparking in her eyes.

"Detective Samantha Ryan," she said, producing her badge.

"Oh." Some of the fight left the woman. "What do you want?"

"I have a couple of questions for you."

Samantha's phone rang. She checked and saw that it was Lance. "I have to take this call."

"Okay," Winona said, her voice now uncertain. "Just knock on the door when you're ready."

"Sure."

Samantha answered the phone as Winona retreated back inside the house. "Hi. What's up?"

"I'm wondering where my partner is. You were supposed to meet me at the crime scene."

"Which crime scene?" she asked.

"Which crime scene? Are you losing it or something? The one from yesterday, the Thai restaurant downtown?"

It was all Samantha could do to try to focus, figure out the best thing to say next. She hadn't heard about a murder at a Thai restaurant in the last few days.

"Right. Can you text me the address again?" she said, scrambling to catch up. "I'll be there as soon as I can. I was just chasing down some leads. Hey, you know the Lightfoot murder?"

There was a pause. "What Lightfoot murder?"

Samantha's pulse quickened. "A few days ago, the body in the Swamp at the Natural History Museum?"

"You mean the place they filmed all those PSAs? 'I'm proud to be a Japanese American' commercials."

"Yeah, only we established that you are proud to be an Asshole American," she said.

Another pause. Then a chuckle. "That's funny. I'm going to use it. As for the homicide, I haven't heard anything about something happening there. You want me to ask around, find out who's on the case?"

"No! I mean, no, that's okay. Send me that address, and I'll meet you as soon as I can."

Samantha hung up, and she could feel sweat dripping

down her back. Was it possible that the murder never happened? Or had she chosen to put her trust in the wrong person . . . again. Could Lance be part of whatever was happening? She double-checked the date on her phone to make sure that it was the day she thought it was and that the whole thing hadn't been some sort of dream.

No. Everything was as she expected it to be.

She called the coroner next. Jada answered on the third ring. "What can I help you with, Detective?"

"Jada, I was hoping you could refresh my memory about something." She stopped, struggling with how to word her question so she didn't sound crazy.

"I'll do what I can."

"You remember the petrification case, the one where the woman's body had been turned solid?"

"Petrification? No. I would remember something like that. How old is the case? It was probably before my time."

"You know what, never mind. I think someone was just teasing me."

"It's always hard to be the new cop in the group. Don't believe a word half those boys say."

"Thanks. I'll remember that."

Samantha hung up. Even if Lance and Jada were both in on whatever was happening, there was one more place she could look. The murder had been big news because Winona was a bit of a local celebrity and because of where her body had been found. Samantha launched her Web browser and did a quick search.

Nothing. No news articles about Winona being dead

or about a body being found in the museum complex. Samantha shoved the phone in her pocket and steadied herself for a moment on the car.

The past had been undone. Somehow Winona was back from the dead and Samantha was the only one who remembered it. How was that even possible?

She took a deep breath and forced herself to walk to the house. Why would she remember when others didn't? Was it because of her powers? If that was the case, though, then how come Robin didn't seem to remember? If she had, she would have recognized Samantha.

She mounted the steps to the front door and knocked. Moments later, the dead woman herself opened the door and ushered Samantha inside. She couldn't leave Lance waiting too long. It was going to take forever to drive there as it was, and he would be chock-full of questions she had no answers to. But she couldn't pass up this opportunity to talk to the living Winona. Just because she was alive at this moment didn't mean someone wouldn't try to kill her again.

They sat down in the living room. She could see Robin in the kitchen, curious, but not wanting to approach too close. It was then that she realized Robin was wearing the same purple T-shirt that was supposed to be in Samantha's washing machine. She rubbed her head.

"What is this all about, Detective?" Winona asked. She still seemed mistrustful, and who could blame her after the scene outside?

"I understand you've been getting some threatening letters."

Winona cast a quick glance over her shoulder, clearly

not wanting Robin to be part of the conversation. The girl didn't take the hint, though, but she still kept her distance.

"Um, yes."

"I'm just following up on a tip we got," Samantha said, struggling to choose her words carefully.

Winona looked at her, eyebrows raised questioningly. Samantha looked from her to Robin.

I can't do this. I can't sit here and pretend everything is okay when it's not.

Samantha cleared her throat. "Okay, look. I know your daughter can sense me, but I don't know if you can. So I'm going to level with you."

There was a notepad and a pen on the far end of the coffee table. She crooked a finger and the pen flew into her hand.

Winona's face hardened. "What do you want?"

"I had a . . . vision." *So much for leveling with her.* "It didn't go well with you. A witch . . . hurt you."

"Dreams and visions should never be taken lightly," Winona said.

"I know. That's why I'm here. I need to know who's been threatening you and if you've been contacted at all by someone like me. Also, does the name Giselle mean anything to you?"

Winona pressed her hands to her face. "I'm sorry. This is a lot to take in. Let me think."

"Of course," Samantha said. She ticked her gaze over to Robin. The girl had drifted slightly closer, her eyes pinned on Samantha. Curiosity and fear vied with each other for the upper hand in the girl's eyes.

"Well, I can tell you that the letters are because I've proposed limiting access to some of our caves here in Santa Cruz. We have some very famous ones that are home to some endangered species. As part of my work, I not only do ongoing research about the early history of the area, I also struggle to maintain it and the culture. These caves were significant to the culture of the early inhabitants for practical and religious reasons. Unfortunately, these caves are being desecrated by kids who think of them as good places to party. We did a clean-up not so long ago of one cave that was full of trash, beer bottles, stuff like that. Of course, many students think of these places as their own party dens and don't want access cut off. Additionally, there are others, those who are into spelunking, that sort of thing, who don't want access to the caves restricted."

"Is Hell Hole Cave on the list of caves you're trying to limit access to?"

Winona shook her head. "That cave is much harder to access. It doesn't need the same kind of immediate protection that the others do."

Samantha noticed that the woman hadn't shown any real reaction to the name of the cave. She took a stab in the dark. "Have you found the book in the university library yet that corroborates what your grandfather told you about the demon that was buried under the mountain in that cave?"

Winona went completely white. "No," she whispered. "It's true?"

"I don't know if it's true, but I know that you read this book before you . . . in my vision."

Winona nodded slowly. "I will have to go look for it."

Samantha was at a loss how to answer. If Winona had never found it and Winona had never been murdered then she and Lance shouldn't have been there investigating and she wouldn't have found the book. So the jackpot question would be: *Where is the book now, in my room or in the library?*

It made her head hurt just thinking about it. She nodded, not sure what she could say.

"As for Giselle, no, I haven't heard the name. And to the best of my knowledge, you are the first person outside of family members I've met with these gifts."

Gifts. That was how Winona truly saw them. Samantha could never see them as that. To her, they were a curse.

"Okay. I appreciate your time." She fished a business card out of her pocket and handed it to the woman. "If you think of anything, or anything new happens, please let me know."

"Thank you. I appreciate the diligence with which you've responded to your vision. I hope it never comes true."

"Me too," Samantha whispered.

She stood up, forcing a smile. She headed for the door. *Just get out of these people's lives and pray that they never have to see you again and vice versa.*

She had her hand on the door when she stopped.

"Is there anything else we can help you with, Detective?" Winona asked.

Samantha set her jaw. "Yeah, actually." She looked past Winona to where Robin was standing and locked eyes with her. "Robin, stop sneaking out of the house to go to the witch ceremonies in Cathedral Grove. They're dangerous people, and they've been using and manipulating you. Anything they've given you, destroy it immediately."

Winona turned to look at her daughter.

Robin was pale and shaking. "How—how did you know?" she whispered.

"It's true?" Winona asked, voice rising.

Robin nodded.

"I know you want your daughter to be a shaman like your father was, but you need to talk to her about what she wants. And both of you need to call me if you see any sign of anyone else with power. Do I make myself clear?"

Both Winona and Robin nodded.

"Good. Now I'll leave the two of you to talk things over."

"Wait!" Robin said, eyes wide.

"What is it?"

"I don't know how to explain it, but it's been like I've been having snatches of a dream or something coming back to me all day. Everything has just felt wrong. And it was like I recognized you when I first saw you. I think you were in my dreams. And . . ." The girl stammered and turned to her mom. "In my dreams, someone had killed you."

Winona put a hand over her heart and stared at her daughter, speechless.

"Thank you for telling me," Samantha said. "If you can think of anything else, please let me know."

Samantha turned and walked out the door, shutting it

firmly behind her. She wasn't sure how it was going to turn out between mother and daughter, or if it would even matter. Come tomorrow, it might be a whole other world again.

She got in her car and headed down the hill for what she hoped was the last time. It would be a miracle if Winona escaped this thing unscathed. For Robin's sake, she prayed that it was so.

She dialed Anthony, hoping he'd pick up.

When she heard his voice on the other end, relief flooded through her. "She's alive! The woman who was killed by witches is suddenly alive again."

"Whoa, slow down. Who are you talking about?" Anthony asked.

"You don't remember either," she said.

"Remember what? Samantha, you're not making much sense. Are you okay?"

She licked her lips. "No. I can't talk now, though. I'll call you later."

She hung up and poured on the speed. She just had to deal with Lance. And after that, she really needed to find a way to get in touch with Trina. Hopefully, the other witch had answers.

When she finally walked into the Thai restaurant Lance had sent her the address for, he looked at her and rolled his eyes. "Nice of you to show up. Sorry to inconvenience you today."

"Knock it off. I told you, I was working."

"Yeah, we should all do that much work," he said sarcastically.

Samantha felt rage explode inside her. He had no idea how much she had been through in the past few days. She wanted to kill him.

She felt energy building up in her body, and with sudden alarm, realized that she was going to kill him. She turned and made it to the door before energy exploded from her fingertips. It arched over a dozen cars and caused a Dumpster to explode. A shower of garbage rained down all over the parking lot.

She stood, dazed, as Lance pushed past her. "What happened? Was that a bomb?" he shouted.

She couldn't speak. All she could do was stare at the charred ground where the Dumpster had been. She had done that. Not because she wanted to, but because she couldn't stop the outburst, just control the direction of it. If she hadn't moved when she had, she would have killed Lance with that energy. She felt sick to the bottom of her soul.

I almost killed him. I almost killed him for being ignorant and sarcastic. Dear God, what's happening to me?

Lance was inspecting the area now. She could see him calling someone on his cell. If he thought it had been a bomb that went off, he was probably calling in the experts. *How could it possibly get any worse than this?*

Finally, Lance walked back to her. He took her arm and led her inside to a booth in the back. "Can we get some water?" he asked the manager.

The man returned in a moment with the water, and Lance shoved a glass at her.

"Helluva day," he said.

She stared down at her water glass. That didn't even

begin to describe it. She forced herself to pick it up and take a drink.

"Hey, you okay?" he asked. "You didn't get hit by anything, shrapnel?"

"I'm fine," she said, licking her lips. It came out as a gravelly whisper. She kept staring at her water glass, looking for answers where there were none.

"Look, if you need something stronger, I get it, but we have to wait until we're off duty. Then the booze is on me."

She looked up at him and realized that he was pale. He lifted his own water glass with a hand that shook. He might not have any clue what had really just happened, but it had rattled him nonetheless.

She nodded, and they sat in silence, sipping their water. Finally, other officers arrived and began investigating the parking lot. Samantha wished she could help them out, explain that they were looking for traces of a bomb that didn't exist, but she couldn't. Even if she did tell the truth, who would believe her?

So she sat, sipping water, wondering what it all meant. Now that Winona was alive, what was she supposed to do? How much of the past few days did that unravel? And was there anyone besides her who remembered?

Lance got up at one point and went to talk to the guy from the bomb squad. When he came back, Samantha struggled to pull it together.

"Any luck?" she asked.

He shook his head. "They can't figure out what caused it. No obvious incendiary device. Apparently, it's a mystery."

She nodded. "What about here? Did you find anything?"

"You remember last night when I said that something didn't feel right about this?"

"Uh-huh," she lied. Apparently, an aftereffect of remembering the past that had been undone was that she had no knowledge of the current past. She didn't think it possible, but her head started to hurt even more.

"I was right. Get this. The guy who got killed here last night was out here on a business trip from Chicago."

"If you tell me he had ties to the Mob, I'm leaving," she threatened.

"Well, then grab your purse on the way out, because bingo! Mob ties."

Samantha put her head down on the table and wondered if it was too late to feign illness and go home, where she could try to sort this all out. Lance went on to tell her what he'd found out from questioning all the restaurant employees while waiting for her.

She got the not-so-subtle dig but let it pass. If she chose to take offense, she might try to kill him again, and that would be bad for everyone. She thought of the little girl in her mind who was the master of temper tantrums. Was she trying to take over Samantha's body just as number eleven had done at the Boardwalk? The thought chilled her to the bone. When Lance had stopped talking, she asked, "So, are we done here for today?"

"I'm calling it. I think I'm going to head home," he said.

She was grateful that he had forgotten about buying her a drink. She was in no mood. She dragged herself to her feet. She made it to her car and drove home. Outside, she noticed there were no longer policemen watching the building. Why would there be? Winona was alive, which meant that everything that had led to their presence on her street and watching Jill had been erased too.

Samantha walked up the steps, reached for the door, and froze. It was ajar. Jill never left the door unlocked. Samantha drew her gun and kicked the door open before flattening herself against the outside wall.

Nothing.

She glanced in and saw the kitchen chairs knocked over and Jill's books and papers scattered all over the floor.

"Jill, are you okay?" she shouted.

Silence.

Samantha rushed in, moving swiftly from room to room. There was no one in either bedroom, and at first glance, it didn't look like anything had been disturbed. She returned to the kitchen, holstering her weapon. She looked down at the scattered books and papers.

A smear of blood was on the table.

Samantha put her hand down on the table and closed her eyes. There was a struggle. She could feel Jill's terror, pain, and confusion, the emotions trapped in the air around her.

Jill had been kidnapped.

Samantha took a deep breath. Witches had kidnapped Jill. Why? What did they think she had? Or was it something they thought she knew?

She should call Lance, tell him what was happening. But how could she explain Jill's being kidnapped without telling him everything? She reached up and grabbed the cross necklace and prayed for strength and guidance.

"What do I do?" she whispered.

Her phone rang and she grabbed at it. It was Lance. She didn't want to take the call, but maybe this was an answer to a prayer; maybe she was supposed to get his help. It would have been easier back when they knew of Jill's connection with Winona's killer. She couldn't worry about that, though. The important thing was to get as much manpower on the hunt for Jill as they could. And the fact that she was hunting for her roommate would help people excuse or ignore the fact that she was going to be checking in less and less until this whole thing was finished.

"Hello?"

"Hey," he said. His voice sounded strained.

"Lance, I just got home. I think Jill's been kidnapped."

"What? Are you sure?"

"The door was ajar. There's stuff knocked over in the kitchen and a smear of blood on the table."

"Have you tried her cell?"

"Not yet. I just saw it when you called."

"Okay, I'm on my way over there right now. Don't worry. We'll find her."

"Okay, great."

There was a pause. "Samantha?"

"Yeah."

"Don't be there when I get there."

"What do you mean?"

He cleared his throat. "I just got a call from the captain. It's why I was calling you, actually. You hear about that thing that happened at the Boardwalk in Santa Cruz last night?"

Her heart began to hammer in her chest. "Yeah, there was something about it on the news update right after the earthquake earlier today."

"Well, they found your fingerprints at the scene."

"What?" she gasped.

"Listen, it's totally bogus. I don't know what's happening, but the captain asked me to bring you in ... for questioning."

"But Jill—"

"I know. I think someone's setting you up. I also think the best person to figure this out is you. So, when I get there, don't be there, okay? I don't want to know where you're going. Got it?"

"Yes," she whispered.

Her world was crashing down around her. Lance didn't know that it was her who'd killed that man. If they had her fingerprints in the system, it would be nearly impossible to convince people otherwise, even with a magical assist.

"We're going to get through this. It's going to be okay."

She hung up and raced to her bedroom. She grabbed her trunk, which contained every bit of her history as a witch. She checked for the book and was shocked to find it still on her nightstand. She threw it in a bag along with some clothes.

She heard a soft mew and looked under the bed to find Freaky and Roxy both staring at her with great, fearful eyes. She couldn't let them be there when Lance arrived, so she passed her hands through both, dispersing the energy. Then she headed for the car.

She managed to throw everything in the backseat and jumped in, grateful that it was still the rental car and it would take them a while to figure out what she was driving.

She slammed her foot down on the gas pedal and was halfway down the street when she saw Lance's car in her rearview mirror.

She hit the highway and made a beeline for Santa Cruz. That was where all of this had started and that was the only place she would find answers. Hopefully, since it was also the scene of her crime, it was the last place they would suspect her of running to.

Even though she felt like time was slipping away from her, she forced herself to keep it under the speed limit. There was a ton of traffic on the roads, and the chances of being able to make it down there without anyone seeing her or any accidents was nil if she tried to speed.

It took forever, but she finally pulled into the parking lot of a small motel not far from Roaring Camp. She put a glamour on the car, changing its color and license plate to the casual observer as a precaution. A quick spell inside the lobby allowed her to get away with paying cash for the room without having to give her name or show any form of identification.

She hauled her stuff inside the room and then sat down at the desk and buried her head in her hands. She should have taken her computer too, but she'd had no time.

Think. You can get through this. You have *to get through this.*

By now cops would be crawling all over her apartment, going through all of her things. Anything personal to her was with her, but it was still an invasion. They'd be going through Jill's things too, and hopefully they'd find something that helped them locate her.

Her phone buzzed in her pocket and she jumped, startled. Like an idiot, she'd forgotten to take out the battery. They could be tracking her right now. She yanked the phone out and saw that the message was from Lance.

Will do what I can to clear you. IA is involved now. U need 2 lay low. They r on a witch hunt.

Samantha stared at the text. Witch hunt. Lance didn't realize how true that was. She yanked the battery out of the phone. This had all started with a witch hunt months before. She had been the hunter, desperate to kill them and save lives. This time was different, though. The witch being hunted was her.

18

Samantha felt sick and dizzy to the bottom of her soul. She couldn't help but feel that this was all her fault. It had been her desire to not use magic that had made her hold back. Although she knew she hadn't been holding back as much as she wanted to, as much as she should if she were truly trying to give it up again. That struggle seemed so pointless at the moment, though. If she hadn't held back at all, if she'd used the magic as much as she could have, then maybe Jill would be here, safe, and the whole thing would be over.

And I'd either be dead or moving on again.

She wanted, needed to talk to someone. She was sure both her adoptive parents and Anthony would encourage her to use her magic, do whatever it took. But she couldn't call them. Even if she could talk to them, none of them understood the danger, how much it took out of her, or just what it would cost her.

"Magic is simple," she told herself as she stared at her phone.

She put the battery back in. She closed her hand around the phone and could feel energy moving from her hand and spreading to the phone and the air around it. "If someone tries to track this phone they won't be able to; they will only get interference."

She turned on the phone and called the only person who might understand.

The phone rang, and the sick feeling spread throughout her body. Finally, a female voice answered. "Hello?"

Samantha licked her lips. "Vanessa? It's Samantha."

"Samantha! How are you? Are you okay?" Vanessa asked.

"Not really. Listen, I need to talk to Ed. Do you think he'll speak with me?"

"He will, if I have anything to say about it," Vanessa said, her voice hardening. "This is ridiculous—you were partners and friends for three years. I know I told you he'd come around in time, but this is getting ridiculous. I'm sorry he hasn't called you."

"It's okay. I understand. Really, I do. But right now I need some advice badly, and he's the only one I want to talk to about it."

"Hold on."

Samantha waited what seemed like forever. She had just decided that Ed was never going to come on the line, no matter how much his wife threatened him, when she heard his voice.

"Hi, Samantha."

The cold, distant tone broke her heart. She and Ed had once been very close, great partners. They had worked together and trusted each other for three years before the events of Salem. Before he found out that she was a witch.

What did you expect? she asked herself fiercely. He hadn't been ready to deal with the realities of the magic world and the things Samantha had had to do, the people she'd had to kill to bring down the coven in Salem.

"Vanessa tells me you need to talk."

"I do."

"Is it cop stuff or is it . . . witch . . . stuff?"

"Unfortunately, it's both."

He swore. There was a pause and then he said, "Go ahead."

"I went out on a homicide call a few days ago. It turns out the woman was killed by witches. There's lots of crazy stuff happening here. I haven't figured it all out yet, but my roommate was just kidnapped. I'm pretty sure the coven wants her because they think she has something."

"So, it's about her and not you?"

"Yes."

"Okay. What do you want to ask?"

"I—I don't know what to do. I just got home and found her gone. And things have gotten crazy and I'm having to hide out. There's no one I can trust, and I can't bring my partner in any further than he already is."

"Because that would mean telling him everything."

"Yes," she whispered. It was because Ed knew everything that they were no longer partners and not even friends. He hadn't been able to cope with a dark Samantha who did terrible deeds even if it was to save the world and even if he had encouraged her to do them in the first place. She'd thought he would have her back, but when everything was over and the coven was dead, he had told her that he wasn't okay with the person she was. It had hurt like the devil. He wasn't the only one on the force who had felt that way. It was one of the key factors for her move to San Francisco.

"These witches you've gone up against. Have you done everything in your power to stop them?"

"No."

"Why not?"

"You know why."

"I guess I do. Last time, you tried to warn me about what it could do to you if you started using your powers again. I didn't listen."

"You were right then. If I hadn't, so many more people would be dead and evil would be walking the earth."

"It walks the earth every day wearing a thousand different faces. I've had a lot of time to think about it. I'm not sure we couldn't have found another way."

"I haven't been able to figure out how," she admitted.

"Me either. I'm guessing you've exhausted every normal option at this point?"

"Yes."

"Are lives in danger?"

"Jill's, at the very least. But these witches have already killed and some of the spells they're doing are causing the kind of damage you'd have to see to believe."

"And you don't want to use your powers?"

"I don't, but I'm afraid. Sometimes I use them accidentally, and then I do use them, but for smaller things, nothing ... lethal." She could feel herself starting to babble. She didn't know what she was looking for from Ed. Forgiveness? Permission? She didn't know. She just knew that it had been important to talk to him.

He sighed. "You know I got Jackson for a partner these days?"

"Jackass Jackson?"

"Yeah, can you believe that?"

She smiled. "My partner's worse. He shoots first and asks questions later."

"God help us all."

"Ed?"

"Yeah?"

"What should I do?"

"Go and be the badass witch you were born to be."

He ended the call, and she dropped the phone onto the table and wrapped her arms around herself.

"God, why? Why do I have to do this?" she asked.

A dam somewhere inside of her broke loose and she could feel the tears rushing down her face. "Why?" she screamed, and pounded her fist into the table with all her might.

The table snapped in half and tumbled to the ground. She stared down at her hand. Three bones were broken, but she could already feel them beginning to heal. Power surged up and down her arm. She felt like she was going to be sick. She also felt like she could fly.

She got up, walked over to her trunk, and threw open the lid.

She conjured Freaky, and the kitten looked inquisitively inside.

"Come on, Freaky, we've got work to do," she whispered.

An hour later, when Trina shoved open the door to the motel room and stalked inside, Samantha was waiting for her.

"What did you—"Trina stopped talking as she looked at the candles arranged on the nightstand. They snuffed themselves out, and she turned to stare at Samantha, arms folded angrily.

Samantha closed the door behind Trina with a wave of her hand and leaned against the wall. "Nice of you to join me," she said, not bothering to hide the sarcasm in her voice.

"Like you gave me any choice. A summoning spell, really? I was in the middle of dinner."

"Like you gave *me* any choice. I had no other way to contact you."

"Fine. What do you want?"Trina asked.

"A lot of things. But let's start with answers. Did you know that Winona Lightfoot is back from the dead?"

"I—what? Wait—what?"Trina said, looking baffled.

Samantha nodded. "Alive and kicking. And no memories of the other side because she was never killed in the first place. And for some reason, no one but me remembers her being dead."

"*I* remember her being dead,"Trina said.

"Great. That makes two of us who are either the only sane ones in town or the only two who have gone batshit crazy."

"What about her daughter?"

"Either she doesn't remember, or she's too scared to admit that she does. All she'd say was that she had some weird dreams."

Trina sat down on the bed and drew a ragged breath. "It's true."

"What's true?" Samantha asked.

Trina looked at her. "It seemed so crazy, I didn't want to say anything until I knew for sure. I think I've finally figured out what's so strange about these earthquakes."

"What?"

"They're not just shifting earth. They're also shifting time. Not uniformly. But what Giselle's trying to do is having, like, a weird ripple effect."

"Timequakes? That's what you think is going on?"

"Yeah. Essentially. It's affecting timelines, but not evenly. Instead, it's showing up in really random ways."

Samantha thought about what Anthony had told her about his Wiccan friend who sometimes felt like he was shifting from one reality to another. She had dismissed it at the time as being crazy or impractical or both. Now, though, it looked like it might actually explain everything that was going on. In this reality, Winona hadn't found the book, hadn't gone to the museum that night, and hadn't been killed.

She looked at Trina. "It would explain how many times something has shifted on me in the last few days. Car, roommate's hair color and degree."

"Exactly! My favorite necklace suddenly changed colors," Trina said.

"I was talking to someone earlier about multiverse

theory, that for every choice we make there's a universe where we made a different choice. It's like a different timeline," Samantha mused.

"Like one wherein the woman who made my necklace picked the purple stones instead of the green?"

"Exactly," Samantha said. "Or my roommate decided to bleach her hair instead of being a brunette."

"Okay, that makes sense," Trina said, nodding. "And, what, only people like us can sense that things are different, changed somehow?"

"Not just people with powers. I think those with a skewed look on the world as well. It would account for why fervently religious people and many of the homeless have been leaving the city in droves. I'm sure they don't know what's wrong, but I think they can sense that something is," Samantha said.

"Like animals taking off before an earthquake?"

Samantha looked at Trina. Clearly the other woman had heard that theory as well. "But these aren't the intended effects? These are more like, what, bleed through? Aftershocks?"

"That's as near as I can figure."

"Well, if these things that keep changing are the aftershocks, what is the main quake supposed to be doing?" Samantha asked.

"I don't know yet. I feel like I'm close, though. There's something they want and they can't get at it."

"I know what they want," Samantha realized. "And now that I know these are timequakes, I know how they plan on getting it."

"What?" Trina asked.

"You ever heard of the Hell Hole Cave?"

"Yeah. One of the coven members went down into it a couple months back, told us all about it."

"Have you ever heard what's down there?"

"I'm guessing you mean besides a bunch of clay faces and a guestbook?"

Samantha nodded.

"No, not a clue."

"Supposedly, centuries ago a demon was captured and buried down there. The Hell Hole Cave was an access point so that once a year someone could go down and check that it was still there. Over time the earth shifted, cave-ins happened, and it became impossible to go down deep enough."

"Do you think that's what Giselle could possibly be referencing whenever she says 'the last grave'? Maybe it's the creature's grave?"

"That makes more sense than anything I've been able to come up with," Samantha admitted. "If so, she wants to crack that grave open."

"Are you telling me they're trying to shift time in that cave so it resembles the landscape from centuries ago?"

"That's what I think."

"So, they can, what, go down and have a peek at this thing?"

Samantha couldn't help it; she started laughing.

"What's so funny?" Trina asked, eyes narrowed.

"How naive you are. You really think they just want to have a peek at it?"

"You don't think they'd actually try to release it, do you?" Trina asked as the color drained from her face.

"I most certainly think they would."

"Then we have to stop them."

Samantha nodded. "Time to take down a coven."

Trina grew even paler. "They're meeting tonight. It's the full moon."

"I know. And I can't think of a better time to try to pull off what they want to do."

Trina put her hand over her mouth, and Samantha could see that she was shaking. She waited a moment and then she asked, "Is this your first rodeo?"

Trina shook her head. "My third. But the others, what they were doing was illegal, immoral, but nothing like this. And Randy was with me. He was a senior agent in the group. I'm one of the newcomers. This was my first solo assignment. It was supposed to be an easy one, mostly just keeping tabs. Not all dark covens become a true problem quickly. It can take years for the power to corrupt, new ideas to emerge. There's been an active coven here for decades, dabbling in dark magic, doing things that might be immoral but weren't illegal and certainly weren't seen as a threat by the government. I was just supposed to observe for a couple months, make sure nothing had changed."

"Well, something changed in a big way."

"I know. And now there's not even time to get someone else out here to help."

Samantha stepped forward and put her hand on Trina's shoulder. "You've got me," she said softly.

Trina grabbed her hand. Samantha could feel the other woman's fear and self-doubt. But beneath all that, she felt the surge of power, real power, raw and untamed.

In a flash she saw snatches of Trina's life. She had been raised without others of their kind. She hadn't found anyone like her until she went to college. Right out of college she'd been recruited by Randy for this task force. She was still learning, growing, and she had no idea how far she could go, how much power she could harness. She might be a great agent, good at infiltration and under- cover work, but she had no idea just how much power she had and what she could do with it if she unleashed it.

"You're strong. Powerful," Samantha said. "I can feel it in you. You've never really had to push yourself, though. That's going to change tonight, but you don't need to be scared. You have all the talent, all the ability you will ever need for this work. You are the right person in the right place at the right time."

I just hope it doesn't get you killed, she added silently.

Trina nodded. "Thanks. I needed to hear that. It's true. I've never pushed myself. I've never really had to be- fore."

"Know your enemy and know yourself and in a thou- sand battles you will always be victorious," Samantha said.

"Sun Tzu. Butchered a bit, but still fitting."

Samantha forced a smile before she turned away to hide the worry in her own eyes. There was every possibil- ity of Trina truly discovering herself tonight, but Saman- tha worried that she was going to lose herself.

"Ouch!"

Samantha turned. Freaky had emerged from under the bed and taken a swipe at Trina's ankle, startling her and drawing some blood.

"Freaky, play nice," Samantha said.

The kitten jumped onto the bed, where he proceeded to try to stare down Trina.

"Your cat is . . . disturbing," Trina said at last.

Samantha smiled. "Freaky has been with me on and off for years."

"An energy pet. That's brilliant. When this is over, maybe you can show me how to make a ferret."

"I will. I promise. Now, it's time to prepare for tonight. You might want to go and get your gear."

"It's in the car. I never travel without it."

"All right. Let's get started."

Trina walked outside and Samantha's phone trilled. She had left the magic scrambler on it so she could receive any calls or texts she needed to. "Hello?" she asked cautiously, not recognizing the number.

"Detective Ryan? This is Winona Lightfoot."

"Winona. How can I help you?"

"After you left, I had to go into the city for a meeting. I'm at the Museum of Natural History and I had the creepiest feeling."

Like you were walking over your grave? Samantha thought but didn't ask.

"I was thinking about what you said about the mountains and the cave. On a hunch, I went to check on this one geology exhibit that's always fascinated me. There's a stone tablet with very faint writing on it that I've never been able to make out. There's never been a translation or anything on the plaques about it. None of the curators I've talked to over the years have been able to really tell me anything about it."

"And?" Samantha asked.

"It was gone. There was a break-in at the museum a few nights ago and until now they didn't think anything had been taken. It felt like it might be important, so I called."

"Thank you. You were right to do so," Samantha said as Trina walked back into the room carrying a black duffel bag. "You say you couldn't decipher the writing?"

"No. I'm supposed to meet with a grad student at the university to help her with some research for her dissertation. It's my understanding that she knows a thing or two about some of the older languages, and I had been thinking of asking her if she could read it."

"Jill," Samantha whispered.

"Yes. Do you know her?"

"Yeah. Listen, let me know if you think of anything else."

"I will."

Samantha hung up.

"What was all that about?" Trina asked.

"Apparently the reason Giselle was at the museum was to steal a tablet with some ancient writing on it. I guess it's Winona's luck that somehow she wasn't there to try to stop her this time. I'm worried, though. Apparently, my roommate reads ancient languages. I'm wondering if Giselle figured that out and kidnapped her, hoping to get a translation of the tablet."

"Stop Giselle and hopefully we'll find Jill," Trina said.

God, let that be true, Samantha prayed as she touched her cross.

*   *   *

A couple of hours later, Samantha was following Trina through the forest, headed for Cathedral Grove. They both were dressed in black cloaks and were carrying athames. Fortunately, they were able to park their car within a half hour's walk of the grove. They were set to arrive early. Coven rituals happened at midnight.

She could still sense the fear and doubt that were assailing Trina. Samantha toyed with trying to calm her down, but knew that could backfire on them. Instead, she just hoped that if anyone noticed, they were also feeling the same way and took it as normal.

Around them the wildlife of the forest hushed as they passed by. The air was incredibly still. Inside her cloak, Samantha couldn't feel the biting cold. It never got nearly as cold there as it did in Boston. Still, the temperature had crawled down to around thirty degrees, which was lower than it usually dropped. It was cold enough that her breath crystallized in the air, and she was grateful that she was wearing shoes and not going barefoot.

As they neared the circle, the air around them began to change even more. There was a sense of anticipation, of nature's collective breath being held. It was hard not to hold hers as well. *Spooky* was the only word that came to mind.

Trina had told her that members of the coven didn't have to ask permission to be absent from circle meetings. She had arranged for someone from her department to call one of the members of the coven with some fake news about a relative having been in a car crash and being in a coma in the southern part of the state. It had been enough to get the woman out of the way so that when Samantha joined the circle, no one would notice an extra person.

They were the first to arrive at the circle, just as they had planned to be. With regret, Samantha took off her shoes and socks. The ground was cold and hard, and she fought the urge to use magic so that she felt neither.

Then Samantha faced the circle. Remembering the lesson learned from her last visit there, she focused on her belief that she belonged inside the circle. When she finally stepped forward, it did not reject her. She passed through the energy barrier and stood on the inside.

She could feel the trees around her and the earth beneath her feet thrumming with energy. She thought about the ghosts that haunted this place, wishing she'd stopped to think about them earlier. She glanced around, hoping that the pervert ghost didn't show up and cause trouble.

"Can you see them—the ghosts?" Trina asked as she stepped into the circle and stood next to her.

"I have, but I don't see them now. I'm really grateful for that."

"There's such a sad one, a young man. I feel sorry for him."

"Don't. He's not worth it. And for heaven's sake, don't do anything to attract his attention."

Trina looked at her in surprise.

She regretted not having found out how to kill that particular ghost.

"Now what?" Trina whispered.

"Now we soak up all the energy that we can, because we're going to need it."

They began moving around the circle in opposite directions, going from tree to tree. At each tree, Samantha stopped and pulled energy out of it and into herself. It was uncomfortable, almost painful. The energy was so strange, tainted with darkness, stained with blood. Beggars couldn't be choosers, though, and the more energy the trees gave to her, the less they could possibly give to anyone else.

She couldn't worry about the trees outside of the circle. With any luck, no one would make it out of the circle to try to get it.

When they had finished, they both took some energy from the earth, but not nearly as much. Coven members who entered the circle would not necessarily touch the trees to feel the difference in them, but they would be touching the ground.

"Okay," Samantha said at last.

"Do you think it's enough?"

"It will have to be. Remember, once the fight starts, suck as much energy from the earth as you can. It will help us and prevent them from using it against us."

"And now we wait," Trina said. "Unfortunately, this is one thing I've gotten very good at doing."

Samantha couldn't help but smile at that. A hundred questions crowded her mind about Trina and the program that she was working for. Randy had said there were other front lines. Just how long had this section of the FBI been in existence? And what was their ultimate goal?

Now was not the time for questions, though. She and Trina stood, waiting patiently as the moon climbed higher and higher in the night sky. She could feel its pull on her just as the oceans did. Big magic was often reserved for the full moon, when there was more energy in the air and chaos was running rampant. It had the added bonus of making it easy to see what you were doing without the requirement of artificial light in the circle.

"Someone's coming," Trina whispered at last.

Samantha nodded. She could feel it too. A minute later, another cloaked figure stepped barefoot into the circle. Samantha wished she knew who it was. If it was Giselle, she could strike at her now and save a lot of time and effort. *Take her down when she's alone.*

But whoever it was didn't carry themself as a leader. Instead they stood silent, head bowed, not in prayer but in respect, in submission.

And the part of Samantha that she didn't want anything to do with recognized weakness in the other and wanted to exploit it.

Steady, she cautioned herself. It would do her no good to take down this witch and expose herself prematurely. Fortunately, she could see others approaching the circle. The time for waiting was almost over.

One by one cloaked figures stepped inside. They began to stand in a loose ring shape. Samantha and Trina were positioned at the farthest end from the entry point. It wasn't ideal. She would have preferred to be blocking the exit, but then she risked others getting too close to her as they entered and discovering who she was. Giselle, particularly, would likely be able to discern her presence at such close range.

It appeared that all had arrived, but clearly they were still waiting for someone.

Finally, Giselle entered the circle. Samantha could tell that it was her by the way she walked. The high priestess didn't join the others by standing in a circle but instead moved into the exact center of the grove, allowing them to ring her just as the trees ringed them.

"Welcome tonight to this grand moment that will witness our triumph," she spoke. She tossed back her hood and Samantha tensed, waiting to see if the rest did likewise. They didn't.

"All our preparations have been for this night," Giselle continued. "At last you will all see the fruits of your labors and you will be rewarded."

Having witnessed firsthand what trying to raise a demon could do, Samantha would say that what was coming to all those assembled was anything but a reward.

Giselle raised her hands, and the dirt in front of her erupted upward, forming the mound that Samantha had seen the echoes of. She now realized it was representative of the mountain the cave was in, inside of which the demon was trapped.

A line in the dirt formed, cutting across much of the circle, including the mound itself. *A fault line,* Samantha realized.

The witch raised her athame high in the air and then plunged it down into the mountain. "Tonight we release enough energy to return the Hell Hole Cave to its previous form from three hundred years ago, and then one of us will be able to reach the creature and speak its freedom with these words." She pulled a stone tablet from under her cloak.

Speak its freedom.

Samantha blinked as she suddenly understood. The point of expanding the cave and not just cracking the mountain open was that the binding spell on the creature had to be undone by words and they had to be physically heard by the creature. That was diabolically clever of whoever had locked him up in the first place. It also explained why there'd been a yearly pilgrimage to see if he was still locked up.

"And we have someone who can read it for us," Giselle continued.

She gestured, and one of the cloaked figures seemed to float closer, until she stood next to the high priestess.

"We have taken that which belonged to our enemy and made it to serve our purpose," Giselle chortled. She threw back the hood, and Samantha's worst fears were realized.

Standing there, eyes dilated and completely dazed, was Jill.

19

It took all of Samantha's self-control not to leap forward, grab Jill, and try to run with her. That, she knew, would only get both of them killed. She gritted her teeth. She had to wait, pick her moment. Her body was already gearing up for it. Without even intending to, she was pulling energy again from the earth beneath her, preparing to make her move.

Next to her, she could feel Trina's anxiety. The FBI agent was having even more trouble biding her time than she was. At this point, she might very well jump the gun. Samantha regretted now that they hadn't worked out a prearranged signal, but she had honestly expected that Trina would follow her lead.

Giselle raised both hands toward heaven, and even though the night was perfectly clear, lightning flashed down, touching her hands and channeling through her and into the mound at her feet.

She felt the mixed emotions of those around her. Excitement, fear, jealousy, and anticipation mingled with her own anger in the air.

Even though it was not the first time Samantha had seen Giselle channel lightning, she still marveled at it. The amount of neurological damage she had to be doing to herself alone should have been a warning sign. What made the other witch so fearless? She thought of what her eight-year-old self had said.

"It's amazing how much more you can accomplish if you don't care if you live or die."

Was that what made Giselle so formidable? In the end, did she not care at all for her own life? Samantha had a hard time believing that.

"We seek to restore the cave to its old form," Giselle intoned.

Around the circle, the cloaked figures stretched out their arms and clasped hands. The mingling of their energies would make them stronger.

Samantha grimaced but took the hand of the person on her right. She stretched her hand toward Trina, but she did not allow their hands to actually touch. In the darkness, it would be hard to tell that from just looking.

More lines appeared in the dirt, radiating from the mound like the spokes of a wheel to each person standing in the circle. They began to shimmer and pulse with energy. Giselle began chanting.

Samantha gave up any sense of subtlety and was pulling energy from the earth below her and the witch beside her.

"What on earth?" she heard the witch beside her mutter in a deep, male voice.

Giselle stopped in midsentence. "Who here works at cross-purposes to us?" she demanded.

Samantha remained still, motionless. She had learned from experience that it was better to wait and see who was accused than to give yourself away. There was a strong chance Giselle would pick someone else.

"I do," Trina said, stepping forward and lowering her hood. "What we're doing is wrong. Thousands of people could get hurt, killed. You wouldn't want that, would you?" she asked as she moved her head, clearly trying to reach the hearts and minds of the cloaked figures around them.

Samantha could sense it wasn't going to work. Unlike Jill, the others were here of their own free will. And unlike Salem, they knew what it was they were there to do.

Samantha wrapped the fingers of her free hand around her athame, waiting, ready.

Giselle laughed. "I'm afraid you're going to find yourself very much alone."

Trina lifted her chin even higher. "I'm not alone. I have my coven brothers and sisters, and they will support me because they know in their hearts that what we're doing is wrong and will have very deadly consequences."

The witch who had been standing on Trina's left lunged forward, athame in hand, and prepared to plunge it into Trina's back.

Samantha threw her own athame and it buried itself in the attacker's chest. That was the signal everyone seemed to be waiting for. In a moment, fireballs were streaking through the night.

Samantha hadn't been sure how many of the witches would actually fight. She was dismayed when she realized the answer was *all of them*.

Two witches leaped on her, bringing her to the ground. One began to stab at her with an athame while the other put his hand on her stomach and began pulling something out of her. For a moment Samantha thought he was trying to grab energy from her, but it felt different, strange.

Suddenly her mouth became very dry and her skin felt sunburned all over. She fought against them both, sending energy blasts into them. It did no good. Both witches just seemed to absorb what she sent at them.

Samantha's lips felt incredibly chapped, and a moment later she smelled blood as they split.

He's pulling all the water out of me, dehydrating me, she realized. She redoubled her efforts, determined not to end up as a petrified corpse in the middle of the Redwoods.

She threw her hands up toward the sky like she had seen Giselle do. Lightning came down, hit her. The electricity rushing through her body hurt worse than anything she'd ever known. But the resultant shock threw the two witches clear of her.

She could feel her body begin its rapid healing, desperately trying to fix the damage as fast as it could. She needed water and badly, but that would have to wait. She stumbled over to the one who had been doing that to her, and while he was still on the ground recovering from the electrocution, she broke his neck.

The other witch, she stabbed through the heart with her athame. The dagger was supposed to be a ritual tool to help focus energy. In a pinch, though, it killed someone pretty quick.

The energy she had soaked up before the coven had arrived was gone, the majority of it focused on healing her body. She needed more fast.

And then something the ghost had said came back to her. *In the end, we're all just energy.* She looked around with new eyes, and instead of seeing ghosts, shadows of people that had once lived, she saw energy. And with crystal clarity she knew what she had to do. "Show me the ghosts," she whispered.

And then the spirits were swirling around her, reenacting their death throes. Trapped energy.

"What is going on?" the ghost who had kissed her demanded as he strode up to her.

She thrust her hand into the middle of his chest and pulled the energy into herself.

"What are you doing?" he asked, voice rising in panic.

"Saving the world," she said. "And stopping you from hurting anyone else is an added bonus."

He thrashed and screamed, but rapidly faded until she could barely see him and could no longer hear him. She closed her eyes, gave one last pull, and all the energy was hers. She could feel the moment he left and knew that it was forever.

She opened her eyes and directed a lightning bolt at a witch battling Trina across the clearing. It struck the man in the chest, and he fell to the ground dead.

Samantha spun and plunged her hand into another ghost, draining it as well. She used it to down another witch. Trina saw and immediately began to copy her. The ones they were battling had yet to figure out what they were doing. Samantha waded into a small cluster of them. She slashed the throat of one woman with her athame and stopped the heart of another with a well-placed jolt.

She saw Giselle leave the circle, Jill on her heels.

"No!" Samantha screamed, heading for them.

Two more witches ran toward her, and she yanked out their intestines. *Just like my younger self did to the witch at the Boardwalk,* she realized as she ran past them.

She paused in front of the ghost of the little girl she had seen before. She was a recording only, not sentient like the young man had been. But as the last of the energy drained from her into Samantha, something stirred in her eyes and she looked up at Samantha.

"Thank you," the ghost child whispered.

Samantha nodded and then drained the energy of the girl's ghost attacker.

Out of the corner of her eye, she saw Trina go down, and she ran to her. The FBI agent had her stomach slashed open, and her eyes were starting to roll back in her head.

Samantha killed the witch who had done it before he could attack Trina again.

"You're going to be okay!" Samantha told Trina.

Trina handed Samantha car keys. "Go stop them. Don't worry. Enough energy here to help heal me."

Samantha shook her head fiercely. "We drained all the ghosts."

"The old ones, not the new ones."

Samantha turned and looked. Everywhere in the circle, ghosts were standing up from their bodies wearing various expressions ranging from vacant stares to bewildered frowns.

"Go get 'em," she whispered to Trina, and then Samantha crammed her shoes on her feet and took off at a run.

She had paid attention to the way they had come to get to the grove. Trina had told her everyone parked in the same place. It was close and isolated. Giselle would be heading for the Hell Hole Cave, and she would need her car to get her and Jill there quickly.

I'm coming, Jill. Hold on.

Samantha ran with everything she had in her, hoping she could catch the others before they made it to the cars. Tree branches reached out for her, trying to entangle her. She pushed them back with small, measured bursts of energy. When roots reared up to try to trip her, she leaped over them.

An enormous felled tree suddenly appeared across her path. Samantha knew it hadn't been there earlier. Going around would take too much time. Climbing over it would present its own challenges.

It's not real, just an illusion. She was willing to bet everything on that. So, she ran straight into it and then through it. As she emerged on the other side, she fought the urge to shout with triumph. Her instincts had been right. It had been nothing more than a mirage.

A fireball exploded into a tree two feet away from her, and she forced herself to keep running. She couldn't see Giselle and she was willing to bet Giselle couldn't see her either.

The closer they got to the cars, the more fireballs

whizzed around her. She knew she was gaining. She could feel it.

Then a wall of energy seemed to hit her hard, propelling her backward. She flew through the air and landed on her back with a grunt. She jumped to her feet, her own hands forming fireballs that she then had to release out to her sides. She couldn't risk hurting Jill.

She made it to the parking area just in time to see a silver car speeding away. Samantha slid into Trina's car and floored it. Tires squealed as they sought to gain a purchase on the ground beneath.

Giselle knew the roads better than she did. Samantha could see her taillights ahead of her, but she could never quite catch up to her. Every time she pushed the accelerator too hard, they'd hit another sharp turn and her car would swerve out of control.

For a moment she panicked, thinking she'd lost the other car. She rounded two more turns and then saw it parked off to the side of the road. Samantha parked her car and leaped out. Giselle and Jill were already gone.

Samantha ran up the side of the mountain and reached the Hell Hole Cave. She stared at the opening. There was no grate partially covering it now, but that made it no less frightening. She touched the rock inside and could feel the subtle vibrations. Giselle and Jill had gone inside. Samantha couldn't risk trying to incapacitate Giselle from where she was because it might hurt or even kill Jill, depending on where they were in the climb and how completely Giselle had control over her mind.

Samantha was going to have to go in after them. She

formed a ball of light with her hands and dropped it into the cave so that she'd be able to see what she was doing.

Samantha got down onto her stomach and shimmied backward into the cave opening. The way was narrow, and when she'd gone just a couple of feet, she couldn't see outside anymore. She felt completely claustrophobic and wanted nothing more than to crawl back out.

You can do this. You have to, she told herself. She forced herself to keep backing up, scooting over rocks. Then she reached a place where she could stand up. She turned to look around. The reddish brown rock had a few salamanders crawling over it. She kept going but tripped painfully over some tree roots in mud. She came to a rope that led down to what had to be an eighty-foot drop. She held her breath as she climbed down.

The walls closed in again, and she had to twist sideways to get between them. When she emerged into another larger cavern, her heart was racing. She wondered how far the cave extended. She guessed that depended a lot on when the cave was created. The older it was, the farther it should go, free of rock slides.

At last she made it to the cavern of clay faces, and she shuddered. There were only a handful there, leading her to believe this couldn't be the modern form of the cave. Also, there was no guestbook to sign. On the far end, another incredibly narrow passageway led deeper into the earth.

After she squeezed through a particularly tight place, the tunnel seemed to open up again. It was still steep, but at least it was slightly wider.

If something happens to this cave, I'll never make it out alive, she realized.

Her shins and ankles were completely bruised, but her body was too busy still working on the other injuries to be of any help. She started limping. And then, at last, she heard something ahead of her in the darkness.

She paused and listened.

Footsteps. She had to be getting closer to Giselle and Jill. She dimmed the light as much as she could and continued to move forward as carefully and quietly as possible.

The rocks on either side brushed against her shoulders, and she had to start walking stooped over because the ceiling was getting lower. Another long slope presented itself, and she started down it, twisted her ankle, and fell hard.

She slid down the rock slope on her chest, trying not to scream in pain. When she landed at the bottom, she pushed herself up off the ground with arms that were shaking uncontrollably.

Why had Giselle come here? They hadn't completed the ritual. There was no guarantee this cave as it was would get her within earshot of the demon.

"Do it!"

She jerked, smacking her head against the rock, startled at the sudden command. It was Giselle's voice and it was close by. She crept forward slowly, praying she wouldn't be discovered. She reached up to touch her cross necklace only to realize she had lost it somewhere, probably when she had been sliding on her chest.

Although it wasn't as precious to her as the one that

witches in Salem had stolen months earlier, it had still made her feel better and she mourned its loss.

Maybe there was nothing really down here. She hoped that was the case as she tried to creep up on Giselle. A dim light appeared ahead. That one would belong to Giselle and Jill. Samantha extinguished her own and felt her way slowly along the ground.

Finally, she could see the two figures, haloed by the light. Jill was holding the tablet and staring at it intently. The smell of sulfur assaulted Samantha's nostrils, and she began to pinch her nose shut, struggling not to sneeze.

And she could feel something down there in the bowels of the mountain, something that wasn't human.

The hair rose on the back of her neck. The legend was right. There was something trapped down here. She couldn't let Giselle unleash it on the world.

Jill began to speak haltingly. Samantha didn't recognize the language. The words were supposed to be spoken within hearing of the creature that was trapped. Could it hear them? To the best of her knowledge, there hadn't yet been another earthquake after the ceremony in the grove. Maybe it wasn't too late.

"That's right; keep going!" Giselle shrieked. "As loud as you can!"

The witch was so focused on listening to Jill reading that she didn't see Samantha coming until she was on top of her. Samantha snatched the tablet from Jill's hands and did the only thing she could think of. She smashed the tablet against the rocks, and it shattered into a hundred pieces.

Giselle turned on her with an angry shout and pushed her hands against the walls, making them vibrate.

She'll bring the whole cave down on top of us, Samantha realized in horror. A moment later, though, she realized that wasn't their biggest problem.

An earthquake was coming. Here in the bowels of the earth, she could feel it so clearly and plainly. And this wasn't going to be a small quake. This was going to be the one this coven had been trying to cause for days. This time they would return the cave to the oldest form they needed to, so they could see and hear the creature and it could see and hear them.

Samantha prayed there was no other way of releasing it than through the words on the tablet she had smashed.

If Giselle was smart, she made a copy of them.

Giselle laughed again.

The energy was swirling, building, it was ready to rip free.

It was coming. The mother of all earthquakes was coming. And it was going to rip apart earth and flesh and even time itself.

"Can't you feel it?" Giselle screamed above the rising roar. Her grin was wide, but her eyes held horror and something more, pleading.

Samantha blinked. She remembered the moment the grove had shown her, the one the ghost had said was important and had changed things. Trina had told her the coven had been fairly low-key until very recently.

And the pleading look Giselle was giving her she'd seen before, in the eyes of someone who was possessed. And suddenly everything she'd done made sense. She'd had several chances to kill Samantha and had been about to do it when she'd vanish or run off.

And as the energy of the earthquake, the result of the greatest timequake ever conjured, continued to build and swirl around them, Samantha knew that Giselle wasn't behind it all. She was just a puppet. And somewhere, the invisible puppet master was pulling her strings. That was how she could do the magic she was doing when it was so destructive to her.

The puppet master doesn't care if he destroys his puppet.

"We have to get out of here!" Samantha screamed.

"It's too late for that now," Giselle said.

"I don't want to die here. Not now, not like this. They'll never find our bodies." As panic flooded Samantha, she realized that there was truly only one thing she could do. But in order to do it, she was going to have to be calm and centered. And she was going to have to remember the two rules: *Magic was easy and magic cost.*

But Giselle, or whoever was controlling her, wasn't going to let it be that easy.

Giselle lunged at her with a blade, and in the tight quarters, Samantha was forced to take the blow. She fell backward and Giselle fell on top of her, gouging at her eyes with her fingernails, biting and slashing at her.

And then Samantha managed to get ahold of her arm and pin it between them. They thrashed around on the ground, smashing into the stone walls and breaking each other's bones. And then Samantha got hold of the knife and stabbed the witch through the stomach with it.

Just like she made Robin do to me.

Samantha pushed the witch off her and Giselle landed, half propped up by an outcropping of rock as around them the earth rumbled and the thing beyond them in the dark continued to growl.

She looked at Giselle. The woman was dying, her blood rushing out all over. But her eyes were clear.

"Someone possessed you, made you do all this, didn't they?" Samantha asked.

"Yes. I didn't want to," Giselle said. "Thank you for putting an end to it."

The energy around them was still swirling, building, but Samantha didn't have the heart to tell that to her.

"The last grave. What does it mean?" Giselle asked.

"You tell me! You're the one who's written it all over the Bay Area."

"I don't know what it means. It's the only thing that I get off her mind, the only impression of the one who did this to me. It's in her thoughts constantly. The last grave—it's what she thinks about over and over."

"I don't understand," Samantha said.

The woman coughed hard and blood bubbled up on her lips. She was dying, and she didn't have much time left. Samantha was getting desperate.

"The last grave. Who's in it?" the woman asked.

"You tell me!" Samantha demanded.

"I wish I—"

And then she was gone.

Samantha stared down at the lifeless body in her arms. She grabbed the woman's head, struggling to sense anything she was thinking, feeling.

Death and pain swirled through Samantha's mind, causing her to cry out in anguish and terror. But there, she could hear the words.

The last grave.
The last grave.
The last grave.

It was like a perpetual echo going around and around in someone's mind, but Samantha didn't know whose.

What is the last grave?

Everything was fading to black, but a whispered word came to her.

Salem.

And that's when Samantha knew. If she survived this, she had to go back again.

She let go of Giselle and grabbed hold of Jill. Her roommate was still dazed, partially mesmerized. "Go back the way you came. Go as fast as you can," she commanded.

Jill swayed for a moment on her feet and then turned and scrambled up the incline.

Samantha heard low, deep growling. And something in her had to know. As if compelled, she took one step deeper into the cave and then another. And a dozen feet in, she found a tiny slit beginning to open in the wall.

She held her breath and put her eye up to it.

She could see a vague shadow beyond. No, not a shadow. That part of the cave was pitch black, but the outline was something that somehow was even darker than the darkness that surrounded it. The light from the energy balls didn't touch the thing sitting there in the dark.

And she had a terrible feeling that she had met it before. No! Not it, but something like it. Flashes of memory seemed to come back to her, and she couldn't help but feel that this creature was somehow linked to the one that her coven had raised when she was a girl.

She heard a deep rumbling noise that sounded more like an avalanche, and in horror she realized that what she initially thought was laughter was actually words. The beast within said, "I know you."

Samantha turned and ran. She clawed her way up the rock incline, moving as fast as her battered body would allow her. Around her the cave walls began to shake, rock dust drifting down to clog her nostrils and choke her. She pushed forward. She had to get out before the cave shook itself apart.

She thought about the creature trapped back there in the darkness. She had to make sure it stayed that way for all eternity. The words that could be used to free it were on a smashed tablet no one would ever likely find or be able to put back together to translate. But that wasn't good enough.

When she made it to the cave of clay faces, she turned and put her hands on the rock wall of the passage she had just been down.

"Restore," she whispered.

And she heard the crashing of rocks as they came down to block the passage. It was taking the last of her energy to do, but she had to fix that which had been undone by Giselle's rituals.

Finished, she turned and then crashed to her knees in the center of the cavern. The timequake was coming and she could feel its size, sense its power. Here in the mountain, it would rip through time and rock, but out there, it would cause an earthquake so powerful the destruction couldn't even be estimated. She thought of Robin's dream and her own vision of it killing George in the center of downtown San Francisco. If the earthquake was allowed to happen, it would destroy tens of thousands of lives just like so many had been predicting. She couldn't let that be. She had to find a way to divert the energy somewhere else, vent it somehow.

"God, please help me. Where can I put the energy?"

And in the silence that followed, she knew there was only one place. She put her hands to the ground on either side of it and reached out. She could feel the fault line. She could feel the energy building, about to explode, and through rock and earth she called it to her. And as the tide came rushing her way, she screamed in pain and terror.

20

Samantha was knocked onto her back. Around her, she could actually see the energy swirling through the air, funneling down into her. It had to be what being caught in a tornado felt like. She screamed her throat raw but couldn't hear herself. All she heard was the roar of the earth venting its wrath on her.

Sparks were flying from her fingertips, and she could see that her entire body was glowing, pulsing with light and heat. She felt like she was being turned inside out. Finally, she lost consciousness and opened her eyes in the hallway of doors. All the little girls she had interacted with were huddled together, holding on to one another.

"You did it now," Five whispered before burying her face in one of the other's shoulders.

"Make it stop!" Samantha screamed, finding her voice here.

None of them answered her. None of them would even look at her anymore. Black and red light shimmered on the door marked TWELVE, which was still shut.

"Somebody help me!" she screamed again.

"There's no help here," someone whispered, but she didn't know who.

How long she was there, she didn't know. But finally she woke up and she was in the cave. The clay faces in the room had all melted. There was a guestbook suddenly, but its pages were blackened and charred. She hoped that meant that time had been set right.

But if it has, what does that mean for Robin and Winona? she wondered.

She couldn't worry about them now. She just had to get herself out of this hole and figure out what she had to do next. She stood to her feet slowly. Every atom of her being hurt. She was thrumming with energy. She felt like she was going to explode.

Despite that, hiking out and climbing the rope ladder nearly killed her. When she reached the entrance to the cave, she noted that the top half was again covered and it was light outside.

She pulled herself out with a gasp and then lay for a moment on the ground outside, struggling to breathe. Slowly, she got to her hands and knees and considered crawling to the car. She forced herself to her feet, though, and began to stagger down the incline, grabbing on to trees for support.

When the cars came into sight, she gave a shout of relief. Jill was sitting on the ground, a blanket wrapped around her. Lance was talking with Trina.

"Hello?" she called, waving.

Lance turned and pulled his gun on her.

"Whoa, easy!" she said, lifting her hands into the air.

She had forgotten that she was a wanted woman due to the killing of the witch on the Boardwalk.

"That's not her," Jill said.

Lance reholstered his gun. "Sorry, ma'am."

She walked over to him. "What's with the ma'am crap?" she asked.

He looked taken aback. "Lady, are you feeling okay?"

"No. I've had one hell of a night. One hell of a week, actually. Tell me you have some good news for me."

He just stood there, staring at her. Finally, he said, "Lady, I don't know you."

"Don't be ridiculous," Samantha said, rolling her eyes. "Look, I'm sure we can work this all out together with a little help from our friendly neighborhood Fed," she said, pointing to Trina.

Trina was staring at her suspiciously. "How do you know who I am?"

"What's going on here?" Samantha asked. "I know I'm pretty out of it, but—" She stopped short as she took a good look at Jill's face. Her roommate's eyes were clear and her hair was blond again, like it used to be. And there was absolutely no recognition on her face.

"Jill, it's me, Samantha Ryan. Your roommate."

Jill looked up at Lance. "I don't have a roommate." Then she turned back to Samantha. "Wait, Samantha?" she asked, recognition starting to dawn in her eyes.

"Yes!"

"Samantha from Boston? What on earth are you do-ing here?" Jill asked, sounding baffled. She glanced at the others. "Samantha and I went to the same college, shared some classes. But I haven't seen her in years."

Samantha stared at her in horror. How could Jill not remember the last three months?

Samantha turned to look at Trina, panic rising in her. "Trina, the coven, they're still all dead, right?"

"Yes, as of a few hours ago, but how do you know any of this?"

"I'm Samantha Ryan," she said, annunciating clearly, like it would help. "I'm a homicide detective for the San Francisco Police Department. I'm your partner," she said pointedly to Lance.

"Wait a minute. I know you," Trina said, her face turning pale.

"Yes! Thank you," Samantha said.

"You're Samantha Castor. You got my partner, Randy, killed. What are you doing here?"

Castor, the last name she'd had when she was a child before she changed it. The name she'd readopted when infiltrating the Salem coven. She had kept her true first name hidden, though, since words had power. The only living people who knew that name were her adoptive parents and Captain Roberts, who had been the cop she had told her story to back in Salem when she escaped the slaughter of her coven when she was twelve.

And as Lance, Jill, and Trina all stood gaping at her, she fell to her knees and began to scream.

Twenty-four hours later, Samantha was sitting in Trina's car at the San Francisco International Airport, pulling up to the departure gates. The timequake that she had absorbed had erased her entire history in San Francisco. No one knew her; no one remembered her. Trina had taken responsibility for killing Giselle and the rest of the coven. She was headed for a promotion at work. At least she had finally come around and believed Samantha's story about what had actually happened the last week. Miraculously, Winona Lightfoot was still alive. In this reality, she'd never found the book, never gone to the museum to try to keep the tablet from being stolen by Giselle. Neither she nor Robin remembered Samantha, though.

"Where will you go?" Trina asked.

"I don't know. Home first; there's a few things I have to check on. I called my captain there and at least they remember me. They have a vague memory of me being on the West Coast, but not being transferred here. He thinks I'm on some sort of leave following everything that happened in Salem."

"I'm sorry, about everything that's happened to you."

"Thanks. Look, you don't remember it, but I made you a promise."

Samantha took Trina's hands and held them, letting the energy build up between them. "Ferret," she whispered, and the energy took shape and a moment later solidified.

Trina squealed with delight.

"And when you need to hide him, just disperse the energy," Samantha said, demonstrating. "Now you try."

Trina put her hands together and crafted the tiny ferret again. The creature ran up and perched on her shoulder. She turned to look at Samantha, tears shimmering in her eyes. "Thank you for this," she said.

Samantha nodded. "Now you'll never be alone."

She got out of the car before she could start to cry.

She had no luggage, not even a carry-on. She had no idea what had happened to all of her things—her cloak, her athame, any of it.

When she finally boarded the plane, she conjured Freaky, putting a glamour on him so only she could see him. She needed him more than ever.

Once she landed in Boston, she'd get a rental car and drive straight to Salem. She had questions that needed answers and they wouldn't wait. As the plane lifted off the runway, she fell into a mercifully dreamless sleep.

Salem.

As Samantha drove her rental car across the town limits, she suppressed the urge to hang a U in the middle of the street and head right back out. She had to keep going. There were questions she needed answered, and there was nowhere else to go for those answers.

She parked at the Hawthorne, praying she wouldn't need to check back in and stay for a few days. As soon as she got out of her car, she headed toward the pedestrian mall. She had to see Anthony. She needed to get that over with first. She owed that much to both of them.

It was still midafternoon, so he should be at his museum. Anthony had owned a museum of the occult when she met him while undercover in Salem. When he had insisted on trying to help her bring down the coven that was sacrificing young women, she had put him in harm's way. He'd nearly been killed, and his museum had been destroyed. She had never asked him how the rebuild was going. She'd felt too guilty about everything that had happened.

As she walked the familiar streets, she tried to breathe

easier. This was the first time she had walked them as something other than a witch. Her past was behind her. That's what she had to keep reminding herself. She was no longer a little girl, manipulated and controlled by members of her coven. Nor was she the undercover cop using magic to infiltrate and take down a later version of that coven. She was just her.

She looked at the stores and all of their witchcraft trappings with new eyes. It was just window dressing for the tourists who expected it. There was no malice behind it. She took a deep breath, forcing herself to stroll calmly. She could pretend that she was also a tourist and that these streets weren't haunted for her. With the afterglow of magic and power faded, it was easier to do.

She rehearsed yet again what she was going to say to Anthony when she saw him. She reached the block where his museum was and she could feel her heart begin to beat faster. Her slow, measured steps quickened.

And then everything stopped. There, where Anthony's museum had once stood, was a new building. She studied the sign with misgivings.

COFFINS. COFFEE AND MUFFINS.

She pushed open the door and walked inside. Rich aromas filled the air, and she breathed in deeply. A girl behind the counter dressed in black with pale white makeup looked up.

"Can I help you?"

"Actually, I was looking for the gentleman who used to have the occult museum in this spot."

The girl wrinkled up her nose. "I don't know about a museum. I've been working here for a couple of weeks."

Samantha felt her heart sinking. So many things had changed in San Francisco. Had the effects reached this far too? She caught her breath. What if Anthony didn't even know her anymore?

"Can I get you anything?"

"Yeah. What's good?"

"Well, we have to get your blood type first."

"Excuse me?" Samantha asked, jolted out of her own thoughts.

"What type of coffee you like. You know, life's blood?"

Samantha raised an eyebrow. "Wow, you guys picked a theme and committed."

"That's the idea. O is our specialty house blend. A is dark roast. B is medium roast. Positive is caffeinated. Negative is decaffeinated."

"In that case I'll take A positive."

"How many millimeters?"

"Just give me whatever a medium ends up being," Samantha said, starting to get frustrated.

"Sure."

She glanced down at the display case and saw muffins shaped like mini cauldrons. According to a sign, you could have molten chocolate, butter, or cream poured in them. Nearby were chocolate éclairs shaped like coffins.

"I'll take a couple of the coffins too."

Five minutes later she was out the door with her coffee and pastries. She headed back toward the hotel parking lot and then drove her car to Anthony's house. She parked on the street and took a moment to refocus herself.

Finally, she climbed out of her car and headed for the front door, coffee and pastry bag in hand.

She rang the doorbell, heart in her throat.

A few seconds later it opened, and she blinked up at Anthony.

His eyes widened in surprise and she took a ragged breath. Somehow "hi" seemed way too casual a thing to say.

He looked down at the bag in her hands. "Traitor."

"So what is the deal with that?" she asked, relieved that he had spoken first.

He sighed and rolled his eyes. "Want to come in and hear the story?"

She nodded, and he stood aside to let her enter. Her shoulder brushed against his, and the contact sent shivers throughout her body.

She turned around. "So—"

He took her in his arms and kissed her. Stunned, she stood there for a moment, coffee in one hand and pastry bag in the other.

He let her go just as abruptly, stepping back to put distance between them. She stood staring, having even less clue what to begin to say to him than she had before.

"Why don't you sit down on the couch," he said finally.

She licked her lips and then did as he suggested, setting down the cup and the bag on the coffee table. She was relieved when he sat down in a chair. Being close to him scrambled her brain and made it impossible to think clearly.

She just had to keep reminding herself that this was a man she had no business being with. She had ruined his life in so many ways. And being with him was a reminder of all the things she struggled daily to forget.

But he was the only one who would understand what she'd been through.

"So, you going to tell me what happened in San Francisco?" he asked. "By the way, I'm fuzzy on how long you were there."

"I'm not surprised."

He listened intently as she told him everything, and then he moved over and sat next to her on the couch and held her while she cried.

"I can't imagine what you've been through," he said. "What a nightmare."

"And it's not over. I know I have to visit the cemetery where my old coven is buried. I think it has something to do with whoever it was that was possessing Giselle."

"And then what?"

She shrugged. "I won't know what comes next until I know what is going on now."

She stood. "I should go. If I don't do this now, I never will."

"Thanks for stopping by."

"Thanks for not giving up on me." It seemed like such a lame thing to say given the enormity of what he'd been through waiting for her.

"Never."

She moved to the door, not trusting herself to say anything more.

"You want some company?"

She shook her head and cleared her throat. "No. This is something I have to do alone."

Half an hour later, Samantha was inside the graveyard, wishing she were anywhere else. She reached the row of graves she was looking for and stopped. Her mother was buried in her own plot, purchased long before her death. She had visited that grave when she had returned to Salem a few months before. Abigail, the former high priestess, also had a grave separate and apart a few rows away. The coven that Samantha had infiltrated had successfully raised the woman from the dead, hoping to use her to help summon the demon that had destroyed Abigail and the rest of Samantha's coven. Samantha shuddered as she remembered the horror of being part of the resurrection process and magically bound, unable to stop it and instead compelled to give her energy to aid it.

How ironic it was that the two women who had seemed most indomitable, most sure of their own immortality, had been the only two who had planned ahead for their deaths. The rest of the coven was buried here, in this row. The tombstones had pentagrams in enclosed circles placed at the top. It was ridiculous. Real witches never used that symbol, shunning it at best as a joke and at worst as a Christian artifact. But then, whoever had buried these people, who'd had the tombstones made, had not been a witch.

She began to walk, turning her face away to look straight ahead. She didn't read the names as she passed grave after grave. She didn't have to.

The dead were calling out to her. She could hear them, feel them. There was John, whom she'd always thought had to be the oldest man in the world and whose dentures had once fallen out during a very serious ritual, much to his chagrin. Louisa, who taught kindergarten. Kym, who had purple hair before it was popular. Byron, who had spent the most time instructing the younger witches with a harsh word and a cruel hand. Samantha resisted the urge to spit on his grave as she passed it. It was his voice that had haunted so many of her nightmares, commanding her to turn and keep turning, spilling her own blood in a circle of protection as a hellhound charged at her.

Fiona had run a candy store. When Samantha first heard the story of Hansel and Gretel, she had thought it was a true story about Fiona. Up until the part about the children burning the witch in the oven. Fiona was far too clever to have been caught that way. Instead she met her fate at the hands of a demon.

Finally, she came to the last grave, and it was as silent as mortals imagined graves to be. No voice called out to her; no memories stirred. A chill ran up and down her spine, and fear knotted in the pit of her stomach.

She forced herself to turn until she was standing, facing the tombstone.

Desdemona Castor.

The last grave was hers.

She crashed to her knees, sick and dizzy all at once. How had this happened? Why was there a grave with her name? No one was even supposed to know that name. She had kept it hidden for so long.

Before she even knew what she was doing, she was digging into the earth, clawing at it. She was sobbing. There was so much dirt. It would take so much time to dig up the grave.

Not for a witch, she realized.

Energy thrummed through her body as she plunged her hands down hard onto the earth. It erupted upward and outward in a shower of rocks and dirt that rained over the entire area, leaving the grave uncovered.

Samantha struggled to her feet and stared down at the wooden coffin. *Her coffin*. At least, it was meant to have been.

She stretched out her hand, compelling the lid to raise as she braced herself for what she would see inside. The hinges groaned as the coffin opened. When it had revealed its secret, she felt her heart begin to pound.

She jumped down into the coffin and picked up the single sheet of paper. There was so much power radiating off of it that merely holding it caused her entire arm to shake. It was a picture of her stolen cross necklace. Beneath it someone had left her a message written in blood.

Come and get it.

Her mind went numb. Someone knew who she was. Someone had been planning this for a long, long time. Who could it have been? It was someone who had known her as a child; she could feel it.

And standing there in the empty coffin, Samantha suddenly realized she was inside her own mind again, staring at the hallway of doors. The girls she had met were sobbing, crying, pleading with her.

She walked toward door number twelve, always glowing, always pulsing with red light streaming out from underneath. The other girls didn't know who could have done this, but Twelve would.

She shook off the small hands that grabbed at her clothes, trying to hold her back. At last she stood in front of the door they had warned her about for so long. It was time.

"I have to remember who I was," Samantha insisted as she reached toward the doorknob.

Before she could touch it, the door flew open on its own and a girl in a black cloak stepped out. "No," the girl rebuked her. "You have to remember who you *are*."

And she remembered . . . everything.

And when she climbed out of the grave, she moved her hands to form the energy ball that would become her cat. And when she was finished, she looked down at Freaky, who was no longer a furry black kitten but instead a sleek black panther. Freaky's eyes were glowing red. Just like Desdemona knew hers were.

Don't miss the next novel in the
Witch Hunt series by Debbie Viguié,

Circle of Blood

Coming from Arrow Books in 2014

The room was dark. No one was home, but that didn't mean that she was alone. Shadows slithered down the walls and voices whispered all around her. They told her to stop, told her that she was a fool and that she didn't know what she was doing. Something deep inside her was thrashing like a dying animal and it took everything she had to keep her concentration.

Sitting on the floor of her bedroom, she sliced her hand open with a butcher knife she'd gotten from the kitchen. It wasn't a ceremonial object, but the important part wasn't the blade itself; it was the blood. Her blood.

She smeared the blood on the floor around her until it formed a circle. When it was completed, she wiped her hand on her skirt and took a deep breath.

It was now or never. If she didn't do this she'd be a prisoner forever, and she wanted so desperately to be free. But the thing that slithered around inside her hated the very word. It made her hands shake so badly she almost couldn't light the candles that were around her.

On top of the circle she placed two candles. One was blue for protection. The other was yellow for memory. Then she lit a white candle and placed it inside the circle in front of her. The candle represented her, her higher self, who she wished to be.

Next she lit three black candles and placed one behind the white candle and the other two to the left and right of it. Black candles repelled negativity and were used for protection and binding.

Her hands were shaking so badly now that she knocked over the third candle. She quickly snuffed the flame that leaped to life on the carpet. And she understood exactly what the thing clawing at her stomach wanted. If it couldn't have her, it would kill her.

But she wouldn't let it, not today of all days. It was her birthday. She was thirteen. Mr. and Mrs. Ryan were at work but they had already given her the present she had asked for. She picked up the necklace that had been sitting next to her on the floor. It was a silver cross, and they hadn't even balked when she'd asked for it to be made for her based on a centuries-old design.

She twisted the top of it off, revealing a tiny hidden chamber in the heart of the cross. It wasn't large, but it didn't have to be.

She shuddered as she felt the shadows reaching out to her, touching her with icy hands that inspired dread and sorrow and terror, as they always did. But now, for the first time, they also inspired anger.

She wouldn't let them control and manipulate her anymore. Everyone was dead; her mother, Abigail ... all killed when their coven had tried raising that demon, which had destroyed them.

She would not be joining them. She was choosing life. A new life. New family, new religion. Even a new name.

"I put away the old self, the old life. I renounce the witchcraft and the acts of evil I have witnessed and participated in."

Around her she could hear screaming. Inside her belly the creature that had been with her for what felt like a lifetime writhed in agony. It needed her fear, her will to survive, and she was going to deny it those things.

"I seal myself to God and as Christ shed his blood on the cross, I too shed my blood on this image of the cross to bind my life to him."

She lifted her injured hand and squeezed three drops of blood into the hidden chamber of the cross. Three, a holy number, a sacred number to so many different peoples. She screwed the top of the cross back on and put it around her neck.

She could feel heat radiating from the cross into her skin.

"I turn my back on the darkness."

Things were throwing themselves at her now, but her circle of protection kept them at bay. There was howling and scratching outside the circle. Inside the circle the thing within her was making her sick, trying to confound her mind so she couldn't remember what it was she was doing, so she couldn't remember how to rid herself of it once and for all.

"I choose a new life, a new world. And nothing of the

old belongs in it. I am no longer Desdemona Castor. I choose to forget the evil that she has done. I am Samantha Ryan. Behold, I am become new."

She blew out the white and black candles and then immediately doubled over in pain. She wretched and something black oozed out of her mouth and slid across the floor, seeking escape. She picked up the blue candle and set fire to the black slime incinerating it. And slowly the screams faded from her mind.

When it was gone she blew out the flame on the blue candle and then the yellow candle. Yellow, for memory. Very deliberately, she took the knife and cut the candle in half. The two pieces toppled to the floor and she slid to the ground as tears of relief burst from her.

Desdemona Castor sat up with a shriek. She had been dreaming about the moment where she ceased to be, and the impostor known as Samantha Ryan had taken her place. She put her legs over the side of the bed and put her hands together, forming a ball of energy between them that grew and twisted until finally Freaky, in the form of a sleek black panther, was sitting on the ground staring at her with eyes that glowed red. She reached out to pet his head as she shook off the remnants of the nightmare.

"Never again," she promised the big cat.

They were in an abandoned house on the outskirts of New Orleans. A little magic when they arrived the night before had made it habitable and obscured them from detection. On the nightstand was a picture of the cross necklace from her nightmare. *Come and get it* was written in blood on it. The cross had been stolen by witches months before, when she was a homicide detective in Boston and had still been going by the name Samantha Ryan.

Whoever had stolen it had left the picture for her in a grave in Salem, taunting her, daring her to come and find them. When she did, she would destroy both the cross and the witch who had stolen it.

The night before, when they had arrived in New Orleans, she had attempted a summoning spell to bring the witch to her. It had failed. The witch in question was either very powerful or had taken precautions against such spells. It was no matter; Desdemona would find her and when she did, and nothing on earth would save the witch who had crossed her.

Desdemona rose and got dressed. It was time to hunt a witch.

An hour later she was haunting the dark streets of the French Quarter. The bars and clubs had emptied and the shadows reigned supreme. She stalked through them, unafraid of anything that might be lurking within. No mere mortal was a match for her, and few witches had enough power to pose any kind of threat.

A gunshot rang out through the air, and she tensed. She started to turn toward the sound, but she forced herself to continue walking on her path. She wasn't a cop; that was the usurper's job and self-identity, not hers. That wasn't who she truly was. Local police could handle the human drama just fine. Besides, what did she care?

As she walked, she searched for evidence of the witch

she was seeking. She would head to the Garden District next if she couldn't find what she was looking for. Witches, by their very nature, loved places steeped in history. A police car sped by a few minutes later, followed by an ambulance.

The streets were grimy, and without throngs of people the place felt desolate. She stepped over a puddle that seemed to be congealing blood. The energy in the place was palpable and so very different from other places she had been.

There was no sense of the earth beneath her, just concrete. Instead the energy was pulsing off the buildings, the collected fears and dreams of so many creative and desperate people. Life was one big party until you died, and here sex, death, and jazz seemed to permeate the air.

It was nearly dawn when she finally felt power shimmering in the air. She walked into a small café that was open for early-morning breakfast. She took a table and her eyes zeroed in on an older man with gray hair who was engrossed in his breakfast. She ordered beignets and coffee.

When they came a few minutes later she was still closely watching the man. So far he had refused to acknowledge her presence even though he most surely had felt her power as well.

She considered confronting him then and there, but the importance of keeping magic a secret had been well drilled into her as a child. She had once blinded a schoolyard bully, only to be tortured by her mother as punishment. She could wait until the man left the café.

The coffee was only lukewarm, but she had no need

of distracting herself by yelling at the waiter. Instead, keeping her eyes focused on her quarry, she wrapped her hand around the cup and pushed energy out of her body through her hand and into the cup. She could hear the liquid begin to boil, and she released it.

Twenty minutes later she was finished eating. He finally got up and exited the café in another ten minutes. She waited a beat and then rose to follow him.

She stayed about a block behind. He couldn't help but know that she was following him. She would let him choose the place of their confrontation. She could feel power vibrating through her and struggled to hold it back. Finally she saw him turn up an alleyway between two buildings.

She tensed, the energy ebbing and flowing through her. She debated briefly about how to enter the alleyway in case he was waiting to ambush her. Finally she took it slowly, hand raised, fire dancing along her fingertips.

She stopped a couple of feet in.

The man was standing over the body of someone else sprawled on the ground. The stench of blood filled the air and she could feel the person on the ground as he died.

She stared with narrowed eyes at the man she'd been following. He just shrugged his shoulders and looked at her with steely eyes. "And what, then, is it you'll be wanting of me?" he asked in a lilting Irish accent.

"What are you?"

"A man, last I checked," he said, a smile twisting his lips.

"Are you a witch?"

"Druid, actually," he said shortly.

A surge of power rippled through the air, followed by a gasp and the sound of shattering glass.

Desdemona turned impatiently. There, standing behind her, was one of the magic users whose life she had spared back in Salem, a young girl with flaming red hair who was shaking uncontrollably, a broken vase with fresh flowers at her feet.

"Please, please don't kill me," the girl begged.

Desdemona turned back. The man had vanished, and she recognized instantly the body of the dead guy and blinked in surprise.

It was her waiter from the café.

The 13th Sacrifice

Debbie Viguié

THE PAST CAN KILL

Samantha Ryan is plagued by nightmares. Horrific memories lie in wait – of dark magic and crippling fear, of strange creatures and blood-soaked walls. Because Samantha grew up in a witches' coven, enslaved by power and greed.

But now Samantha must go undercover to confront the horror of her terrible past, and protect her home town against a newly awakened heart of evil.

'One of the most beautifully written and scariest books I've ever read' – Nancy Holder, author of *Buffy the Vampire Slayer*

'Dark, bloody, emotional and scary, and so darn well-written that it's almost impossible to put it down... this novel is an insanely good read.' – *USA Today*

arrow books

ALSO AVAILABLE IN ARROW

The Swedish international bestseller

The Circle

Sara B. Elfgren & Mats Strandberg

One night, when a strange red moon fills the sky, six schoolgirls find themselves in an abandoned theme park, drawn there by a mysterious force. A student has just been found dead. Everyone suspects suicide. Everyone except them.

In that derelict fairground an ancient prophecy is revealed. They are The Chosen Ones, a group of witches bound together by power, one which could destroy them all. But they soon learn that despite their differences they need each other, in order to master the forces that have been awakened within them.

'Rightly destined to be the next cult read.'
Sunday Telegraph

'Impossible to put down'
QX

arrow books

THE POWER OF READING

Visit the Random House website and get connected with information on all our books and authors

EXTRACTS from our recently published books and selected backlist titles

COMPETITIONS AND PRIZE DRAWS Win signed books, audiobooks and more

AUTHOR EVENTS Find out which of our authors are on tour and where you can meet them

LATEST NEWS on bestsellers, awards and new publications

MINISITES with exclusive special features dedicated to our authors and their titles

READING GROUPS Reading guides, special features and all the information you need for your reading group

LISTEN to extracts from the latest audiobook publications

WATCH video clips of interviews and readings with our authors

RANDOM HOUSE INFORMATION including advice for writers, job vacancies and all your general queries answered

Come home to Random House
www.randomhouse.co.uk